Tiare in Bloom

Also by
Célestine Vaite

Breadfruit

Frangipani

Breadfruit

*A wise, enchanting tale of Tahitian-style romance, introducing Materena
Mahi, whose cleverness, generosity, and appreciation of island traditions make
her one of the most appealing heroines in contemporary fiction*

"Like Alexander McCall Smith in his No. 1 Ladies' Detective Agency
series, Vaite excels at depicting the warm sense of community that
pervades her Tahitian island setting. . . . In charming fashion, Vaite
conveys universal truths about men and women and the mysteries at
the heart of every romantic relationship."

—Joanne Wilkinson, *Booklist*

"Vaite's focus is on how one woman's strength can affect the lives of her
family and the community. . . . She writes about real people coping and
caring and somehow getting along."

—Ginny Merdes, *Seattle Times*

"Peppered with witty encounters between Materena and her nosy
family. . . . When combined with Vaite's light touch and the exotic
setting, the result is redolent of the No. 1 Ladies' Detective Agency
series — a delightful diversion."

—*Publishers Weekly*

"*Breadfruit* is as much about the culture of Tahiti as it is about Materena
and her impending marriage."

—Rebecca Stuhr, *Library Journal*

. . . and Frangipani

*A tale of big dreams on a small island — in which Materena Mahi,
professional house cleaner and "the best listener in Tahiti,"
becomes a radio talk-show host*

"What a gorgeous, evocative novel! It charmed me from beginning to end."

— Sophie Kinsella, author of the Shopaholic series

"A winning tale of mothers and daughters. . . . An engaging debut."

—*People*

"This delightful novel speaks to the universal nature of the mother-daughter experience. Even though Célestine Vaite writes of Tahiti, a place I've never been and a culture with which I'm entirely unfamiliar, I felt as if she were writing about me, my own daughters, and my own mother."

— Ayelet Waldman, author of
Love and Other Impossible Pursuits

"Vaite takes us beyond the resort compounds into the rhythms and rivalries of a tropical culture. A novel about two strong women, *Frangipani* testifies to the necessity of upholding traditions and defying them too."

—Carrington Alvarez, *Elle*

"I read *Frangipani* in one sitting, falling in love with the characters. Célestine Vaite writes about the bond between mothers and daughters with such truth and tenderness. I loved reading about the struggle between Materena and Leilani, even when it made me cry. There are no hopes and dreams like those of a mother for her daughter, and Ms. Vaite made them so real, I found myself missing my mother terribly."

— Luanne Rice

"Vaite serves her culture well by taking us into the kitchens of those fibro shacks where we can hear the characters' travails in a chatty narrative. Generously, *Frangipani* gives us Gauguin's women in their off hours."

—Victoria Kelly, *San Francisco Chronicle*

"A lovely and transcendent mother-daughter story. . . . An intriguing slice of Tahitian life."

—Debbie Bogenschutz, *Library Journal*

Tiare in Bloom

a novel

Célestine Vaite

BACK BAY BOOKS
Little, Brown and Company
New York   Boston   London

Back Bay Books
Little, Brown and Company
Hachette Book Group USA
237 Park Avenue, New York, NY 10017
Visit our Web site at www.HachetteBookGroupUSA.com

First United States Edition: June 2007

Originally published in 2006 by
The Text Publishing Company

The characters and events in this book are fictitious. Any similarity to real persons, living or dead, is coincidental and not intended by the author.

Cover illustration and interior art by Philippe Lardy

Library of Congress Cataloging-in-Publication Data
Vaite, Célestine.
[Tiare]
Tiare in bloom : a novel / Célestine Vaite. — 1st U.S. ed.
p.   cm.
ISBN-10: 0-316-11467-7
ISBN-13: 978-0-316-11467-7
1. Women in radio broadcasting — Fiction.
2. Tahiti — Fiction. 3. Domestic fiction. I. Title.
PR9619.4.V35T53 2007
823'.92 — dc22   2006034791

10 9 8 7 6 5 4 3 2 1

Q-MART

Printed in the United States of America

For my sons: Genji, Heimanu, and Toriki.
"A happy woman means a happy household."
Remember this, boys.

Tiare in Bloom

Pito's Congratulation

Pito Tehana steps off the truck at the petrol station facing the bakery in Faa'a. His calico bag is thrown casually over his shoulder and a smile is on his lips because work is over. Still smiling, he gives a little, slow nod to one of his wife's many cousins walking to the Chinese store, meaning, *Iaorana,* you're fine?

The woman shrugs an insolent shrug, flicks her hair, and keeps on walking.

"You need something, you," Pito mutters under his breath.

Another of his wife's relatives walks past, but this one has already done her grocery shopping at the Chinese store. Today, that means a family-size packet of disposable diapers and ten breadsticks. Pito gives another *Iaorana,* you're fine? nod. She raises an eyebrow, gives Pito a long look, and turns away.

"*Iaorana,* my arse!" Pito calls out, thinking, Here, now you have a reason to be rude to me.

He is puzzled, though. It's not that he expects Materena's relatives to be overwhelmed at the sight of him, they never are. But give him a nod at least! A little nod, where's the politeness, eh? It's not as if he was asking for a salutation to the sun!

Then Pito spots Materena's cousin Mori playing his eternal accordion and drinking his beer under the mango tree near the petrol station.

"Mori!" Pito calls out. "*E aha te huru,* Cousin?"

"*Maitai, maitai!*" Mori calls back, putting his accordion down.

Mori never ignores Pito. *Enfin,* Mori never ignores anybody. The two men shake hands.

"Eh?" Pito asks Mori, who sees and hears everything from his mango tree. "What's the story with the Mahi family this time?"

Mori considers the question. "Well, it's about you, *hoa hia.*"

"It's always about me, what did I do now?"

After a moment of hesitation, Mori spills the bucket. "The family says that you don't care about Materena's new job because you didn't invite her to the restaurant and she's been at the radio for a year."

Pito gives Mori a blank look.

"Twelve months, Cousin," Mori continues. "And you know about Materena's radio program, it's a success, it deserves champagne, an invitation to the restaurant. It's the most listened-to program in Tahiti, Cousin!" Seeing Pito's incredulous face, Mori asks, "You didn't read *Les Nouvelles* on Tuesday?"

"*Non.*"

Mori shakes his dreadlocks, meaning, You don't read the *news?* "There was an article, it's official, nobody can say it's just stories. Materena is the star of radios! But she hasn't turned into a *faaoru,* a show-off, she's still the same Materena that I know. She says good morning, she talks to you."

There, Mori has spoken the truth.

"What else are they saying about me?" Pito wants more information. What he's just heard isn't enough.

"You're a big *zéro.*"

"Eh oh," Pito protests, looking wounded.

"You're thirsty, Cousin?" Mori hurries to ask, as if to make himself forgiven for the harsh comment.

"*Oui,* my throat is a bit dry," Pito admits, and sits down on the concrete. He never refuses a beer with Mori. It is so rare. It's not that Mori is tight with his beer, but when you drink thanks to your mother's generosity, you can't distribute like you want.

Pito takes a few sips of his warm beer and explains his case. He doesn't like to eat at restaurants, it's simple, *d'accord?* He doesn't want somebody coughing on his food, spitting on his food, talking over his food. When you eat at a restaurant, you don't see what's going on in the kitchen. And anyway, he likes to eat at home, his wife is a number-one cook...

"Where's the problem?" Pito asks Mori.

"Cousin," Mori says nicely. "Women like to eat at the restaurant now and then. It's an occasion. They put on a beautiful dress, makeup, shoes... They feel special and they have a rest."

Pito shrugs. He'd like a rest too, and not having to work eleven months of the year. Everybody would like a little rest, but it doesn't mean people can tell stories about him.

"It really annoys me," Pito continues, "when people talk like they know what they're talking about and they don't even know."

By *people* Pito means women, because they're always talking, those ones, they never shut up. "My husband did this, my husband did that. My children talk back to me. Tonight we're going to eat breadfruit stew..." They talk in the truck, outside the Chinese store, inside the Chinese store, over hedges, under trees, by the side of the road, on the steps of the church, on the radio... Even when they have the flu and their voice is croaky, they talk and talk and talk.

Mori chuckles.

"I'm sure women are born with a special mouth," Pito says, pretending he doesn't see the cranky look another relative by marriage fires at him as she walks past with her breadsticks. Mori gets a friendly wave. Mori always gets a friendly wave.

"Cousin," Pito says.

"*Oui,* Cousin."

"What else are they saying about me?" Pito mentally prepares himself for another story. With the Mahi women, there's never just one story. But Mori has said enough for today, perhaps even too much. His lips are stitched.

"*Cousin?*" Pito repeats.

"That's all I know."

Fine. Since Mori doesn't want to speak, Pito will say a few words. In his opinion, Materena's relatives have never liked him. He understood this during his first official visits to Materena at her mother's house. Before that, Pito's visits to Materena were behind the bank, under a tree, in the dark, and in total secrecy. Then Materena fell pregnant and... welcome into the family, eh? The moment he arrived in the neighborhood, the Mahi family felt they knew Pito Tehana. "I hope you're not going to abandon Materena after what you've done to her," one of Materena's relatives would greet him. "You better recognize Materena's baby." "You better not make Materena cry."

The first time Loana met Pito, her greeting was much shorter. "Ah, you're here." She did her little eyes at Pito as if he were a nuisance and not her potential son-in-law, the father of her unborn first grandchild. "Take your thongs off before walking into my house."

Pito never stayed for too long back then, ten minutes was enough. He had to save a bit of energy for the journalists waiting for him by the side of the road. "You don't care about Materena's baby," they said. "We see it in your eyes. Have you bought any blankets for the baby, at least? We don't dance the tango alone, you know. It takes two."

Pito couldn't believe his ears! In his experience, a Tahitian man who does the right thing (by this, Pito means visiting the girl he got pregnant) is feted like an *ari'i,* a king! The girl's relatives give the father of the unborn baby a chair to sit on, and somebody (usually the grandmother) gives him something nice to eat like cookies — fried prawns if he's lucky. This happened to two of Pito's brothers. But all Pito got from Materena's family, he tells Mori, was *tutae uri.* Dog shit.

"I bet I could write a book on all the stories your family has told about me over the years," says Pito.

"It's true." Mori smiles. *Aue,* if Pito only knew! He could write a whole encyclopedia!

"Unbelievable." Pito finishes his beer, thanks Mori, and gets up. "Your family can say what they want, I don't care."

"Maybe you should, Pito." Mori's smile drops.

"A man can congratulate his wife in other ways. There's no need to go to the restaurant."

"True, Cousin," Mori agrees, feeling friendly towards Pito again. "A bouquet of flowers, a —"

"I congratulate my wife in my own way," Pito goes on, with a smirk that tells long stories. "And no complaints so far."

Pito walks home, his head held up high.

You talk of a congratulation, Mori says to himself, and, picking up his accordion, he attacks a love song, the one about Rosalie and how she left.

"*Rosalie,*" sings Mori. "*Elle est partie . . .*"

He doesn't know why that song came into his mind. It just did.

"*And if you see her, bring her back to me.*"

All the Confidence Required

With her first driving lesson fresh in her mind, Materena opens her radio program at eight p.m. on the dot, straight after Ati's love song dedication program.

"*Iaorana,* girlfriends!" comes Materena's cheerful greeting, followed by a special thank-you to all the women who called last night to share their stories on the radio, moving on to the necessary technicalities such as the radio's two telephone numbers. Then she jumps straight into her opening story.

"Girlfriends," Materena laughs into the microphone, "I had my first driving lesson today and let me tell you... *Aue* ... this is something I've wanted to do for a long time but I didn't have the confidence to do it until today..."

In fact, Materena's foot was jumping on the clutch, she was so nervous. But she got through the lesson, managing to change gears seven times and stall only five, and with one satisfactory reverse park in front of a snack filled with people eating sandwiches.

Well anyway, this is Materena's story and she now appeals to her listeners to share their own stories of overcoming fear, their stories of moving forward and getting confident. "Let's

inspire ourselves, eh? And thank you in advance, girlfriends."
Materena used to appeal to the male listeners too but has since
given up on the masculine sex. Never once has a man picked up
the phone to ring her, in fact Materena wouldn't be surprised if
men didn't even listen to her program.

She plays a soft song to give the listeners an opportunity to
grab their telephone, then she leans back and anxiously looks at
her two assistants behind the glass, thinking, as always, What
if nobody calls? She often has nightmares of this happening.
She's in the studio waiting and waiting but nobody is calling
because the movie on TV is much more interesting.

But tonight, as usual, all is fine. Her two assistants are giving her the thumbs-up, meaning, We have calls.

The first caller confesses to Materena that three months ago
she got confident enough to set her ex-husband's snack on fire,
as she'd been dreaming to do for years. She didn't do this out
of revenge and hatred, she insists. She just wanted to show her
ex how well their son had turned out. It was her way of telling
him, "Do you remember what you told me when you left with
that skeleton woman who can't cook? That my son was going to
be a good-for-nothing? My son is a fireman, he has medals and
he has letters of recommendation! Who saved your snack today,
eh? It's not my son by any chance?"

Another caller got *fiu* of complaining to her husband about
her Christmas present from his mother. "A cheap bottle of
shampoo! Is this all I'm worth in her eyes? Me, the mother of
her grandchildren? The woman who cooks, picks up, washes,
who does everything?" And the husband would say, "*Aue,* it's
the thought that counts," but for Materena's listener, most
of the time it's the thought that's the problem. So she finally
got the courage to give the mother-in-law a bottle of cheap
shampoo on her birthday, her way of saying, "*Voilà,* this is how

much you're worth in *my* eyes: less than three hundred francs, one and a half packets of rice." This past Christmas the caller got some very nice pearl earrings.

More stories follow. These are stories of women getting themselves a new job, whiter teeth, a business, new shoes, a child, a checkbook, a new meaning in life.

"*Iaorana,* Juanita!" The calls are still coming in. "And what's the big change in your life?"

"I'm divorcing my husband."

"Juanita," Materena says as if she were speaking to a friend, "what made you decide to divorce your husband? Tell us your story." Materena leans back in her chair and listens.

To begin the story, Juanita would like to inform Materena and the other women listening that she's been married for six years and has been planning to divorce her husband for the past three years. But she kept thinking about what people were going to say — her family, his family, their friends. And what about her marriage vows? To love and obey her husband and stay with him no matter what, in sickness and in health, till death, et cetera. But she never said it was acceptable for her husband to treat her as if she had the word *idiot* tattooed on her forehead.

"He's only my husband on paper," says Juanita. "If he was really my husband, he wouldn't leave me at home with the kids all the time to go surfing. Sometimes I feel that his surfboard is his wife. He tells me, 'Surfing is my religion,' but when he gets his needs, it's me that's his religion. Get lost! And he never helps me with the house, the kids...*rien de quelque chose.* It's like I'm his slave."

Two months ago in bed, the day before Juanita's husband went for yet another surfing holiday, Juanita told him that she wanted to talk to him about their marital problems. Next second, he was shouting at her, "*Merde!* You are a real boil, you know? Stop masturbating your mind!" Then he kicked the quilt and turned his back on his crying wife.

So Juanita is divorcing her husband. She knows her mother will be very disappointed because she's from the generation that doesn't expect much from their husband. But this is Juanita's *life*. She wants a real husband, a real man, not a living room doll. Juanita keeps on talking and Materena keeps on saying *oui*. Her *oui* says, "I hear you, girl, go on, give me more information." Meanwhile Materena's two assistants behind the glass window are slicing their throats with their fingers, meaning, Cut! Cut now!

Ah hia hia, this is the hardest part of the job for Materena. Cutting people off, especially cutting off a woman pouring her heart out, but Materena has to be fair to the other women calling, she can't keep them waiting for too long. Otherwise, they'll hang up and switch to another station.

Ati explained when she started working at the radio that the time limit for someone to be on air is forty-five seconds because that's how long it takes to tell a good yarn. More than that and it's just blabbing. Juanita has been talking for nearly one minute and a half. Materena leans forward and softly, diplomatically, says, "Juanita, let's see if our next caller has a story that might help you. Keep listening to Radio Tefana, we need to help each other."

"Pardon," Juanita cackles. "I talk too much, Heifara always says that."

Ouf, Materena is so relieved Juanita didn't get cranky, unlike one of her callers, an old woman who went on and on about how these days old people are not respected when Materena told her (diplomatically) that her time was up.

Eh well, you can't make everybody happy.

Materena thanks Juanita, presses the button, and is immediately connected to the next caller, who doesn't want to give her name and who only has one thing to say to Juanita.

"Life is not a fairy tale, the Prince Charming doesn't stay charming forever, he turns back into a frog."

The following caller urges Juanita not to throw the pillow out of the window and to remember what attracted her to Heifara at the beginning of their story. Wasn't it his surfing? The salt on his skin? Didn't she brag to her girlfriends, "Guess what! My boyfriend is a surfer!"?

"It happens," the caller continues, speaking with a maternal voice, "that the thing that attracts us at the beginning is the thing that annoys us later on, but it doesn't mean we should divorce, my *chérie.*"

The next caller has a solution. "Speaking of pillows, I've been married for eleven years, and my husband is a real husband, not a work in progress. He sweeps the floors, he hangs the clothes on the line, and he's a father hen with the children, it's like he's the one who gave birth to them!" The woman sighs like she can't believe how lucky she is. "As soon as he does his *parara,*" she continues, "like go out with his friends, waste his money, tell the children to go away, mock my war wounds —"

"War wounds?" Materena wants to know.

"Well, my stretch marks," the caller explains, cackling, with Materena joining in.

She continues, "So, when my man is like that, I get my bottle of ylang-ylang and sprinkle a few drops on his pillow at night while he's asleep." The woman swears that the scent of the ylang-ylang does something to a man's brain, because when her husband wakes up in the morning, he looks at her with surprised eyes and exclaims, "Who is this beautiful woman in my bed?" After that, he's like hypnotized, he gives her compliments and does all that she asks. Sometimes, she doesn't even have to ask. It's the world in reverse!

The lucky woman has been using that trick for ten years now, and for your information, sisters, here's the address where she religiously buys her magic potion twice a year.

Next morning, passing the very tiny Oils and Soaps shop, Materena finds fifty women, many with babies in their arms, squeezed against each other and spilling out onto the footpath. There are big women, little women, middle-aged women, young women, women who'd never heard of the magic ylang-ylang until last night on Materena's program. Materena rarely gets to see her audience. That is the reason she's here. She doesn't need a potion, her kids have all grown up. For some reason, she's also suspecting that the woman who called last night is inside that shop, behind the counter, at the cash register.

"Eh," Materena asks a young woman nearby, "you're here to buy ylang-ylang?"

"*Oui,* but it's not for me, it's for my sister." She takes a step forward without a glance at this woman twice her age.

"Ah, and she has children?" Materena asks.

"*Oui,* five, but it's not the potion that's going to save her."

"*Ah bon?*" The next question on Materena's lips is, And what is going to save your sister? But you can't ask too many questions to people you don't know. It's not proper. On radio it goes, but not on the streets.

"Men are like fruit," says the young woman with her serious face like she really knows what she's talking about. "As the French say, there are ripe ones and there are not-ripe ones." She glances to Materena and nods a firm nod, meaning, yes, this is what I think. "Potions," she spits, "are for the superstitious. Me, I believe more in the power of the head."

Still the Man

The main story on the coconut radio in the Mahi *quartier* is still how Pito doesn't deserve Materena. For a start, she's very nice compared with her husband, he hasn't been raised well, that one. You'll never hear *"Iaorana,* my arse" coming out of Materena's mouth! Also, the house where Pito lives belongs to Materena — part of her heritage from her mother — whereas Pito doesn't have even a handful of soil to his name. Plus, Materena still looks young, you would think she was in her thirties, but the relatives can't say the same about her husband — he's not aging well at all. And now Materena is learning to drive!

The story also goes that Materena tolerated her good-for-nothing husband for years and years because she wanted a father for her children, having grown up without her own father, only uncles. But her children are adults now, they are living their own lives. Materena doesn't need Pito anymore.

Ah, just as well Pito isn't the kind to take gossips seriously. Another man would have panicked, crumbled under the pressure, and complained to his wife about her relatives being horrible to him. But Pito has nerves of steel. It will take much more than gossips to knock out his confidence.

And so today, with his usual confident demeanor, Pito steps down from the truck — not in Faa'a, but in Punaauia, where he's from — to see how his mother is and everything; to make sure Mama Roti is still alive.

Here's the Ah-Ka Chinese store by the side of the road and Pito instantly feels at home, because he is. He bought thousands of Chinese lollies at this Chinese store when he was a kid. It was much smaller then, and back in those wonderful days the owners of that Chinese store trusted the little people, they gave them credit. These days, they want their money up front.

But at least children aren't allowed to buy wine for their grandparents anymore. Pito remembers going to that Chinese store as an eight-year-old to buy a liter of Faragui red wine for his grandfather. He'd say, "It's for Grand-père," and Ziou, the Chinese man, would exclaim in disbelief, "Your grandfather is still *alive* with all that he drinks?"

Pito stood near the banana tree over there one hundred thousand times, waiting for the truck to go to school, the market, or to see his *copain* Ati or a girl he liked. But the old man who used to drink vodka and talk to himself beside the banana tree died — in his bed — when Pito was about ten. He was a great-uncle, a well-known singer through the whole of French Polynesia, admired for his tenor voice. He really had extraordinary lungs, but then his woman ran away with a gardener. End of career. The singer became a drinker.

Otherwise, nothing much has changed around here in the Tehana *quartier*. Aunties, older now, are still hanging clothes on the line, watering flowers, gossiping over hibiscus hedges, raking the leaves, minding the great-grandchildren, keeping busy. Pito walks past the row of neat, proud fibro shacks, his eyes firmly on the dirt path. He's hoping to pass unnoticed, but of course this is impossible.

"Pito, *iti e!*"

Pito looks up and waves to his auntie Philomena, one of his father's eight sisters, and the one Mama Roti likes the least because she talks to say nothing and asks too many questions. Apparently, Auntie Philomena used to be very reserved in her youth, although this is hard for Pito to believe.

"Come here a little," Auntie Philomena cackles, opening her fat arms to her nephew. "What's this walking with your eyes on the ground, eh?" She squeezes Pito tight, strangling him almost. "So? How's life in Faa'a? How's Materena? How's her mother? How's Ati? How are you? I hear Materena is a big star now, eh? How much are they paying her at the radio? More than when she was a cleaner, that's for sure, eh? I wanted to work at the radio when I was young, but your uncle said it was not a place for a woman, can you believe it? The world has changed, eh? When are they going to give Materena a limousine? When I was young I wanted to drive a car, but your uncle said cars are not for women, can you believe it? The world has changed, eh? *Aue,* we're all getting old, Pito, and you too! I remember when you were a baby, you ate a peg, and it came out with your *caca* two days later! I know you don't believe me, because your mama told you it's impossible for a baby to shit out a peg, but I saw that peg with my own eyes. *Enfin,* you're here to visit your mama? That's nice. She looked a bit sick last time I saw her. But how does it feel to be married to a star?" The auntie stops talking and she's now expecting her nephew to answer.

"A star?" Pito chuckles. "Materena is still the same."

"Stop doing your idiot, Pito, everybody who works at the radio is well known, but Materena is the most popular. And she's only been at the radio for one year! Imagine a little in ten years! She's going to be better known than Gabilou. I like Materena's radio program, it talks about things I understand, like life, love, youth. I told Tonton to listen, but you know your uncle, he just wants to listen to his doum-doum music." Auntie Philomena stops talking to take a deep breath.

Okay, it's now or never! *"Allez,* Auntie," Pito jumps in. "I see that you're busy. I leave you." Before she starts up her speech again, Pito walks away, nodding in agreement to the words she's calling out to his back.

Auntie Maire, watering her flowers with her latest great-grandchild fast asleep in her carriage nearby, stops him two yards further. The eldest sister and the skinniest, she's the sister-in-law Mama Roti likes the most because she doesn't talk to say nothing.

"Pito!" Auntie Maire bends her hose to stop the water flowing and gives her nephew a big kiss on his cheeks. "It's very nice of you to visit Mama, *haere,* go... don't let Mama wait, and give my felicitations to Materena for her first year at the radio."

Pito gives his promise and keeps walking, only to be stopped yards later by another auntie, and another auntie, and another. At last he reaches the house where he took his first steps, drank his first beer, smoked his first *paka,* and lost his virginity with a friend of a cousin.

He was about sixteen and she was more than twenty. It was the big love for Pito, but she dropped him for an older man who worked at the bank. Pito was heartbroken for months, and after that he was a little obsessed with older women for a while. Sitting across from an older woman in a truck, he'd be trans-fixed, watching as she rolled a cigarette, licking the paper and telling him with her eyes, I bet you'd like me to do that to you, eh, kid? Pito would swallow hard. He'd fantasize about that sexy mama for weeks.

Enfin, here's Mama Roti at the door, warned of her son's visit by the exclamations of the sisters-in-law. As he gets closer, she looks Pito up and down and says, "You're getting fat." There's no *Iaorana,* how are you, thank you for remembering that I'm alive.

"I'm the same as last week when you saw me."

"Where's my Materena?"

Your Materena, eh? Pito snorts, thinking back to the night when he overturned his mother's kitchen table after she said words about Materena that did not please his ears. Plates and glasses smashed on the floor right before Mama Roti's horrified eyes, but at least she got Pito's message: Don't talk bad about the mother of my children. Pito was drunk and Mama Roti not too far off, and it's very possible that the words got a bit exaggerated, but they both learned a valuable lesson that night: Don't drink together. "Materena is in town for her driving lesson."

"Driving lesson?" Mama Roti cringes as if she's just been told an absurd story. "And after? A passport? She has a car at least?" Mama Roti knows many people who take driving lessons and they don't even have a car. What's the use of that? Pito informs his mother that actually, yes, Materena has a car. She bought Mama Teta's Fiat two days ago, to be paid for little by little as per the Tahitian finance tradition. Mama Teta didn't need the Fiat anymore, having upgraded to driving a minibus since starting her nursing home. That way, she can take her clients to Papeete for their medical checkups and to special outings like bingo.

"You have lots of gray hair, Pito." Mama Roti doesn't care about Materena's car. "What's the story? You're stressed?"

"I've had gray hair for the past three years."

Mama Roti looks into her son's eyes. "Maybe it's time for you to put your flag down and do something."

"Do something?" Pito asks, wondering what his mother is going on about. "What?"

"It's not up to me to tell you," Mama Roti snaps. "Materena isn't my wife. I don't know what she loves. Pito, eh, you were so handsome before, but now you look so old and you're not even a grandfather yet."

"Eh?"

"When I look at you," Mama Roti sighs with deep concern, "it's like you have ten grandchildren."

"Eh?" Pito repeats, thinking, Is this a son's reward when he remembers that his mother is alive? Criticisms and guessing games?

"*Aue,* Pito." More sighing from Mama Roti. "Look at yourself in the mirror now and then, hum?"

Two hours later, in front of the mirror, Pito is shaving. He shaves when there's a funeral, a wedding, a baptism, a meeting at work, and when he wants his wife. After the shaving, Pito scrubs his body clean with soap, dabs eau de cologne on his neck... in brief, he makes himself beautiful like a prince.

He thinks fleetingly of how when it's the wife who's in the mood, she doesn't have to use any tricks to interest her husband. She just gives him the look, the look that says, *Coucou,* look at me closely, I'm interested! And the husband better be interested too, otherwise she gets suspicious. "How come you're not interested? You have a problem? Another woman?" It's a cruel world, *oui,* but Pito isn't going to waste time philosophizing about it. He's too busy getting prepared.

When Materena walks into the house, carrying a big box, Pito — shaved, smiling his *uh-huh-huh* smile, and puffing out his bare chest — is posing for a Mr. Universe photograph on the sofa.

Materena bursts out laughing.

"What?" Pito asks, sucking his belly in. "What is funny?"

Still laughing, Materena delicately puts the box on the ground and massages her sore arms. "I'm not telling you," she says. "But that box was heavy."

"What did you buy this time?"

"A thing to put things in." What Materena means is a multiple-tray rack. "It was reduced by eighty percent."

"With you, it's always reduced by eighty percent," Pito chuckles, but when he sees Materena rip the box open, his heart sinks. "You're not going to do this now!" Out come pieces of metal and plastic. "It can't wait a little?"

Materena reads the instructions with Pito looking on, amused.

"Okay, okay," Materena says, grabbing one of the pieces. "*Oui,* I put that with that." She grabs another piece. "Then I do this... All right, then, it's not the right piece, maybe it's that piece. *Non,* it's not that piece either, okay, how about I try with another piece... *Merde!* Okay maybe I'm going to read the instructions again, eh?" She reads. "Okay, *oui,* I put that piece with that piece, and then *non,* ah, *oui,* silly me, it's that piece... *non*...But! Who wrote these stupid instructions? Okay, let's start from the beginning again."

"You've got two years?" Pito asks, letting his belly out a bit.

Materena looks up and starts laughing again. "I can't look at you, Pito, you're making me laugh with your belly like that...Okay, Materena, concentrate."

Pito looks on, stroking his smooth chin. Materena doesn't understand instructions, it's like with plumbing, electrical wires, digging holes... Pito isn't making fun of his wife though, it's not the moment to annoy her.

"You want me to help you?" he asks sweetly, sucking his belly in again.

This..., says Materena to herself, goes here or here?

Half an hour later she cracks. "I don't understand your instructions!" she growls at the piece of paper.

"You want me to help you?" Pito asks again as he gets off the sofa as naturally as possible. The trick here is not to look like he's superior. Pito knows from experience (though very limited) helping Materena that when he puts his I'm-superior look on his face, Materena changes her mind about being helped.

Materena passes him the instruction sheet.

"Let me see," Pito says, also as casually as possible, still careful not to look too confident. "Maybe this piece goes there…" Pito lets his voice trail off. Of course he could assemble that plastic piece of shit in less than a minute, but he knows that it is in his interest to show a bit of a struggle. "Maybe it goes here instead." He lifts his beautiful eyes to his wife for a few seconds to see if she's watching him. "I wonder," Pito continues, glad that Materena is paying him undivided attention, "if this piece and this piece are not a couple, by any chance?"

By the time Materena's multiple-tray rack is half built, Materena is sending her husband very positive signals. A little smile, soft eyes…

Eh, eh, Pito cackles in his head. I'm still the man, don't you worry about that!

Breathing Like You Want

Ah, a man doesn't need much to be happy. Food, sexy loving, peace and quiet at night. He can breathe like he wants. His wife is at work.

Tonight, for example, Pito can relax in front of the TV without having to listen to Materena's sighs and comments every time she walks past about how she can't believe he's wasting his life watching a movie that has no tail and no head. He can watch a *good* movie and there will be no distractions from Materena, ironing in front of the TV because she also wants to watch the movie. He can rest his eyes on the sofa for a while and Materena won't tap him on the shoulder and whisper in his ear, "Pito! You're sleeping? Go to bed now, *allez*, I don't want to carry you."

When Materena got that job at the radio Pito was scared she was going to start speaking high class, become a *Me, I* person, but she's still the Materena Pito has been living with for almost a quarter of a century. She runs around the house with the broom, though less than she used to do — at least now the broom has a rest. She lends eggs to relatives who didn't have time to go to the Chinese store before it closed. She cooks, laughs, complains, rakes the leaves, and stresses out when her banana cake comes out of the oven bizarre. She goes to mass, talks to her relatives, weeds her ancestors' graves, regularly visits her mother...She's a typical Tahitian woman.

And she's not home. So, whistling because he has no one to answer to, Pito steps out of the house to attend the very important nocturnal rendezvous with *les copains.*

Meanwhile, in the studio of Radio Tefana, Lovaina, the fifth caller tonight, is telling Materena that her father is French.

"He came to Tahiti a young man and —"

"For military service?" Materena asks without thinking, then realizes she has interrupted her caller. "Oh, excu —"

"*Ah non!*" The caller interrupts Materena's interruption, sounding very offended by the question. "I know that there are a lot of children born in Tahiti from French *militaires* and Tahitian women meeting in bars, but my father *is* educated." For the record, Lovaina informs all listening that her father was actually in his third year of legal studies at university when he came to Tahiti for a three-week holiday. But he met a beautiful Tahitian woman one day at the market where she was selling her vegetables...and he never left, that's all.

"Ah, okay," says Materena.

"We can say that Papa is now a French *tropicalisé,*" Lovaina continues. "He speaks Tahitian, he eats *fafaru,* grows taro, he wants to be buried on Tahitian soil.... He feels more Tahitian than I do."

"Do you think of yourself as French?" Materena dares to ask.

A silence. "I don't know who I am," Lovaina whispers at last. "I'm so confused about my identity. My father, who is French, acts like he's Tahitian. My mother, who is Tahitian, acts like she's French. She does the *reuh-reuh* when she speaks, she's a Madame, she's always quoting French sayings, and as soon as she meets someone, the first thing she says is, 'You know, my husband is French, his family owns castles...'" A big sigh from Lovaina. "Who am I?" she asks. "Half Tahitian, half French...but where do I go?"

After this the switchboard goes crazy, and half an hour later the calls are still coming in about identity, Tahitian identity especially. The Tahitians who don't speak Tahitian have their say. The Tahitians who don't have tattoos, who don't like raw fish, who don't look Tahitian, the list goes on and on. But all these confused women want to know one thing. What does make a person Tahitian these days?

"Listen," says one caller, "from my point of view, to be Tahitian, you must be able to talk Tahitian, that's the most important thing." But other listeners insist that speaking the language means nothing, because anyone can learn a language but not everyone can have more than fifty percent Tahitian *toto,* blood in the veins. "Oh," an old woman snorts, "blood is just liquid, what you need is a Tahitian heart, *c'est tout.*"

"*Ah bon?*" the following listener challenges. "A Tahitian heart? I don't think so. The heart is just an organ. For me, to be Tahitian means fishing and growing taro...living like in the old days. No TV, no stereo, no car. *Aue,* be proud to be Tahitian, walk or paddle a canoe!"

Finally, one of the listeners wants to know Materena's thoughts on this serious topic. Does she consider herself Tahitian?

Words fly out of her mouth before she can think. "*Ah oui!* My father is French, but I feel one hundred percent Tahitian because..." Materena stops to think for a moment. She doesn't want to divulge too much information about her situation on the radio. Like how she's never met her French father and has Father Unknown written on her birth certificate. "...Because I was raised the Tahitian way," Materena says, hoping her listener will leave it at that.

"And how are we raised the Tahitian way?" the listener asks.

Materena leans away from the microphone to weigh her words. When you work for a radio that supports independence, you've got to be careful of what you say. Materena doesn't want to sound political. She just wants to express her personal feelings. After a quick look at her assistants behind the glass window, Materena carefully begins to explain what the Tahitian way means for her.

It means not eating in front of people if she can't share; showing respect to old people, to all people; remembering and honoring the dead; not whistling at night; and not marrying a cousin. It means helping the family; planting the child's placenta in the earth, along with a tree; singing; nurturing the soil and the ocean; doing your best by your children. It means *belonging to* a family. It also means being strong and getting up after each fall. And loving the broom — all Tahitian people, especially women — love their broom. With the broom a woman can get rid of unwanted guests without hurting their feelings by sweeping under their feet, and she keeps her floor clean too. Tahitian women are proud of their clean floor. And being Tahitian means... being diplomatic with the relatives, because you're going to bump into your relatives day after day after day until you die, so it's important to get along. Then of course, there's the respect for the mother.

When Materena finishes explaining herself there's a long silence and Materena hopes her listener isn't going to burst out laughing, "This is not Tahitian, all this! This is Christianization!"

To Materena's greatest relief, the woman, moved, simply whispers, "It's very beautiful what you've just said."

"Maururu," says Materena, and before her listener can fire another question, she hurries on with her usual line: Let's see what the next caller has to say.

By eleven o'clock Materena is bewildered. She thought Tahiti was only filled with brave women who didn't mind sharing their wonderful stories on the radio. She didn't know about these half-caste women confused over their identity and feeling like they were being cut in two.

When Materena gets home, kindly driven by Cousin Mori, she tiptoes in and gets her never-to-throw-away box from under the bed. She is careful not to wake up Pito. Being Tahitian, she thinks to herself, is also respecting people who sleep. Even when they snore like a pig because they have been out drinking all night with *les copains.*

This is the box where she keeps birth certificates and drawings by her children, along with their first tooth, their first lock of hair, and more treasures alike. She sits at the kitchen table, opens the box, and takes her birth certificate out. She lays it on the table, straightening it with the palms of her hands, and stares at those words Father Unknown. She looks away, and looks back to that sentence again, all the while thinking about the French man who gave her a dimple on her left cheek and almond-shaped eyes: Tom Delors.

Tom Delors came to Tahiti for military service and met Loana, Materena's mother, at the Zizou Bar. That night, these two eighteen-year-olds danced nonstop, fell in love, and moved in together not long after. The local people gave Loana dirty looks because back then, local women who played with *popa'a* — worse, *militaires* — had a bad reputation. They were considered sluts who were only after a ticket out of Tahiti.

Pah! Loana didn't want a ticket anywhere. She just loved Tom. But Loana left Tom six months after they had become an official couple when he criticized her chicken with split peas in front of their guests. She was so humiliated. Also five weeks pregnant with Materena, though she didn't know that yet. Loana waited for Tom to come and say *pardon* to her, and then she would have told him, I forgive you but don't you dare ever criticize my food again.

But Tom didn't come, and since Loana wasn't the kind to crawl back, she got on with her life. Later, when she found out that there was a seed growing in her belly, she cried her eyes out. But she knew there was no going back and resigned herself to her fate as a single mother.

Materena keeps on staring at her birth certificate and declares out loud, "Papa, I've been longing to know you since the age of nine years old. I'm nearly forty-one now, and I'm ready!" She even bangs a determined fist on the table.

At this precise moment Pito walks into the kitchen.

"Did I wake you?" Materena asks, ready to apologize.

"What are you doing?" he slurs, still drunk.

"Pito..." Two big tears plop out of Materena's eyes. "I'm going to look for my father."

"That *popa'a?*" Pito snorts, filling a glass with water. "You think he's going to want to know you?"

And with this declaration, Pito drinks his water and goes back to bed, unaware that he has just hurt his wife so deep she can't breathe.

A Woman — but Not Any Woman

As soon as his head hits the pillow, Pito is unconscious. He wakes up the following morning fully rested and in a cheerful mood, no hangover at all. Materena is not in bed, it means she's in the kitchen. Pito hops out of bed. He is famished! He wouldn't mind a ham omelette.

"*Chérie!*" he calls out sweetly.

No answer. That's strange.

Pito finds his wife in the living room, sitting straight like a statue on the sofa. "You've already eaten?" he asks, still being sweet.

"I'm not hungry."

Oh, Madame doesn't seem to be in a good mood. "You got up from the wrong side of the bed?" Pito teases.

Materena shrugs.

"You're cranky?"

Again Materena shrugs, and Pito understands that his wife is not talking to him. All of Materena's silent treatments begin with a shrug, and most times Pito doesn't know the reason. He just lives with it. He understands that it is something Materena does when...well, when it takes her. The best thing to do is not to insist and to leave the woman who's not talking alone until she feels better and starts talking. So Pito goes off to eat.

He's at the kitchen table with his coffee and buttered Sao biscuits when Materena decides to clean the house, dragging chairs that way, this way, with the radio switched on full blast, and Pito has one word on his mind: *escape*. He scarfs down his biscuits, gulps his coffee, delicately puts his bowl and plate in the sink, and flees out of the house through the back door just as his best friend, Ati, arrives in his car.

"Pito!" Ati calls out, switching the engine off. "What are you doing today? You want to come for a speedboat ride?"

Pito is already in Ati's car, fastening his seat belt.

And now, on this beautiful, sunny Saturday morning in Tahiti, two childhood friends are enjoying the smooth ride in the crystal green lagoon, passing women sunbaking naked on a pontoon, who shriek and hurry to cover up. Pito and Ati chuckle. When they were younger, they used to whistle and call out sweet words. Older, they might only just smile with nostalgia.

"My mama came to see me this morning," Ati says.

"Ah, and she's in good health?"

"She had a dream."

Here's the story . . .

Ati opens the door of his apartment and his mother barges in without waiting for the please-come-in invitation.

"Eh," he says, surprised, "you're not with your sister today?"

Saturday is the day Mama Angelina spends with her sister. It's been like that for as long as Ati remembers.

"*Aue!* Look at all that *bordel!*" Mama Angelina ignores her son's question and marches straight to the kitchen. She picks up an empty can of pork and beans from the bench. "You ate this last night?" Next second, Mama Angelina is at the sink doing the dishes, shaking her head at the pile of newspapers shoved in a basket. "Why do you keep all these newspapers? They attract mice. It's not as if you're in the newspapers these days. How come you're not in the newspapers anymore? You were in the newspapers all the time before."

The dishes are done and Mama Angelina wipes the bench. "I can't believe a good-looking man like you is still *célibataire*. Is it so hard to find a good woman in Tahiti? They're all over the place, open your eyes. You don't want to die without heirs." On and on Mama Angelina goes with her litany as she transforms her son's kitchen with her magical motherly hands.

Then she stops in the middle of a sentence to look at her son, who still hasn't said a word. Whispering, she asks him if he has company. "There's a woman in your bedroom? Who is she? I hope she's not married. Did you meet her at the nightclub? What did I tell you about women who go to nightclubs? What family is she from?"

Ati shakes his head. "Do you think," he says, "I would have opened the door if there was a woman in my bed?"

"Ah." Mama Angelina sounds disappointed. "You spent last night alone then? What did you do? Watch TV? All on your own..." She looks at her son with pity. "Come on, we sit, I have to talk to you about something."

"I'm going to see Pito soon."

"Leave Pito and his wife to do their things," Mama Angelina says, dragging a chair to sit on, "and think about your future."

Ati sits facing his mother and taps his fingers on the table to pass the time.

"Don't tap your fingers on the table like that. It's not po-lite." Ati stops tapping and leans back on the chair. "Don't lean on the chair like that, you're going to fall and crack your head open." So Ati stays still like a statue, his eyes on the clock slowly going *ticktock*.

"Mama?" he says at last. "And my future? It's for today or for tomorrow?"

"When was the last time you watered your plants?" Mama Angelina asks, scanning the dying potted plants scattered in the living room. "They look a bit sick to me."

"Mama!"

"Okay..." Mama Angelina takes a deep breath. "*Voilà,* last night..."

Ati waits, feeling a bit anxious now.

"I dreamed," Mama Angelina continues.

Ah, Ati is relieved. His mother only dreamed. She's always dreaming. She could write a book about all her dreams.

"I know you're thinking that I can write a book about all the dreams I have. It's not my fault I dream a lot." Mama Angelina reminds her son that dreams are messages, and her dreams have been right many times. Like when she dreamed of Ati holding a newborn, and a week later Ati was the godfather of Pito and Materena's daughter. Then there was the dream of Ati speaking into a microphone, and less than a week later, he got a job at Radio Tefana. Mama Angelina reminds her son, presently doing his I'm-getting-bored expression, of how she dreamed of him packing his suitcase days before he moved out to live in this apartment without a view.

"And last night," she continues sadly, "in my dream, I saw your sister and her husband and —"

"She was yelling at him," Ati says.

"*Non, non,* she wasn't yelling at all, she was sitting under a tree with her husband and their eight children and they were smiling, they looked very happy and you —"

"I was dancing with a pretty woman," Ati chuckles.

"Not at all . . . you were crying."

"Eh?"

"You were crying," Mama Angelina repeats, teary now, "and there was nobody with you and you were old." Mama Angelina takes her son's hand. "Ati, maybe it's fun what you're doing now, one woman, another woman, lots of women, but who is going to look after you when you get old?"

"Myself!" Ati takes his hand away.

"How come you can't stay with a woman for more than two weeks?"

"Mama, it's not your onions."

"And what about your political career?"

"What about it?" Ati snaps.

"Ati, listen to me." Mama Angelina has her serious voice now. "We don't vote for politicians who don't have a wife, children. A politician without a family can talk and promise things but nobody is going to believe him and . . . Anyway" — Mama Angelina waves a hand in the air — "I didn't come here to talk about your career, I came here to talk about your situation."

"I'm very happy with my situation."

"You're happy now, but in a few years —" Mama Angelina sighs like she's so stressed by her son's situation. "Find yourself a good woman, Ati."

"Hum," Ati agrees, thinking that the problem with good women is that they're already taken.

"Do you want me to find you a good woman?" Mama Angelina asks eagerly. She insists that she knows what a man wants in a woman. She knows because she's lived with a man for more than thirty years.

According to Mama Angelina, the first thing a man wants in a woman is for her to be nice, but she's got to be nice to look at too. Not too beautiful though, otherwise he'll be spending his time being jealous.

A good cook, but there's no need for her to be a *cordon bleu* — when food is cooked, it's edible. Tidy, but there's no need for her to be a neat freak, because men are not obsessed with tidiness as long as they can find socks and towels.

Not the kind who plays games. Men don't like women who play games, they like women who say what they think, easygoing women, someone you can laugh with after work and have a few drinks. A bit masculine on the surface and —

Ati gets up, meaning, Thanks for your visit. To make his message clearer, Ati kisses his mother good-bye.

Mama Angelina slowly rises and leaves. But not before telling her son that with all the women he's had in his life none have truly loved him because none have wanted to have his children.

"When a woman loves a man," she says, stopping the door with her foot, "she wants his children. Hurry up, Ati. Find that woman."

As the door closes, she adds that he's forty-three and that soon he's going to be infertile.

This is Ati's story for the day, and from now on, so Ati tells Pito, he might have to start meeting women in a restaurant. In his mind, the restaurant is a great place for a man to get intimate with a woman. You don't get distracted like you do (and so easily) when you're in bed and she has you by the *couilles.* Now, Ati is not saying that a man can't get intimate with a woman in bed (because he does), but he's looking for something else these days.

Ati has never invited a woman to the restaurant, he continues. To the bar, *oui,* the hotel, *oui,* his mother's house, *oui,* his apartment, *oui,* but never to the restaurant. For him, restaurants are for couples who have been married for too long and for friends who are not that close.

"Oh," Pito shrugs, "me and restaurants —"

Also, Ati continues, he must stay clear of married women. Married women are very discreet, and they are, well, very, well...no need to draw a picture. What Ati means to say is that when a married woman decides to fool around, the man she chooses will be spending a very pleasant evening indeed, and then there's no harassing him the morning after. She doesn't ask, "When are you going to call me? Are you going to call me?" She just gives him one last passionate kiss, her hands firmly grabbing him on the arse, then she winks at him, blows him a kiss, and leaves.

Oui, Ati has a very weak spot for married women, but he wants something more now. "Ah, you're lucky, *copain,*" he sighs, one hand on the motor gearshift and the other resting on his knee. "How come a woman like Materena never came my way?"

"Try living with her," Pito grunts.

A Story of Arse

Usually, cleaning the house calms Materena. She has used that technique many times in her life as a mother *and* a wife, but the problem is that there's not much cleaning to do since her three children have left home. So Materena, now picking up fluff off the carpet, is still shocked and fuming about the words that came out of Pito's mouth last night. He did well to disappear before she picked up the kitchen knife and killed him.

She doesn't understand his meanness. Why wouldn't her father want to know her, eh? She's not a beggar, she's not living in the streets. And her parents' story — it wasn't just a story of arse. They had tender moments together, Tom and Loana... Could it really be true that her husband thinks so little of her?

A tear rolls down Materena's cheek. She wonders if she will ever forgive Pito completely.

The phone rings and Materena goes to answer it, dragging her feet with her carpet fluff rolled into a ball. She's not in the mood to talk, but it could be one of her children calling.

Sure enough, as she picks up the phone, she hears the international click before her daughter's sweet voice calls out, "*Iaorana,*

Mamie!" Out of three children living away from home, the one calling home the most is the daughter.

"Eh!" Materena immediately feels much better. "You're fine, *chérie?*"

"I'm fine, Mamie, and you?"

"All is fine, *chérie. Alors,* what is the news?"

Well, the news is the same — studies are getting harder, four more students have dropped out, but Leilani is determined to get her medical degree — she knows she was born to save people's lives. Otherwise, she's still enjoying her part-time job at the bookshop, caught up with brother Tamatoa, and made a new friend...Leilani rambles on, and Materena knows that it's only a matter of time before she comes back to her favorite topic of conversation: the ex-boyfriend she left behind so that she could fulfill her purpose in life.

Hotu, sexy dentist: good-looking, down-to-earth young man who has already spent years studying overseas. Hotu this, Hotu that, fabulous rowing champion, more sexy than him you die. Hotu, whom Materena is not allowed to call because he might think Leilani is spying on him, but at the same time, should Materena see something about Hotu in the newspapers (like a marriage announcement, for example), Materena is to immediately report the news to Leilani.

And Materena is to definitely go and see Hotu in the flesh if Leilani dies — Leilani said this two weeks ago as a joke! She'd like her body repatriated back to Tahiti, of course, and for Hotu to dig her hole. She wants sweat pouring down his sexy back and she gives him permission to give her one last passionate kiss on her mouth. He doesn't need to act proper at her wake, kissing her on the forehead. Kiss her on the mouth!

"Mamie," Leilani gushes, "I bought the cologne that Hotu uses.

"*Ah bon?*"

"*Oui,* and I spray it on my wrists when I go to bed, I smell my wrists and inhale him . . . I close my eyes, and I see —"

"And what do you see?"

"I can't tell you!" Leilani exclaims.

"Ah . . . it's like that, eh?"

Cackling, Leilani also admits that whenever she sees a man of Hotu's build, her heart goes *bip-bip!* Here, yesterday she was walking to the bookshop where she works, when she saw a man hailing a taxi. He was tall, with a newspaper tucked under his arm, and from behind he looked a bit like Hotu. Leilani froze, right there in the middle of the footpath with people walking past and knocking her on the shoulders. She was like a coconut tree. And her heart was going *bip-bip!*

She was so tempted to phone Hotu afterwards just to hear his voice, but they had agreed not to call each other because it would make things difficult but . . . Ah, she misses him like crazy. "Mamie, I'm sure you know what I'm talking about, it must have been the same for you when Papi was in France for military service."

"Girl, that was a long time ago," Materena says, though she still remembers those days. *Ah oui,* she was obsessed with that boy Pito Tehana she used to meet in secret under the frangipani tree behind the bank. That was before he left for military service in France. And for the two whole years, Materena stayed faithful. She didn't look at any other boys. She wasn't even Pito's official girlfriend back then, just this girl he knew and who was crazy about him.

For two years Pito was constantly on Materena's mind. She'd be slicing onions or folding clothes and she would see him, just like that. Sometimes he was smiling, sometimes he was winking. Other times he was kissing her on the mouth. And every day, for two whole years, Materena asked God for signs that Pito was thinking about her too. She even prayed.

"You prayed?" Leilani sounds like she thinks it's funny her mother prayed.

"*Oui,* I prayed. I kneeled in front of the Virgin Mary, Understanding Woman, and prayed the same prayer. 'Please make Pito come home to me, please don't let him fall in love with a girl there in France, Amen.' You know your grandmother was very worried. One day, she said to me, 'Girl, that's a lot of praying you're doing, I hope you're not asking the Virgin Mary, Understanding Woman, for a miracle.'"

"Well, your prayers were answered," Leilani giggles.

"Your father didn't even send me a postcard."

"Oh, Papi isn't the kind to send people postcards, that's all. I don't even know if he can write." Leilani hurries to add, "Not like you, I mean. For someone who left school at fourteen to clean houses, you write well, Mamie, and you never make spelling mistakes. And you are so strong, everybody likes you, and you have fans —"

"I don't have fans," Materena laughs.

"You do, stop fishing for compliments, of course you have fans. If you didn't have fans, your program would have been already axed."

"Ah." Materena has never thought of her listeners as fans.

"And what else are you up to?" Leilani asks.

"Well, I'm learning to drive."

"Mamie! You are a champion! *Eh-eh,* poor Papi, he must be feeling so intimidated by you, but he's proud of you, he told me when he called me last week —"

"Papi called you?" Materena asks, surprised.

"Well *oui!* I'm not just your child, you know." Leilani continues her story. Last week, when her father called for the first time, he said that he was very proud of Materena for her radio program and that he had listened to it once. *Enfin,* ten minutes of it. A woman was complaining of an article in the newspapers about a fisherman who had caught a four-hundred-pound tuna. The lucky fisherman was beside himself, he was going to get lots of money for his fish. But then he found out that his fish was pregnant, it had eggs, and the value of the fish dropped dramatically. "What are men trying to tell us?" the enraged woman shrieked at the top of her lungs, hurting Pito's ears. "That when a woman is pregnant, her value drops?" Pito switched the radio off, telling himself, It's not true! Women are taking themselves for fishes now?

"You see?" Leilani cackles. "You can't say that Papi isn't trying to be supportive of you." In her opinion this is a big step for her father to be taking, considering that he must be feeling a bit threatened at the moment. "But you know Papi, he's a good man, he has his heart on his sleeve."

"Oh," Materena says vaguely, "when he wants to." She can't believe Hotu isn't dominating all of today's conversation.

"It's like with Hotu and me."

He's back!

"You intimidate him?" Materena asks.

"But *non,* he's confident, he's living his dreams, *non,* we've never intimidated each other, but look at us now — I'm here, he's there. Doing sexy loving with a COCONUT-HEAD!"

"Oh, how do you know this?" Materena does the reassuring voice. "He's probably crying on his pillow for you."

"Mamie, he's a man," says Leilani, her sigh filled with resignation: you can't change the world, men are like that, they need action, whereas women can go the distance with the memories and scents that go straight to the head.

"Ah this, you said it, girl!" Materena exclaims. She knows what she's talking about. While she was in Tahiti dreaming about her boyfriend Pito night and day, that *con* was doing romance with French girls. According to Pito, Tahitian military servicemen were very popular with the French girls — they found them exotic, with their smooth chocolate skin. Pito (still according to Pito) only had to wink and the girls jumped on him.

"But not all men are the same," Leilani adds. "Hotu and I had something very special."

"True."

"Our story wasn't just a story of arse . . ." Leilani's voice cracks. "We had our ups and downs . . . like you and Papi."

And Materena sighs, a heavy sigh from the soles of her feet.

"Like everyone, *chérie.*"

Bread Crumbs

When Pito came home from his speedboat wandering with Ati on Saturday, Materena wasn't home, and by the time he went to bed after a frugal dinner (corned beef straight out of the can), Materena was still not home. It was a nice surprise for Pito to open his eyes on Sunday morning and see Materena next to him. He was very tempted to try his luck, but decided otherwise — Materena never wants to do sexy loving before mass. But then Pito thought, eh, maybe she's going to be interested if I do this...

Then the phone rang and Materena sprang out of bed to answer it. Bloody telephone, Pito told himself, there's never a moment of peace, it's only quarter past five! Later, in the kitchen, he overheard part of Materena's conversation with Rita. "Eh, eh, Cousin," Materena was saying, "you got your period again... Rita, don't worry, okay? Baby is going to come when he's ready, eh? You've only been trying for the past five months, sometimes it takes a bit longer... True, at least it's a lot of fun trying! *Oui,* Cousin, I see you at mass."

At the church, Materena completely ignored Pito as she always does — when her relatives are around, her husband doesn't exist — and left with Rita immediately after mass.

By the time Pito went to bed after yet another frugal dinner (corned beef straight out of the can), Materena still wasn't home and he didn't hear her get into bed in the middle of the night. She must have sneaked in.

When Pito gets up next morning she's still in bed, fast asleep, her eyes closed very tight. It's not like Materena — Madame Énergie — to be in bed after six thirty in the morning. Even the next day after coming home from the hospital with a new-born baby, Materena would be up at five getting things done; *café,* breadsticks, omelettes; watering plants; being busy.

Pito watches his wife for a while, thinking how tired she looks. He bends down to kiss her on the head, then pauses; he might wake her up. So, walking very quiet steps, Pito leaves for work, worried a little and starving hungry. He didn't have much to eat this morning. There was nothing in the fridge.

Now, lunchtime, he's devouring his sandwich as if his life depended on it. All the colleagues are — working does make a man hungry — except for Heifara, sitting with his mouth shut, his eyes staring at the sandwich bought at the snack nearby. He's been weird all morning, actually. It's not like him not to talk.

"Heifara," Pito says, "*tama'a.*"

Heifara looks at him for a minute before deciding to spill the bucket. "I'm in a difficult situation."

"*Ah oui?*" Pito asks, to show some interest.

"*Oui,* I'm in a very difficult situation," Heifara says. He looks at his colleagues to see if they'd like to hear about it, and they seem interested. So Heifara tells his story about his difficult situation with his wife.

When he came back from his two-week surfing holiday in Huahine, relaxed and in a very good mood, things weren't quite right. There was no "Oh, *chéri!* Welcome home! I missed you so much, make love to me!" from his wife. *Non.* Instead, what she actually said was, "I want a separation."

Heifara admits to his surprised colleagues that *oui,* of course he was shattered. *"Salope,"* he spits.

"Just like that?" Pito asks, confused. The last time Heifara talked about his wife, she couldn't keep her hands off him, she was wild with desire. Okay, that was about six months ago, but still, eh? Now she wants a separation?

Heifara confirms the fact with a sad nod and raises his left hand, the one with the missing finger, the finger he lost years ago when his wedding band was caught in the machine, shredding it to pieces.

Heifara always raises his left hand (since he lost the finger) whenever he talks about his wife. My wife, he says, winking and raising his left hand as if to say, My wife is worth me having nine fingers instead of ten. But today the raised hand looks more like it's saying, I lost a finger because I married that bitch!

Pito remembers when Heifara joined the company and how much he got on everyone's nerves. When a colleague gave the young recruit advice regarding work safety, Heifara would say, "Yeah, I know." Soon Heifara's nickname was "Monsieur I Know." Then he lost a finger and the colleagues said, "Serves him right, he never bloody listens," but they kept an eye on him for months after the unfortunate accident. Nobody wanted another lost finger.

Heifara, sad-faced, still has his mutilated hand in the air.

Purée, Pito thinks, looking at his colleague from under his eyelashes as he finishes his sandwich, is this what a man gets when he goes away on a short holiday after months working like a dog in the heat and the noise, and for the lowest pay on the island? "Your wife," Pito asks, curious, "she was cranky with you when you took off to Huahine for two weeks?"

Heifara informs his audience that *non,* his wife wasn't cranky at all, and in fact, she had a smile from one ear to the other. "Have a wonderful time!" she said sweetly when she dropped Heifara off at the domestic terminal. "I hope you're going to catch millions of waves!"

Millions? Pito tells himself. This is an angry woman talking.

"She said..." Heifara's voice trails off. He needs to find the correct words to express his disenchantment, and the colleagues aren't going to hurry him up. They just look at him with compassion because he's young. If Heifara were their age, they might have said, "Ah, pull yourself together, *copain,* you're going to give us a bad name." But right now, the colleagues, Pito included, are thinking, Take your time, kid, if we ever came back from holiday and the wife said, "I want a separation," we would... Well, *purée de bonsoir,* there would be holes in the walls.

Anyway, Heifara continues, she told him that she'd been unhappy for the past two years and has tried to tell him about it but he didn't listen. "She's talking *conneries,*" Heifara spits. For instance, his wife said that she'd tried — millions of times — to make him understand that she needed help around the house. But when Heifara did help with the housework on the weekend, his wife would always get cranky. "Get out of my way!" she'd growl. "You're only making things more difficult for me. I have other cats to whip."

Heifara used to help his wife doing the shopping too but everything he'd put in the cart was the wrong thing. "I never buy that brand!" she'd snap, putting whatever he'd picked back on the shelf. She said that she'd tried — millions of times — to tell Heifara that she needed him to spend more time at home.

But when Heifara would make an effort, sitting on the couch with his wife to watch TV instead of going out drinking with his *copains,* she'd say, "Stop touching me! I'm watching a movie! If you think it's easy looking after two small children all day, you have nothing in the head!"

Anyway, the wife told Heifara all of this the day he came home from his wonderful surfing holiday. She also criticized his hair (not combed), his breath (foul), his table manners (worse), his dressing style (*zéro*), his snoring, and the way he listens to her with only one ear... She called him selfish and then hit him with the news of the century: "I want a separation. Read my lips. It's finished. I don't want to be jam given to pigs anymore."

"What am I supposed to do, eh?" young Heifara asks his colleagues. But the older men have nothing to say, not even Pito, the colleague who has been with the same woman the longest. But they're all thinking the same thing: Is this what my woman thinks about me?

"How come you didn't ask your wife to go with you on your holiday?" This question just popped into Pito's head. He doesn't know why, especially when he already knows the reason why Heifara went on his holiday alone, and presently the colleagues are giving Pito strange looks, meaning, What? Are you insane? If the wife comes, the holiday isn't a holiday anymore!

"My wife coming with me?" Heifara laughs a faint laugh. "Are you insane?" He explains that firstly, his wife would have commanded him to leave his surfboards at home, and secondly, she would have changed the holiday destination to a place like Hawaii because of the shopping. And then Heifara would have had to spend his hard-earned holiday following his wife from one shop to the next, carrying shopping bags filled with cheap *conneries.*

"She loves cheap *conneries,*" Heifara says. "She's always buying cheap *conneries,* like plastic baskets, there are plastic baskets all over the house, and they are filled with cheap *conneries* like plastic fruit. Who keeps plastic fruit in plastic baskets? Plastic apples? Plastic bananas? She loves plastic containers too, but how many plastic containers does someone need, eh? I don't think hundreds. She's obsessed with plastic things."

The colleagues nod, but it's time to get back to work. They don't get paid to listen to complicated stories.

Half an hour later, Heifara is still talking about his wife to Pito, the colleague nearest to him, but the sad voice is now bitter.

"And then she said," Heifara spits, sweating away over a plank of wood, " 'Smile! Stop doing that sad face. When I look at you, I want to give you slaps!' And then I said, 'What's there to be happy about? You ruined my life, you *salope.* You've got the house, you've got the kids, I've got *peau de balle et variété!* Peanuts!' And then she said, 'You should have listened to me when you had the chance to.' Then I said, 'I was always there for you, *salope,* I paid for all those plastic things.' Then she said, 'Women don't care about things! Women want love! They don't want to be the bread crumbs!' And then I said, 'Women don't care about plastic things?' And then she said, 'Ah, for once you're not deaf!' So I grabbed all of her stupid fucking plastic things, her stupid fucking plastic bananas, her stupid fucking plastic apples, and I threw them out of the kitchen window, and next thing, she was yelling her head off, 'Stop! My fruit didn't do anything to you! Stop!' And then I said, 'I thought you said that women don't care about plastic things?' She spit in my face, so I grabbed her by the hair and —"

Pito, worried, looks up.

"And," Heifara continues, breathing heavily, "and then she said, 'Touch me and my father is going to turn you into mincemeat.'

44

I let go of her hair and went to bed, and the next day this *salope* said —"

"Heifara," Pito, relieved, interrupts. "Concentrate on your work."

"I'm concentrating," Heifara reassures his colleague, and continues, his eyes on the plank he's cutting. "And then she said that her lawyer informed her that she was entitled to sixty percent of my pay. And then I said, 'Tell your lawyer to go fuck himself.' And then she said, 'If you don't give me sixty percent of your pay, I'm reporting you to the tribunal.' And then I said, 'You *salope*,' and then she said, 'You better mind your words or you can forget about having the children on the weekends.' And then I said..." Heifara's voice trails off.

Pito looks up.

"And then I said nothing. If I don't see my kids, I die." Heifara's lips quiver.

The young father is about to do his crying cinema, so Pito gives him a quick, affectionate tap on the shoulder and goes back to work. Meanwhile, tears are plopping out of Heifara's eyes. "And then I said, 'Please give me one more chance,' and then she said, 'Where were you when I needed you? I've tried to save our marriage but you didn't care, and now it's my turn not to care.' And then she went on and on about things that I told her years ago when we were just boyfriend and girlfriend... But I never told her that I was going to take her to Paris one day. I never told her that I was going to write her name on my surfboard. She's crazy. I said to her, 'You're fucking crazy.' Next thing, she was yelling her head off, 'Don't tell me that I'm crazy!' I said, 'Shut up, you *salope*.' And —"

"You know, she's right," Pito says.

"Who?" Heifara asks.

"Your wife, what's her name again?"

"Juanita?"

"*Oui,* her, your wife."

"What about my wife?"

"She's right."

"About what?"

"Do you listen to yourself talk sometimes?" Pito looks at his colleague, thinking, This kid needs a bit of education. "Rule number one: never call a woman *salope* to her face."

"What if she is a *salope?*" Heifara asks.

"Rule number two: learn to shut up and listen."

"Is this what you do?" Heifara asks, very seriously. "With your wife?"

Pito has to think about this one. "It depends on the situation."

"Do you go on holidays with your wife?"

"My wife likes nothing I like." By this Pito means fishing, soccer, reading comics in bed, and drinking at the bar.

Later, in the truck on his way home, Pito thinks about that holiday he took years ago...it must be twelve years ago, because Moana broke his arm the day before...Anyway, when he came home, Materena gave him the silent treatment for three days and he didn't ask her why. He just lived with it. And there was that other time...Meanwhile, the seven-year-old opposite Pito is telling his mother that he has to wear red clothes tomorrow at school. "You're telling me this now?" the tired mother says through clenched teeth.

"I told you about the red clothes on Sunday, but you were on the telephone with your boyfriend!" The kid doesn't care there are people listening.

When Pito hops off the truck, his mind is made up. Yes, he will spend his next holiday, which is in a few months, with his wife. They will go to the cinema and watch a kung fu movie;

they will go fishing, share a few drinks at the bar, read Akim comic books in bed, and have sex. Whatever they do, they will have a lot of fun.

There, it's decided, and since Pito is very serious about this, he will reveal his wonderful plans to Materena as soon as he gets home. He will commit himself. True commitment — in Pito's opinion — is not given for peace and quiet and it's definitely not because there's something to gain at the end. When commitment is given, words become sacred, they're not just words.

For example, when Pito tells Materena he'll take the garbage out, he isn't really committing himself, it's just words so that she'll get off his back or so he can get into her pants. When he tells Materena he'll climb up the breadfruit tree to get her a breadfruit, it isn't commitment either, it's just words so she'll get off his back or so he can get into her pants.

Pito would be the first to admit he's told Materena, "*Oui,* I'm going to do it," many times but didn't get around to living up to his promise because, well, because he got satisfied, or he forgot.

But when Pito says something he really means, you can rely on him one hundred percent. When Pito says he'll put food on the table, he will. When Pito says he'll keep his job until retirement in loving memory of his uncle who got him that job, he will. When Pito says he'll mow his mother's garden until the day she dies, he will. And when Pito says that he'll spend his next holiday with his wife, that's what will happen.

Pito finds Materena in their daughter's bedroom staring at the world map taped to the wall. "Ah, you're feeling better." Pito's voice is full of honey, and he's smiling a big loving smile. "And what country are you looking at, Madame?"

Materena, with pursed lips and dangerous cranky eyes, shrugs her shoulders and leaves the room, flicking her hair in her husband's face on her way.

"I was thinking of spending my next holiday with you, *chérie!*" Pito calls out, following his wife out of the room.

"*Non merci!*" And the door slams shut.

Pito stands by the door, stunned. Bloody women! It doesn't matter what we do, it's always the wrong thing. Angry now, Pito opens the door and heads to the kitchen. Materena is at the kitchen table, munching on a piece of bread.

"If I understand," Pito says with a cold voice, "you don't want me to spend my next holidays with you."

Materena swallows her piece of bread and shrugs. "You know, Pito, I used to wish that you spent your holidays with us, with the kids and me... Actually, I used to wish for a lot of things." She brushes the bread crumbs into her hand. "Now, I wish for nothing."

Silent Treatment

This has never happened before in their life as a couple — a five-day silent treatment. Three days is the furthest Materena has ever gone before she cracked and made some remark about the weather, giving Pito the chance to redeem himself for whatever he did or didn't do.

Those other times, Pito never got sad when his wife gave him the silent treatment, because he could do whatever he wanted and she wouldn't say a word about it. He could lie on the sofa like a statue for hours and Materena would act like he didn't exist. Still, by the third day Pito was always glad when it was over. It's not much fun when your wife doesn't speak to you.

But five days! Five days — and for what? Pito is so confused. And lately Materena has been doing a lot of sighing, not the annoyed sighing she does with the eye rolling when she's . . . well, annoyed. *Non.* Her sighing is deep and long like Pito's mother used to do — a lot, in between yelling — when Pito was a child. His mother would sigh deep and long sighs, one after another, and yell, "When the heart sighs . . . it means it doesn't have what it desires!"

Pito even asked Materena this morning why she was so cranky at him, and she gave him a long look, the look that says, If I have to explain everything to you...

Puzzled, Pito left for work not feeling one hundred percent, and while waiting for the truck, he noticed Loma on the other side of the road, waving a big friendly wave to him. Pito thought it was very strange, Loma waving at him like that, so he didn't wave back. Then she called out, "You're still on the horizon? I thought Materena replaced you with a rich Chinese man!" Then she laughed her head off as if it were a joke.

Luckily Pito is used to big-mouth Loma spurting out stupid remarks, otherwise he would have gotten black ideas and started to hassle Loma for information about that Chinese man. Still, Pito's face must have had a crushed expression, because later on in the truck two women looked at him with pity.

As soon as Pito got to work, he put on his normal work face — the kind that reveals absolutely nothing. He never takes his trouble to work, unlike some people he knows. As far as Pito is concerned, whatever happens at home (good or bad, especially bad) is nobody's onions.

Safely positioned behind the cutting machine, Pito throws himself into his work, ignoring Heifara's miseries; each to their own miseries *s'il vous plaît*.

Now, later in the day, Pito is in the reception office to use the telephone.

"And hurry up, okay?" Josephine the receptionist says. The reception telephone is for brief messages only, not long family legends. Pito reassures Josephine. He never talks on the telephone for more than thirty seconds anyway. He's not a telephone man.

"Who are you calling?" Josephine asks out of curiosity, since Pito has never used the reception telephone before.

"My wife." That's all Pito is going to say. Josephine doesn't need to know that he's calling his wife to see if she'd like him to get her something at the market. Like taro...or a big juicy watermelon.

"Ah." Josephine goes back to her typing. "Everything is all right?"

"*Oui,* of course." Pito is firm about this.

"Ah...that's good." Josephine adds that she's relieved to see that Materena is still her wonderful self. She hasn't let fame go to her head (and she's kept her husband, who doesn't earn much money and who's not very intelligent, which Josephine doesn't say).

But, she tells Pito, Materena must have a lot of men admirers now, eh?

"Eh?" Josephine asks again.

"She's always had men admirers." Pito forces a chuckle. "It's not just from today."

"And she still cooks for you?"

"*Oui.*"

"That's nice." Josephine smiles. "You are very lucky. Another wife would have told you to cook your own food now that she's a star and she can have any man cook her any dish she likes and kiss her feet at the same time." Josephine pauses to ponder a little. "I hope you appreciate Materena."

"I appreciate." And with that statement Pito dials home.

"Tell Materena I said *bonjour,*" adds Josephine.

Nodding, Pito waits for Materena to pick up the phone, which she does after the third ring. "*Iaorana!*" Materena sings with her good-mood voice, making Pito feel very relieved.

"Materena," Pito whispers sweetly into the telephone, his back turned to the big-ears receptionist. "I'm calling you to see if you —" Pito stops; something is bizarre here. Materena is still talking. "I'm not at the house at the moment, or maybe I'm just outside watering the plants, or maybe I'm at the Chinese store, but I'm not going to be too long. Leave a message after the beep. And don't forget to tell me your telephone number!"

Beep. Pito hangs up.

"What happened?" the receptionist asks.

"It was a machine."

"Why didn't you leave a message?" Josephine does her big eyes, shaking her head with disapproval. She also has an answering machine, she tells Pito, and she detests it when people hang up instead of leaving a message, as if leaving a message were like asking for the moon. Josephine continues on and on about how many of her relatives have told her off for getting an answering machine but any Tahitian with the right mind knows that when it comes to telephones, you must be selective, otherwise nothing would ever get done. It shouldn't be that way, really, Josephine explains to Pito, standing still like a statue at the door. Ah, *oui alors,* people who have telephones shouldn't have to answer their telephone praying it is someone they want to talk to and not a cousin who needs ears for hours, eh?

"...Eh?" Josephine demands.

"*Oui,*" he agrees, escaping through the door.

After work, Pito decides to visit his brother Frank, and here's the Range Rover parked in front of the house, so he's home. Good. Sister-in-law Vaiana is on the veranda drinking a martini with her *copines.* She's wearing a gigantic pandanus hat and waving one hand around to show off her rings, while the other hand is delicately placed on her chest as if to say, "I couldn't believe it...they were actually talking about *moi!*"

Pito knows where to find his brother, but when you visit Frank Tehana, you must first report to Madame, otherwise she complains, whining for days and days about his family's lack of respect.

"He's in his tomato plantation," Vaiana coldly advises her brother-in-law. She used to adore Pito and call him sweet names, "my little cabbage, my little treasure," until one night after a few drinks, she tried to jump on Pito for a bit of beefsteak and he pushed her away. She's never forgiven him.

Pito sneaks in between the row of banana trees and finds his brother comfortable on a mat smoking *paka,* a family-size packet of chips and a big bottle of Coca-Cola nearby.

"Pito!" An embrace, friendly taps on the back, and a *paka* cigarette. Frank knows how to greet family. Anyone, actually.

"Your wife still thinks you're growing tomatoes?" Pito asks, lighting up.

"I don't talk about my plantation with Vaiana."

"Ah. Otherwise, all is fine?"

"All is fine, little brother, and you? All is fine?"

"All is fine," Pito says.

End of conversation. The brothers smoke away. They've never been big-mouths, these two. As children, Frank, the eldest of the tribe, and Pito, the youngest, talked to each other with hands, eyebrows, eyes, and grunts, and they always understood each other.

"Come eat."

"Go and get me a glass of water, *ha'aviti,* quick, I'm thirsty."

"Shhh, not a word to Mamie about my plants, otherwise I'm going to give you one black-buttered eye."

Despite the limited *parau-parau,* Pito has always felt very close to Frank. Pito felt the same with his other two brothers, Tama and Viri, too. But then the sisters-in-law arrived and everything changed. If Pito wants to talk to Tama he can, but only at the gate of Tama's wife's house — she doesn't like visitors. If Pito wants to talk to Viri he can, but only on Viri's wife's telephone — she doesn't like visitors. At least with Frank, all Pito has to do is report to Madame.

"You went to see Papi?" Pito asks.

A nod meaning *oui,* a nostalgic smile meaning, I still miss Papi.

Pito sighs: Me too.

Their poor father couldn't sit for two minutes without his woman yelling at him to go and do something. It seemed to Pito that his mother's mission in life was to see sweat on Frank senior's forehead twenty-four hours a day, it wasn't enough that he had three jobs so that she could buy herself the beautiful things she felt she deserved.

One morning a week after Pito's circumcision, when a boy supposedly becomes a man, Pito told his father (springing to his feet at Mama Roti's shout *"Frank!"*) to have a rest if he wanted.

The father replied, "Son, all a man wants in life is peace." Three months later he was dead.

After his wake, Mama Roti put their mattress next to the coffin and lay there staring at her dead husband and crying her eyes out. She cried nonstop for two whole weeks. She sat at the kitchen table with her red wine and caressed her shiny new wedding ring, singing the praises of her Frank *chéri* who had married her on his hospital deathbed. "My love, come back to me," Mama Roti lamented. "I'm the sky without stars, the tree without roots, the flower without petals."

Pito's ears were hurting. For him, all of this was hypocrisy. His mother was just repeating words from a song.

Pito digs a hand into the packet of chips his brother is holding out to him, thinking, what a miserable life his father had. Then again, maybe he was just one of those men who can't function without a woman to issue commandments and instructions.

"Huh?" says Frank, handing Pito the bottle of Coca-Cola.

Pito takes a sip, relieved he hasn't turned out like his father. Unlike his three brothers, who can't fart without their wife's permission. Ah true, he nods to himself, he can be proud. He fought hard to be where he is today as the man of the house.

But did he really? Or did he just slip into this man's act because Materena let him? Because... well, because she's not the kind to shout and order people around like his mother.

Now that the *pakalolo* is taking effect, Pito realizes quite clearly that Materena is everything his mother isn't. To begin with, she's a very good cook, and she's tidy and neat. She smiles a lot, she's patient... and she doesn't judge people. She is, without exaggerating, the most loving person Pito has ever known in his whole life.

Later, walking through the door of his house, spaced out a bit but very relaxed, Pito finds himself wishing his wife *would* yell at him for once. He wants to know what he's done wrong.

Love for a Man

Materena bumps into Cousin Tapeta on her way into the Chinese store; Tapeta, holding breadsticks, on her way out.

"Cousin! *E aha te huru?*" Two big kisses on the cheeks follow, with a big warm hug.

"And how is our Rose in the country of kangaroos?" Today it's Materena's turn to begin the interrogation about the absent daughters.

"Kangaroo, kangaroo," Tapeta laughs. "I tell you one thing, Cousin, the only kangaroos Rose sees are on postcards and tea towels. Otherwise, my Rose is still walking around Sydney with baby Taina-Duke in a pram, hoping to bump into someone from the island."

"*Ah oui?* And?"

"So far, because our Rose is counting, she's bumped into twenty-five Maoris and twelve Samoans."

"Really? No Tahitians?"

"All the Tahitians live in Tahiti or in France, my poor girl, eh? But the story I wanted to tell you today, Cousin, is that last Saturday Rose drove to the Fijian market to buy a breadfruit."

Materena cackles. Rose used to complain about the bread-fruit diet, and Materena would tell her niece, "One day, Rose, you are going to love the breadfruit like your mama and I do."

Well, after years growing up complaining of the breadfruit diet (even if Tapeta has always gone to great lengths to vary the menu, alternating it from fried breadfruit to barbecued bread-fruit to baked breadfruit, et cetera), Rose suddenly felt the urge to reconnect with the food of her childhood. Her stomach yearned for breadfruit. Her mouth could even taste the warm, soft flesh of cooked breadfruit when it melts on your tongue and you want to eat more even if you're full.

But when she finally got to the Fijian market after the three near-miss accidents (because, so Tapeta explains, they drive on the wrong side in Australia), Rose was very disappointed to see a yellow squashy thing that didn't look like a breadfruit at all. In her experience as a Tahitian, breadfruit is green and firm, and it's round like a little soccer ball or a big mango. It's not yellow, and it doesn't have a bizarre shape.

She asked the shopkeeper, "Are you sure this is a breadfruit? It's such a bizarre shape." Next thing, the little Fijian man was yelling at Rose, "Of course this is a breadfruit! Do you think I don't know what a breadfruit looks like?" In the end, Rose bought the yellow squashy thing, baked it, ate it, and spat it out. She's not sure if the weird taste had something to do with cooking the breadfruit in an electric oven instead of gas, or if that breadfruit was just plain rotten. "What do you think, Cousin?" Tapeta asks.

"I'm sure that breadfruit was fine, but it wasn't to Rose's taste because it wasn't the same breadfruit she's eaten all her life."

Tapeta nods knowingly. "Our breadfruit is special, eh?"

"*Ah oui,* I think so."

"You know I'm saving for my daughter and granddaughter's fares," Tapeta continues. "Every payday I hide a few coins in a sock and I hide that sock in a paper bag and then I hide that paper bag in —" Tapeta stops. "This is a secret, okay, Cousin?"

"Of course!"

"I hide that paper bag under the mattress because if my good-for-nothing husband sees the money, it's for sure he's going to drink it."

"Why don't you just put the money in a bank account?" Materena seriously suggests.

Tapeta admits that so far she has saved only about two thousand francs and it isn't much, considering that the plane ticket costs about three hundred thousand francs. However, it's a start. "I don't want my daughter and my granddaughter to be stuck in Australia because of a money problem," she says. "If Rose wants to come home, she can. The money is my problem. Rose says to me, 'Mamie, I love my husband.' But Cousin," Tapeta says, looking very concerned, "love doesn't last."

"Hum."

"Love for a man, I mean," Tapeta explains.

"I understood you."

"I call to my daughter every day, and every night." In her head, Tapeta asserts, not on the telephone. In her head and in her heart.

"Maybe it's best you stop calling, Cousin." This is Materena's piece of advice for the day. "Her life is in Australia now. Give Rose the chance to adapt."

Tapeta sighs, meaning, *Oui,* I know. "But I'm so worried, Cousin. My girl is all on her own there. She has no job, no money, she has nobody to help her with the baby, nobody to defend her. She's at her husband's mercy. He can do whatever he wants to her and she can't say nothing."

"Cousin," Materena says, putting a reassuring hand on Tapeta's shoulder. "You know your Rose. She's not the kind to let people walk all over her. When she doesn't agree, she opens her mouth."

"*Eh hia tamari'i...*" Tapeta forces laughter. "And how is our Leilani in France?" It is Tapeta's turn to show some interest.

"*Aue,* same, Cousin. She feels lonely."

"She doesn't have any friends?"

"*Oui,* she has, but what she really wants is family." Materena continues about Leilani growing up complaining that she had too many aunties, too many spies, too many ears, too many questions, but now Leilani wishes she had a few relatives living around the corner. Oh, Leilani wouldn't appreciate them visiting every day, but it would be comforting knowing she had some cousins or aunties not too far away. She'd like to see Tamatoa more often too, but he's very busy with his military commitments. Materena won't say a word about Tamatoa's dancing disco moves in nightclubs, which Leilani reports to her. Tapeta might take her nephew's hobby for something else.

"*Eh-eh.*" Tears well in Tapeta's eyes. "And Hotu?"

"They have their pact."

The whole family knows about the don't-call-don't-write-don't-visit-me pact between Leilani and Hotu.

"Ah." Tapeta nods knowingly. "It's for the best. Leilani has her studies, she can have as many men as she wants when she gets her degree. Hotu isn't the last man on Earth... but I've been thinking, Cousin." Tapeta looks over her shoulders for a few seconds. "Don't laugh at me, I'm only asking you because you know so many things... When someone dies overseas, how does the soul find its way back to the birth land? When I think about my daughter's soul wandering and wandering for eternity and never making it home to Tahiti, I get so sad."

"Souls never get lost, Tapeta," Materena says firmly. To reassure her cousin, Materena tells her the story of a Tahitian woman who was buried in Canada, her husband's country, where she'd lived for fifty years.

Three days after the funeral, her sister saw her in Tahiti — standing in the garden next to the kava tree where they used to play as children. The dead woman was wearing a bright yellow dress with her hair all beautiful and her face made up with lipstick, and looking so much younger than seventy years old. And she was smiling the smile we do when we know we're in a good place.

The sister called out, "Teuira is home! Teuira is home!" The whole family gathered to celebrate the safe return of Teuira's soul back to the homeland. They got the ukuleles out, they sang and drank and ate. No expenses were spared. It was as if the woman had come home alive.

When Materena finishes telling the story, tears are falling out of her eyes, and Tapeta, hiding her face behind her breadsticks, is crying her eyes out too.

Meanwhile, people are walking in and out of the Chinese store, throwing the usual curious glances. As well as laughing and gossipping, women have been crying outside the Chinese store for centuries.

Materena walks back to the house with her cooking oil, still feeling emotional from her discussion with Tapeta. She pictures herself trying to tell Pito what he has done to her, but when it comes to hurt (the kind that cuts deeply), Materena finds it hard to express herself. Most likely she'll just burst into tears and Pito will laugh and say, "That's the reason you're not talking to me? I thought it was something serious." Then Materena will slap Pito across the face and —

And here he is, lying stoned on the couch like a zombie.

Non. It's definitely in that man's interest that Materena

doesn't talk to him today. Putting her cooking oil away, Materena remembers a conversation she had with her mother a few days ago about how in her next life she might come back as a lesbian.

And her mother said, "Why wait?"

Ah, *oui alors,* why wait!

Calling Out the Faithful

The first time Materena asked Pito to accompany her to a nightclub — the Zizou Bar, where French *militaires* and Tahitian women get acquainted, and a special place for Materena because it's where her parents met — Pito said, "I'm not putting my feet in that bloody bar." So Materena had her first life experience in a nightclub with her cousin Mori and had a very good time, or so she told her husband when she came home at about ten o'clock.

Well, tonight Materena is going out dancing again. Her soon-to-be-second experience in a nightclub is going to be at the Kikiriri, a nightclub open to all nationalities (especially to Chinese men with thick wallets, Pito knows this). Materena is not asking her husband to accompany her because, so she announced to her husband earlier, she's going out with a *copine*.

"Who?" Pito asks with sugar in his voice, ready for Materena to snap at him. She's been doing a lot of this lately. He's still waiting for that saying "After the storm there's the good weather" to come true.

But Materena doesn't say a word as she slips into a dress Pito has never seen before. It must be new.

"You bought a new dress?"

"I've had this dress for five years!"

"Ah." Pito can't believe he didn't notice that green dress before, but it's very hard for a man to keep track of his woman's dresses. They have so many! Dresses with thick straps, thin straps, red dots, black dots, flowers, squares, drawings... You need a big memory to remember all of this. "Who's your friend?" Pito asks again.

"Tareva," Materena replies nonchalantly, spraying eau de cologne on her wrists. "She's from the radio station."

"She's pretty?"

"She likes to dance."

"*Oui,* but she's pretty?"

"It's important that Tareva is pretty?" Materena snaps as she puts her shoes on, her favorite ones because they're so comfortable.

"You're wearing those shoes?" Pito says to say something.

"*Oui,* and so? They're comfortable."

"They're a bit old."

"People aren't going to talk to my feet." With this tired declaration and an approximate time for her return (ten o'clock), Materena makes an exit.

Pito grabs himself a beer and wanders around the house like someone who has nothing to do. He stops in front of the framed wedding photograph proudly displayed on the wall in the living room. There's him, his wife, their children, when they were younger.

Pito goes to the fridge, opens a new beer, and continues his wandering. He inspects himself in front of the mirror (full front and both sides). "Not bad, my friend." He does ten push-ups on his knuckles. "Not bad, my friend," he smiles, rubbing his sore knuckles. He admires himself in the mirror again. "Hum... not bad at all." He wanders around the house, thinking about this, that, his wife dancing in her new dress.

Eh, Pito is going to call Ati, see what he's up to. They might go for a little drive.

Ati picks up his phone on the third ring. "*A-llo.*" He has his telephone voice on, a mix of mystery and sexiness, in case it is a woman calling.

"It's me," Pito says. *Purée* — is that a hymn being sung in the background?

"Eh, Pito, *e aha te huru?*"

"What's that noise? It's coming from your apartment?"

"*Oui,*" Ati says, resigned. "Mama organized a prayer night at my place." Then speaking between his teeth he adds, "It's to help me find a good wife. All my aunties are here, they're driving me mad with their church songs."

"What's a good wife these days?" Pito asks, forcing a laugh.

But here's Ati's mama yelling out, "Ati! We're not going to do all the singing by ourselves! It's not us who need a wife!"

"All right then, *copain,*" Pito says. "I'll let you go back to your singing."

After a few words of encouragement, Pito stares at the telephone for a good moment, then returns to his wandering around the house, checking this and that, the spotless bathroom, the sparkling white fridge, and the potted plants hiding the holes in the walls...Pito turns around and around, goes to see the president...While he's in the bathroom he might as well have his shower. Then he knots a towel around his waist and wanders some more.

After a while, he starts imagining his wife dancing with a rich Chinese man (old, of course, and decrepit) and comparing him with her idiot husband who's let her go out on her own, thinking she's with a friend from work. She's laughing too, throwing her head backwards to show the rich Chinese man her throat, and you know what it means when a woman shows a man her throat, eh? It means she wants to be nice to him, of course!

"So? What do you do?" Materena could be asking her dancing partner right now, as they waltz around the dance floor, twirling this way, that way. "Oh," the Chinese man casually replies, "I own ten pearl farms and two music shops." Then Materena would give him her most charming smile, and he'd say, "That's a cute dimple you have on your left cheek —"

Pito drags his feet to the bedroom, sits on the bed, and glances at the clothes for mass tomorrow, which Materena has ironed and neatly laid on the ironing board. My wife is so organized, Pito thinks with pride. He's quite surprised to feel proud about this. Ironed clothes lying on the ironing board have never had this effect on him before, but here he is, proud and impressed. He lived with a chaotic and disorganized mother for eighteen years. That's probably why.

At ten o'clock precisely, Pito switches all the lights in the house off except in the kitchen. He lights a mosquito coil in the bedroom, hops into bed, and closes his eyes.

He opens his eyes, he closes his eyes again, turns to his left, to his right, sits up, stays still like a statue for several minutes, gets out of bed.

He switches the bedroom light on, grabs a comic from his comic box, hops back into bed, fluffs the pillows behind his back, makes himself comfortable, and looks at the pictures. Every now and then Pito has visions of his wife in bed with a Chinese man. Actually, *non,* a Tahitian man, a young and fit Tahitian man.

Pito puts his comic down and stares at the wall. If anyone could see his aura right now, it would be glowing with question marks.

Who is my wife with?

Why does my wife look at me like she wants to give me slaps?

Why, who, how . . . To stop the questions, Pito forces himself to think about family stories. Family stories are good to pass the time. There's the story of his great-auntie Catherine, who left Tahiti as a young woman to follow her American husband back to his country and who came home an old woman and a widow. She spent her days raking the leaves, crying for her island that had changed so much, and calling out to her great-nieces and -nephews to give her a kiss and a hug. But all the children would give the foreigner was an obedient forehead. She died not long after her return and was buried, as per her wishes, next to her twin brother, who had died at birth.

Then there's the story of another great-auntie, who didn't know for two months that her only son, who joined the French army during World War Two, had died fighting the Italians in Bir Akeim. For two months the great-auntie imagined her son alive and breathing, a hero of the Egyptian desert, when in fact he had been struck in the first minute of the battle. She had to get the official letter, the one filled with apologetic words, translated since she couldn't read French. She couldn't read full stop. Despite the time lapse, the Tahitian soldier was given a proper farewell ceremony. It was a tricky situation — a wake without a body — but Tahitians are well known for not letting anything get in the way of their prayers. The soldier's family prayed, sang, and called out to his soul to come home, back to his birth land, the *fenua*.

And there's the story of a great-uncle who . . .

At quarter to twelve Pito is on the phone to the Mamao Hospital's emergency ward. He explains the situation to the nurse on duty, how his wife went dancing with a friend and said that she'd be home by ten but she's not home yet. He explains all of this in a neutral voice. There's no need for the nurse to start thinking he's panicking.

"Maybe she's still dancing," the nurse snaps, angry. "Your wife wouldn't be the first woman to go out dancing at night and come home the following morning. What's her name?"

"Materena Tehana."

"*Non,* she's not on our list, call the hotels. Good-bye."

Next morning, just as the first church bells are calling out to the faithful, reminding them all that mass is in half an hour, so get ready, Materena walks in the door. Pito, sitting on the sofa, is straight onto her with a thousand questions, but she's got to get ready for mass, she says, quickly taking her green dress off and heading to the bathroom with a towel around her body.

"Where did you go last night?" Pito asks, following her.

"I was with my *copine,* you're not going to mass?"

"You were with your *copine* all night?"

"Well *oui!* And so?"

"And what did you two do?"

"It's not your onions." Materena closes the bathroom door on her husband and showers in record time while Pito puts on his navy blue suit. Within five minutes, she's out of the house in her pristine below-the-knees white church dress, running to the church like a good Catholic woman, devoted wife and mother, with husband in tow.

"*Iaorana!*" the relatives cheer the couple outside the church. The kissing and the polite words go on for a minute and now Meme Agathe, one of Mama Teta's clients, can resume her monologue about how singing at mass soothes the soul. Meme Agathe insists that she's speaking from experience here, as a woman who has felt down in her life many, many times and who felt better as soon as she started singing during mass.

"Oh *oui,* my Lord," she whispers with devotion, "you can drink liters of wine, you can smoke all kinds of cigarettes, you can have love affairs, but nothing beats singing at mass with the elders. When words of love, forgiveness, patience, hope, strength, come out of your mouth, you are certain to experience a spiritual uplift. Light will knock your worries away, inundate your soul, and you will get up, you will feel good from your head to your toes, you will —"

To everyone's relief the second bell rings, inviting the faithful to come in right now, right this second, mass is about to start.

"And you will shut your mouth," Meme Rarahu snorts.

Men, women, and children rush in, dipping a finger into the blessed water in the huge clam by the door and crossing themselves with their eyes closed, their heads slightly bent with respect.

Now Pito can take his usual seat at the back near the door with the men, but Materena unexpectedly takes his hand in hers and leads him to where she sits.

The Mahi clan have their seats reserved in this beautiful church — it's an unspoken agreement between this large extended family and the other churchgoers, there's no need to have their name engraved on the pews. It's a known fact that the Mahi clan helped build this church, selling tombola tickets, mapes, mangoes, banana cakes, ice to Eskimos.

This front right part of the church, facing the statue of the Virgin Mary, Understanding Woman, and the huge bouquet of flowers, belongs to the Mahi clan, okay? The left side belongs to the Teutu family, except for the three front pews, which are for the choristers. But the two back parts of the church are for everyone. Right out the back near the door is for people who quietly sneak into the church half an hour after mass has started, or people who must sneak out of the church in the middle of the service for a cigarette. And people like Pito who might feel the need to rest their eyes a little while the priest passionately raves on with his sermon.

"Materena," Pito says, sitting next to his wife. "I feel bizarre —"

"Shush," someone behind says.

Pito turns to see who's just told him to be quiet and meets the smiling eyes of Mama Teta, who puts a finger on her mouth and winks. He looks to his left and meets the very serious eyes of his mother-in-law. On his right, the big eyes of Mama George are saying, "What are you looking at me for?"

Sighing, Pito looks down at his shoes.

"Shush."

Pito half turns but changes his mind, he's not in the mood to look at eyes again.

Instead, he stares trancelike at his immaculate white shoes, his fingers, Jesus Christ half naked and nailed to the cross with blood dribbling down his temples.

He remembers the Easter he understood that Jesus Christ had risen from the dead, oh, the celebration in the neighborhood. "Jesus Christ is resurrected! He's risen from the dead!" And the aunties kissed each other like crazy, crying their eyes out with joy. But Pito thought, It's not possible, when you're dead, you're dead, you can't be alive again.

He asked his mother for some explanation. She said, "Jesus Christ is resurrected full stop, there's nothing to explain!"

The four musicians start jamming; it means the priest is on his way. When music was first introduced at mass, some of the old people complained. "Eh, what's this? Music in the church?

What are we? Savages?" But the young people loved it. "Yeah! Music! I'm going to church!" Anyway, for the record, since musicians have been part of mass, the church has been attracting more followers.

It is now time to stand up to welcome Father Patrice, along with his helpers, and ten old women attack the first line of the welcoming song. *"E te varua maitai...aroha mai ia tatou e... O Lord, have pity on us."* Eyes closed, and a hand on their heart, these respectable elders who have loved once, twice, sometimes three times, are begging the Lord for mercy.

But all Pito can think about is how his wife didn't sleep in their marital bed last night. And the song singing in his ears is — for some strange reason — *Je suis cocu mais content!* I'm cuckolded but happy! He glances over to his wife, singing away her faith with her hands clutched in prayer, a serene and peaceful expression on her face, looking every bit the picture of a devout Christian woman who lives her life by the rules of the Bible.

Pito narrows his suspicious eyes and turns his attention back to Jesus. He's certainly not expecting Materena to be taking Communion today, she didn't have time to confess her sins from last night, and she's not the kind to sin but still go on eating the body of Christ so that people don't ask themselves questions.

Many people do that, Pito knows. He himself has done this several times in his life, but his sins were little compared to big sins like stealing or sleeping around. Actually, there was always only one sin: drinking more than the priest.

Pito expects a lot of people to be shocked when, instead of joining the Communion line, Materena will remained seated, her head bowed in shame. But here she is, springing to her feet, a big, bright smile on her face, and joining the Communion line with great enthusiasm. Pito should be relieved. Instead, he's even more suspicious.

This is why, as soon as Pito and Materena are home from mass, he wants to jump on her.

"I need to do the test," he says, his feverish hand fumbling to unzip Materena's white armor.

"The test?" Materena snaps, slapping her husband's hand. "What test are you talking about?"

"Well, the test!" Pito forces a laugh. "The test a husband does on his wife when she goes out to a nightclub and comes home in the morning!"

Pito first heard about it many years ago in a bar somewhere in Paris, when he was doing military service. Apparently, a man shouldn't trust a woman's eyes, as the eyes of a woman can easily lie (women are born comedians, the stranger told Pito), but the test, *he-he,* it always speaks the truth. Basically, the man gets on top of his wife . . .

"Pito!" There's no way Materena is doing that test. Looking at her husband with sad and wounded eyes, she asks, "That's all I am for you? A hole?"

"A hole?" Pito asks, shocked to hear his wife talk about herself like that. A hole? He's heard of that expression many times before, but it has always come out of men's mouths and always referring to women of bad reputation. "Ah," they'd say, "time goes fast with her in bed, but she's just a hole."

"A *hole?*" Pito asks again.

"*Oui,* a hole . . . do you think a woman just wants a tetanus shot?"

"Materena." Pito is still shocked. "You're not a hole. You're the mother of my children. You're my wife."

"Your wife?" Materena laughs, showing her husband her throat.

When a woman shows a man her throat this way, laughing like she's mocking him, it means *tu peux toujours courir:* "In your dreams!"

Two Nights Ago on the Dance Floor

All right then, you people in the Kikiriri nightclub, make way for the two pretty *cousines, s'il vous plaît.* Materena and Lily look stunning in colorful *pareu* dresses (not too short, not too long) with thin straps, their hair loosely falling on their backs, a Tiare flower behind the ear (the left one, meaning, I'm already taken).

There were meant to be three pretty *cousines* bursting into the nightclub, but Rita — tonight's designated driver, having stopped drinking in her quest of falling pregnant — pulled out at the last minute. She'd rather stay home with her man, watch TV, do normal things couples do, have a rest from the intense two weeks they've just had making their baby.

So anyway, that is why there are only two *cousines* tonight.

Materena is wearing brand-new high-heel shoes, which Lily has kindly lent her. "You're not going out in those old shoes," Lily said when she saw Materena's comfortable sandals. "Not if you're coming with me." Materena certainly feels very privileged. Lily never lends her shoes. In fact, Lily never lends anything.

The tiny dance floor is packed with couples languidly swaying to the sexy rhythm of the Tahitian band's version of

"Guantanamera." Some couples, sitting at tables in the dark, have already proceeded to the kissing stage. Other couples, also sitting at tables but not in the dark, are staring into the whites of each other's eyes — the bored way — in between furtive glances to the lucky couples.

Enfin . . . to the bar!

"You are driving, Materena," Lily says to make sure the new designated driver hasn't forgotten.

"You're not going to drink too much, I hope," Materena replies. "I don't want to have to carry you to the car."

"Eh, maybe I'm not going home with you?" Lily chuckles.

"Lily —"

Grinning, Lily turns to her cousin. "And if I meet Prince Charming tonight?"

"I thought you said your Prince Charming isn't going to be at the nightclub?"

"Oh, maybe he's here tonight, he was so bored at home."

At the bar, a fifty-something Chinese man immediately offers to buy these pretty *mesdemoiselles* a drink.

"*Mesdames,*" Materena rectifies, digging for her purse in her bag. As far as she's concerned, she's paying for her drinks, okay? When a man pays for a woman's drink, she can expect expectations. *Non merci!* But Lily is already handing the barman a five-thousand-franc note, and before Materena can tell him what she'd like to drink (a soda, please), she has a gin and tonic in her hands.

Standing and drinking their gin and tonics, the cousins watch the love movies unfolding on the dance floor. A few couples are kissing shyly, while others are shoving tongues down each other's throat. Feverish hands are going up and down on backs, married hands entwining with single hands. All is permitted at this nightclub.

On the podium, the musicians are achieving their sole objective, which is to get the dance floor packed to the maximum. They are five overweight Tahitian men, but everyone knows that when there's music in the story, Tahitian women will be charmed no matter what the musicians look like.

"Cousin," Lily confesses in Materena's ear, "my Prince Charming is a historian."

"*Ah bon?* How do you know?"

"I went to a clairvoyant two weeks ago, and she told me that the man of my life is a historian. She saw my man in her crystal ball. There were a lot of books around him." Lily is talking about books thicker than the Bible here, not magazines.

"*Ah bon?*" And Materena bursts out laughing.

"Why are you laughing?"

"I don't know!"

"You're drunk already? With one drink!"

Materena looks into her glass. *Oups,* it's empty. She better refill it. Two more gin and tonics, please! Another slow dance, more watching couples kiss on the dance floor, this is getting very boring for Materena.

She scans the nightclub, remembering not to make eye contact with the men. When a woman makes eye contact with a man and he raises his eyebrows or makes a slight movement with his head towards the dance floor, she is obliged to accept his invitation to dance. Well, *non,* she's not really obliged, but she'd better be diplomatic with her refusal. She can't, for example, shake her head, meaning thanks but no thanks, because if the man has issues, he'll come straight to her. He might then start abusing her, tell her that the reason she didn't accept his polite invitation to dance is because she doesn't like Tahitian men, or she's a snob; worse, a slut.

Lily has reminded Materena about these rules in the car on their way to the club. Plus, there's always a cousin to tell a nightclub story about how a real ugly *titoi* or a real old *titoi* insulted her because she refused to dance with him. So, the best way to refuse an invitation to dance is to pretend you didn't see the man raise his eyebrows, you didn't see him make a slight head movement towards the dance floor, or you could just rush to the toilets like it's an emergency. Better yet, simply avoid eye contact at all costs, which is exactly what Materena is doing.

In the meantime, here's another gin and tonic, with Lily's compliments, and Materena is beginning to feel the effect. Oh, she's been drunk before, but never with a live band of musicians playing a love song, a beautiful love song about how wonderful it is to wake up next to your loved one and how mornings are truly made for kisses...Materena is feeling all funny and missing Pito. Not the Pito she's been so angry with for nearly two weeks because of his comment about her father not wanting to meet her, not the Pito who's been an insensitive *merde* for twenty-five years. It's not that Pito Materena misses, *non*. It's the Pito in between. The Pito she loved.

The love song ends, the couples are still holding each other, waiting for the next song, hopefully another slow one, but the musicians attack a frantic *tamure*. It's time for proper dancing. Couples detach from each other, but it doesn't mean the flirting and the teasing are over. *Tamure* dancing is very suggestive, an opportunity for women to show their partner the degree of their sensuality.

Beautiful cousins Materena and Lily rush to the dance floor, and...ah, they are certainly numero uno on the dance floor tonight, dancing close to each other, laughing with their heads thrown back, showing off their throats, hair falling in their eyes.

When the song finishes, they kick their shoes off, hurry to the bar for another drink, and dance some more — *tamure*, reggae, fox-trot, *valse*...Slow dance? No problems, the cousins can dance that dance too, and dancing slowly, their bodies pressed together, Materena's hand around her cousin's waist, Lily's hand on Materena's shoulder, they dance, smile, close their eyes, unfazed at being the center of attention.

Men smirk, women smack their men on the face. Men whistle, women smack their men on the face. Men stare in disbelief, women smack their men on the face. Meanwhile, Materena and Lily continue to please themselves in between dancing, drinking, and celebrating the night. They've come here to have fun, and that is exactly what they are doing.

Hours later, the cousins are exhausted, exhilarated, and the designated driver — way too drunk to drive now — falls on a seat near the dance floor to breathe a little. Cousin Lily, drunk too but still bursting with energy, keeps on dancing.

The band attacks "Les Femmes d'Amérique," an upbeat song about how American women are the prettiest but to have them you must have dollars, whereas in Tahiti, we have them for nothing. Vive Tahiti! The island of love! Tahitian women on the dance floor clap their hands with delight.

Materena, still slouched on her seat, is thinking, Who wrote this stupid song? She quickly rises to her feet at the sight of her cousin barging towards the stage, pushing dancers out of her way. Next, Lily is grabbing the microphone from the fat singer. The music instantly stops as two Mr. Muscle bouncers hurry to get that mad woman off the stage.

"Who wrote this stupid song?" she's yelling. "I demand to know! Women are not free, anywhere in the world! Women are —"

Lily gets carried off the stage before she can finish her passionate feminist speech, straight to the door, where Materena is waiting.

"We sleep in the car," Materena says, taking her cousin by the hand.

"*Ah non!*" Lily protests aloud. "I'm not seventeen anymore. I don't sleep in cars, I sleep at the hotel, *merci.*"

Luckily there's a hotel not far away from the club, a famous hotel — renowned as a place where marriages get wrecked. *Boîte à merde,* women call it: "can of shit." But it's good enough for Lily and Materena, who just need somewhere to put their heads down.

"That would be one room or two?" the wide-awake and smiling hotel receptionist asks politely. In this business, it's best never to assume anything.

"Cousin?" Materena's head is spinning; she's holding on to her pillow tight and wishing she didn't have to put her head down.

"*Oui,* Cousin," says Lily, who's doing the same.

"Have you ever been with a woman?" Materena already knows the answer, but in these situations it's best to pretend you're in the dark.

"Four."

"Four!" Materena didn't know there were four women. Materena knew there was one woman, since she had caught the two of them in the throes of passion a long time ago (it was an accident), and she thought Lily's experience with a woman was a once-in-a-lifetime experience, for something different to do. "Four?"

"Four," Lily confirms, yawning.

"If you had to compare between a woman lover and a man lover, who is better?"

Lily ponders for a while, a long while. Has she gone to sleep? "Cousin?" Materena calls out softly.

"There's nothing to compare." But Lily adds that her women lovers were more affectionate and tender, and they kissed better too, much better. Women put a lot of thought into kissing,

Lily insists, it's not kissing to get to the act in record time, it's kissing to say words. And when a woman holds you in her arms, you know that she really means it, you can feel it with every single pore of your skin. Making love to a woman is, well, in Lily's opinion anyway, magic, sensational, utterly romantic, and sweet. She doesn't make you feel like you're just a hole. The hole is not the center of the lovemaking between women. There's no center because everything counts.

"Everything?"

"Everything," Lily confirms. "They notice the little things, and it's because they pay attention, they don't have just the hole in their mind." Here, Lily elaborates, she has a beauty spot on the left lip of her little sister, and none of her men lovers have ever noticed it, but her female lovers have — the four of them. "And you know that I never make love in the dark."

"*Non,* I didn't know that."

"Well, I detest sex in the dark, I want my lover to see the expression on my face."

"Hum." Well, Materena likes sex in the dark. As far as she's concerned, darkness is a woman's best friend, especially when she's had a few children.

"Anyway," Lily yawns, "you see my point about men not paying attention?"

"Oh *oui,* it's like with Pito —"

"He has other qualities."

"Like what?"

"You already know, Cousin, since you've been with him for so long... How long again?"

Materena delivers the sentence. "Twenty years."

"Twenty years." Lily's voice is full of... is it admiration? "So many couples don't even make it past six months, imagine a little twenty years. What's three hundred and sixty-five days times twenty? Wait, three hundred and sixty-five times ten is three thousand six hundred and fifty, then times this by two...my God, you've been with Pito for seven thousand and three hundred days! You two have walked a very long path together..."

But Lily doesn't want to talk about her cousin's relationship with her husband, how it is nearly a quarter of a century. "I can't believe the love of my life is a historian," she rambles on. "As long as he's wonderful like my father, that's all I ask, and maybe my historian has a bit of feminine in him, who knows..."

Lily is sound asleep again now. Materena closes her eyes and starts imagining this and that, making love to a woman, making love to a rich Chinese man, making love to both of them at the same time...Materena opens her eyes and closes them, and here is her husband making love to a French woman and he's holding her tight...

Materena opens her eyes and closes them. She's an old woman, a very old woman, so frail and fragile, and for some reason, her left leg is bandaged. Each step she takes is a torture, but she stoically keeps on walking to the living room, her trembling hands holding, the best she can, a tray with a plate on it.

"Pito, my husband," she says with her croaky voice to the old man resting on the sofa, "I made you a chicken soup."

The old man looks up, then with his long stick turns the TV off — saves all the trouble getting up — and takes the tray. "*Maururu,* wife."

The old woman bends down for a little kiss on the cheek, grimacing a little because her back hurts, but she wants her kiss so much that she persists. Her dear husband is too busy slurping away at his soup to notice.

Materena opens her eyes and closes them.

This time it is pitch-black. Good, she needs her beauty sleep. Mass is tomorrow.

Man in a Suit Walking in the Rain

According to Heifara, when a woman tells her man that it's finished without even giving him the chance to redeem himself and win her back, there's another man on the horizon.

"Apparently," Heifara repeats to Pito.

"*Oui,*" Pito admits, "apparently, but it's not always true. Sometimes, it's just too late."

"But a man has got to know." And that is why, Heifara explains, he's hired a detective.

"A detective? Why? You don't have relatives who can spy on your wife?"

"I don't want the relatives to be involved, because you know how it is with the relatives, they twist everything, they add information, they delete, they exaggerate...detectives are better, they tell you the truth, they give you evidence." Heifara continues on about how he could have hired two of his cousins who don't work but the problem is that Juanita knows Heifara's family, from the uncles to the aunties, the first cousins, the second cousins, et cetera. When it comes to family Juanita has the memory of an elephant. She remembers likes, dislikes, birthdays, birthmarks — everything.

If she were to notice Heifara's cousins following her around, she'd immediately recognize them, even if they were disguised, and suspect them of spying on her under her ex-husband's instructions. Next thing, she'd be on the telephone yelling at Heifara, calling him *bizzaroid,* and threatening to send a few of her relatives his way...It would come to be a big family mess. So it's best to send the detective into the field.

"And he's got a lot of business in Tahiti, your detective?" Pito asks out of pure curiosity.

"Oh *oui.*" Then, lowering his voice a notch, Heifara goes on. "Do you know that the rate of infidelity in Tahiti is something like sixty percent?"

"Sixty percent?" Pito has always known about infidelity (three of his uncles were caught in the act), but he didn't know the rate to be so high. He thought it was something like thirty percent.

"Sixty percent," Heifara confirms gloomily. "And do you know which one is more likely to be unfaithful?"

"The husband?" Pito is not talking from experience but from what he's heard in the family.

"*Non,* the wife."

"The wife!" *Non,* Pito doesn't believe it. He simply can't imagine his aunties being unfaithful. His aunties are saints! They raised the children, cleaned the house, washed the clothes, cooked, went to church. Then they raised the grandchildren, cleaned the house, washed the clothes, cooked, and went to church.

But Heifara insists that sixty percent of wives are unfaithful because, according to his detective anyway, wives often feel unfulfilled. They are the wife, the mother, the cook, the cleaner, and the day comes when they explode. They go looking somewhere else, pack their bags, or show you the door.

*   *   *

Two days later...

Pito knows for certain that if Materena ever shows him the door, he will not be living with his mother. One night with her nearly drove him mad, he can't believe he lived with that insane woman for eighteen years. Perhaps it's just something you do when you're young — you put up with your mother and her strange ways because you don't know any better. But a man of a certain age, like Pito, who's forty-two, *knows* that the grass is greener on the other side.

Not that he actually packed his bags to move back in with his mother last night; *non,* he just took himself and a couple of beers. Mama Roti was quite shocked to see him at her door. "What are you doing here?" she asked.

"My wife is giving me the shits, I'm sleeping here tonight," he replied.

Mama Roti wasn't pleased at all. *"Aue,"* she said, "it doesn't mean you can come and annoy me. I have my habits. Sort your problems out with your wife. I told you to do something special for Materena."

Pito ignored his mother's remark and stepped into the house. By eight o'clock he was ready to flee, but he stayed because... well, he didn't know where else to go. He thought about staying with one of his brothers, but then there's the problem with the wives. Then he thought about staying with Ati, but Ati is on a mission to find himself a suitable wife, the last thing he needs right now is a mate landing on him. Then Pito thought about staying at a hotel, but he had no money, and payday is not for three days. And so he endured his insane mother.

She burned the stew (and blamed Pito), then she talked during the whole movie. For some reason Mama Roti felt Pito needed to know what was about to happen: "The police are going to find him...His wife is going to die." Whenever Pito exclaimed, "Mama!" Mama Roti said, "I've seen this movie before." And on top of the annoying movie commentary, Mama snores! Pito could hear her from his bedroom, the bedroom he once shared with his three brothers. He finally succeeded in falling asleep at about midnight, only to be woken up at three a.m. by the sound of clanging coming from the kitchen. Pito got up to see what was going on.

"I can't sleep," huffed Mama Roti, rearranging the pots and pans in her kitchen cupboards. "It's like this when you get old, the world is turned upside down." Pito went back to bed, and when he got up this morning, for some reason his knees were hurting him. And his mother said, "It's because you don't want to kneel."

Ah, *non,* there's no way Pito could live with his mother again! And as for living with Materena, it is going to be worse, Pito knows. When Pito came back from his mother's house, Materena didn't look too enchanted. She looked straight into Pito's eyes and said, "You're back? Already?"

So there's only one thing for him to do: visit a real-estate agent.

Pito has never rented a house in his life, but he's feeling very confident. His younger son is renting in Bora-Bora. He has a bungalow by the sea, which he shares with his fiancée. Moana could have had a proper house, and could own it too, with compliments of his rich father- and mother-in-law, but he wants to get his house with his own money.

Ah, if Pito were Moana, he would have accepted the generous offer. Vahine's parents are only trying to thank their son-in-law for having taken their problem daughter off their hands.

As for Leilani, that champion, she used to rent too (with six people, two sleeping under the stairs), but three weeks ago she moved. Now she has a maid's chamber, a tiny bedroom (but big enough for Leilani) above the apartment of an old couple. Leilani looks after them, she cleans their apartment, does their shopping, and cooks for them, and in return they take care of her accommodation, including the electricity bill. In Pito's opinion that is a lot of work for one tiny bedroom, not counting that Leilani also works in a bookshop, but Leilani seemed very pleased with the arrangement when she told her father about it.

"They are such a lovely couple," she said. "They still fight about little things like leaving the fridge door open for too long, they're so cute, they remind me of you and Mamie." Leilani went on about how sometimes that old couple prompted her to visualize her parents old and still together, fighting over little things like they'd been doing for years. Pito didn't have the heart to tell his daughter to stop visualizing, because the way things were going...

Anyway, back to Pito's first-ever visit to a real-estate agent, for which he is dressed in his wedding-and-funeral suit. And his shiny black shoes (also wedding-and-funeral). First impressions count, even Pito knows this, and what an impression Pito is making as he walks down the street in Papeete!

A Tahitian man who wears such a suit on a Sunday is a Catholic going to mass. A Tahitian man who wears such a suit on a Saturday is a Protestant going to *le temple.* But when such a suit is worn on a weekday, there's a funeral on. Or it could just be a very important Tahitian man strolling back to his office to make important phone calls, sitting at his very important desk.

Let's just say, in all honesty, that a Tahitian man wearing a suit is bound to attract eyes. This happens to Pito. Some eyes are sad. They are saying, Eh, eh, my condolences. Some eyes are filled with admiration. They are saying, *Ouh,* you must earn a lot of money!

The eyes that look up at the man bursting into the real-estate office are filled with respect. "Monsieur, *bonjour*," the pretty twenty-something French girl says. "May I help you?"

"I'm looking for a house." This voice belongs to a confident businessman.

"Well, you've come to the right place." Smiling, the receptionist picks up her phone, dials an extension, delivers the magical line — someone is here to see you — and, still smiling, asks Pito if he'd like a coffee.

"Ah *oui, merci*." This is the first time, in his entire life, that a receptionist has asked Pito if he'd like a coffee.

"Sugar? Milk?"

Coffee is on its way, but first things first — an introduction to Robert Matron, head of the sales department, a short, fat man with the biggest grin Pito has ever seen, you would think he's just won the tombola or something.

"This way, Monsieur." A hand goes out to the very important client's back to steer him in the right direction. "*Excusez-moi,* my desk is a mess! Take a seat, please. So —" The head of the sales department hurries to shuffle papers away and rubs his hands together. "What kind of house are we looking for?"

"A small one."

"Ah-ha, and with a pool maybe? For hot days?"

"Okay." Pito can sure visualize himself relaxing by his pool.

"A house by the sea or a house in the mountains?"

"By the sea." *Oui*, a house with a pool by the sea. Imagine that! He hopes the rent isn't too much, though.

"I do have a bungalow on my books but —"

"Ah *oui*, a bungalow!" Pito exclaims. "I want a bungalow! *Oui*, give me a bungalow!"

The head of the sales department grins from ear to ear as he reaches for a black folder on his desk, opens it to a picture of a bungalow by the sea. "Isn't she cute?" He raves about the building materials used to build this little treasure (hardwood, which won't rot away), the luscious garden (the purple bougainvillea vine is, like, fifty years old), the grass (green, well looked after), and...let's save the best for last: a pontoon!

"I'm sure," the head of the sales department winks, "that you will put your pontoon to good use. I can already see your speedboat anchored to it —"

"How much is it?" Pito goes straight to the most important question. He doesn't want to get all excited and find out he can't afford the rent because it's more than his salary.

"The price is negotiable." Robert Matron's voice lowers a few notches. "We're talking twenty percent if not thirty off the market value —" Then, adopting a sad expression, he whispers, "There's a death in the family, you understand."

"Somebody died in the bungalow!" The bungalow has suddenly changed in Pito's eyes.

Robert Matron makes frantic small movements with his hands. "*Non, non,* absolutely not, I guarantee you!" He wipes a pearl of sweat from his forehead, repositions himself in his rolling chair, having just remembered that the quickest way to lose a sale in Tahiti is to mention the word *death.* He'd thought this modern businessman to be over such ludicrous superstitions...but once a Tahitian, always a Tahitian. "Nobody died in that bungalow, in fact, nobody died, it was just a figure of speech, what I meant to say is —"

"How much?" Pito doesn't have all day.

"Thirty." The head of the sales department leans back in his chair.

"Thirty." Things are still not clear to Pito. "Thirty a week? Thirty a month?"

"Pardon?" The head of the sales department doesn't seem to be following his client's thinking.

"Thirty thousand francs a week or a month?" Pito repeats.

"Thirty thousand?" The head of sales now looks very lost. *"Excusez-moi,* but I'm talking about millions... thirty million."

"Thirty million! Where do you want me to get thirty million francs from? I can only pay ten thousand francs a week maximum."

The grin vanishes as the head of the sales department gets up. "Monsieur, there has been a misunderstanding." And to the receptionist bringing the very important client his coffee, he adds, "Monsieur was just leaving."

But Pito isn't leaving yet. As far as he's concerned, he'll leave when he's ready, okay? And pass me that coffee. "Where are your houses for rent?" he asks, taking a sip.

"For rent?" the receptionist says, eyeing Monsieur Matron from the corner of her shocked eyes. "I thought —"

"That's right, Bernadette." Poor Bernadette gets the evil eye from the boss. "You thought."

"So?" Pito tells the stunned receptionist. "Where are your houses for rent?"

She points to a notice board at the far corner of the front office, almost hidden behind a gigantic fake plant. "There, Monsieur."

All right, Pito is going to have a look. He looks and he looks, he sees one ugly house after another, they're all the same. A concrete box plonked down on a small block of land. A clean box, too clean... but houses for rent must all be like that. People move in and out, as he plans to do — six weeks maximum — just enough to make his wife miss him and realize that he's worth keeping.

Every now and then, Pito turns to the receptionist, sitting at her desk, still looking a bit pale, to ask the price. "How much for this one?" The price is the same for all of the houses, too expensive, but perhaps he could take a loan at the bank. Here, this one isn't so bad. Less ugly, more trees.

"I'm going to see my bank," he tells the receptionist. "And I come back."

"*Oui,* Monsieur."

"Do I need to fill out some papers with you?" Pito doesn't want to miss out on his house.

"*Oui,* Monsieur, you do." The receptionist attempts a smile. She reaches for a folder on her desk, and explains the whole rent system, including the condition of one month's rent in advance.

"One month in advance?"

"*Oui,* Monsieur."

Well, Pito might see his bank first. He puts his empty cup on the front desk, nods a sharp nod, meaning, I'll see you shortly, and leaves.

Pito strides into the bank and joins the queue. There's a young man over there at the counter who wants to withdraw three hundred francs.

"Three hundred francs?" the bank teller sniggers.

"It's to catch the truck," the young man says.

"There's only two hundred eighty francs in your account."

"Can I withdraw two hundred eighty francs?"

"You need to leave at least two hundred francs in your account." The bank teller, who's all made up as if she were off to a ball, explains that one should always leave some funds in one's account to prevent the account from closing.

"I close my account, then." The young man sounds like he's getting edgy. "I need the money to catch the truck home. I live in Papeno'o."

"Fine...close your account." The bank teller punches her keyboard, making sure not to break her long nails. "Give me seven hundred and fifty francs, *merci.*"

"What?"

The bank teller repeats herself: seven hundred and fifty francs. "You need to pay the closing-account fees before I can close your account."

"I've got no money!" To prove this, the young man turns out the pockets of his ripped shorts.

"I can't close your account, then," the bank teller says.

"What's this? A joke?"

"I don't make the rules."

"Stick your rules up your fat arse!"

The bank teller throws a death look on that rude customer's back before singing out, "Next, please!" Poor kid, Pito thinks. Eh, he's going to give that kid the fare home. Actually, he's going to do more than that. He's going to give that kid five hundred francs for the fare and something to eat on the way home.

"Eh," Pito says discreetly, the banknote flat in the palm of his hand. "Here."

The desperate young man gracefully accepts Pito's generosity. "*Maururu,* Monsieur, I'm going to pay you back." He asks for Pito's address, but Pito waves a little wave that says, Don't worry about it, kid. It's only five hundred francs. I've got more money coming my way.

"I'm here to take out a personal loan," Pito says to the bank teller, another pretty young woman all made up like she's off to lunch with the president. "For one hundred thousand francs."

"You're in the wrong queue," the bank teller says, apparently oblivious to the customer's shiny wedding-and-funeral suit. She sees all kinds of attire in her job and isn't one to judge a man by the cloth he's wearing. She's more the kind to judge a customer by how much money there is in his bank account, and a customer who needs to take a personal loan for a hundred thousand francs isn't what she'd call financially established.

"The wrong queue?" Pito glances over his shoulder to the queue, which has doubled in size in the past ten minutes.

"The loans department is upstairs."

"Upstairs where?"

"The information desk is over there."

Muttering under his breath, Pito proceeds to climb the stairs, joins the correct queue, lands at the right desk, and gets his forms.

What's with all the questions? Pito asks himself later, filling out his forms at the information desk under the watchful eye of a friendly-looking Tahitian mama. Who needs to know if I own my house, how much I spend a week, if I have savings...question one, question two, if the answer is no, go to question six, question seven...Just give me the money, you idiots!

All these questions are giving Pito a headache, and to make matters worse, he answers question three in the question four box. *Merde!* He puts a line through his answer and rewrites it again neatly, and again next to the wrong question. *Titoi!*

"Forms are really hard to fill out, eh?" says the mama at the information desk, to be nice. She has a very special spot for Tahitian people having difficulty filling out forms, she used to be like that too. Now she's a crack at filling out forms, of course.

"You're not wrong," Pito agrees, wiping sweat off his forehead with the back of his hand.

"Why are you taking a personal loan?" the mama asks nicely. "To buy a car?"

"A car? I don't even have my driver's license." He explains that he just needs about one hundred thousand francs to pay the rent for a month.

"One hundred thousand francs? We don't have loans for one hundred thousand francs, you'd best apply for a *carte bleue.*"

"You don't have loans for one hundred thousand francs? What kind of bank is this?"

The nice Tahitian mama, faithful to her employer, takes on a cranky face. "It's the same with all the banks."

Merde, all of this exercise is getting on Pito's nerves. It's enough that he hardly slept last night, and it's enough that he's sweating away like a sumo in his suit. What he needs more right now is a nice cool beer. Or then again, maybe three.

On beer number six Pito hits the road, walking because all his money is gone, the whole lot. Even when it starts to rain (unexpectedly, as it often does on this fertile island) Pito is still walking, with nowhere to go.

Two kinds of people walking by the side of the road get a lift; the people we'd like to know more, and the people we feel sorry for. You would think that a Tahitian man wearing a suit on a weekday and walking in the rain would fit both of the above categories.

But Pito is still walking. He's not cursing people driving by and not stopping, he just puts one foot in front of the other like a robot. All the way back to familiar Faa'a.

Getting Some but
Not in Your Own Backyard

The expression "Don't shit in your own backyard" means what it says: don't be an idiot or you will get caught, and next thing you know, you will be in the *caca* up to here. To put it simply, don't fool around with someone you know, or worse, someone your man or woman knows. This rule also applies to anyone who lives in the neighborhood. If you must fool around, go somewhere discreet, and pick someone discreet.

When it comes to things like these, Pito is not an idiot. He knows all about the mess and the disaster that comes with shitting in your own backyard. Two of his cousins — sisters — had a combat, and one of them (the sister of the wronged woman) lost an eye. What is a woman without both her eyes? What a waste, and this for a brief encounter with the brother-in-law. As for the sisters, who used to be so close, they haven't spoken a word in twelve years now, despite the aunties' repeated attempts to reconcile them with prayers. And to think that when they were little, they used to tell everyone that when they die they'd like to sleep side by side.

You will never see Pito doing any shitting in his own backyard. But when a man isn't getting any in his backyard, he needs to visit someone else's.

Here, yesterday at the Chinese store, Loma gave him the eye and for the first time ever, Pito found Loma breathtakingly beautiful. Loma! The least attractive woman of the Mahi tribe! But that moment she gave Pito the eye, she looked very interesting and he was just about to give her the eye back, when a voice inside his head shouted, "No shitting in your own backyard! And especially not with big-mouth Loma!"

But Pito found Rita pretty when she came to visit Materena yesterday afternoon, despite her doing her sad face because — so Pito guessed — she got her period. Rita has lost a lot of weight since trying to conceive, and Pito has never seen her look that good. Pito didn't know Rita had cheekbones.

Now, sitting at the bar with his colleagues on this hot Friday afternoon, payday, is giving Pito interesting ideas, and why not? His wife doesn't love him, Pito can see it by the way she looks at him, like he's a noodle, an idiot. Well, let's see what happens when the wife looks at the husband like he's an idiot — he goes and plays!

Pito is more sad than cranky, though. He's sad because . . . well, who knows? He's just sad, that's it. Materena changed so much, or perhaps he's just started to notice things about her, perhaps she's always been edgy and distant but he never paid attention.

When Pito asked Materena to lend him her car for half an hour to go and see his brother Frank, she refused just because he doesn't have a driver's license. Materena didn't care about Pito's driving experience. She didn't care that he drove his uncle Perete's car (on the actual road, Pito insisted, and not on some homemade path) when he was about fifteen years old. The uncle was completely *taero,* having lost a couple of thousand francs on a rooster fight and drowned his sorrow in drinks, and so he said to Pito, "Kid, drive your uncle to the Chinese restaurant. I'm sad. I need to eat some chow mein."

Pito drove his uncle's car again later, but this time it was to a family reunion. The uncle was sober, but his left foot was swollen because he had stepped on a sea urchin. Pito also drove Auntie Lele's car...anyway, to cut a very long story short, Pito has had many driving experiences. But Materena didn't care about all that. It was more important for her to be mean.

And perhaps she's mean because she wants Pito out of her life to make way for her Chinese boyfriend. *Oui*, perhaps that's the reason. Yesterday Pito checked the answering machine — just to see, a question of curiosity. There were five messages, three from his mother asking Materena (three times) if she would like to buy a packet of raffle tickets to help Mama Roti's bingo association. First prize: a healthy piglet; second prize: five kilos of tamanu oranges; third prize — Mama Roti got cut off. The other two messages were from Rita (sounding very sad), asking Materena to call back.

"Jojo!" Pito softly calls out. A nod to the left, a hand around an empty glass, and Jojo gets into action. Jojo, affectionately called Siki — a six-foot tower of black strength complete with two golden teeth—fills Pito's glass.

"Eh, Siki," another regular says in what has become a familiar refrain, "when are we going to see a woman behind the bar?"

"Behind the bar isn't the place for a woman." Jojo gives the same answer he's been using for the past twenty years. In Jojo's world, women are to sit comfortably at the tables enjoying their drink, and not behind the bar serving drunken men. Jojo once got very mad at one of his clients who dared mention that he was cutting off both his legs by not having a woman behind the bar. The client said, "A woman behind the bar brings in business. A beautiful woman, of course, and young too, because nobody wants to be served by some *meme*, some old hag."

Jojo lifted that client (literally) and threw him out of his bar. In Jojo's world, *memes* are not old hags, they are respectable grandmothers. That client wasn't a regular, otherwise he would have known about Jojo's sacred and sanctified respect for women. Criticize this respect at your own risk, it has made Jojo a very rich man. A poor Kanak waiter when he emigrated from New Caledonia, Jojo now owns a bar, and he paid the fares of his three brothers and their families to Tahiti. Jojo's brothers are replicas of Jojo, and women know that if they want to enjoy a few quiet drinks without being pestered, go to Jojo's.

Take tonight, for example. There are about fifty women scattered across the large drinking area, along with eighty hopeful men. One of them is Pito's colleague Heifara, who has been busy planting his seeds in anything that moves lately.

"Jojo," Pito softly calls out again. He needs a refill, but all he gets is a glass of water.

"Drink this first," Jojo commands with his don't-argue-with-me booming voice. "Then we'll talk."

Pito drinks his glass of water in one go. You have to do what Jojo says, otherwise he just picks you up and throws you outside.

"How's everything, my friend?" The booming voice is now a concerned whisper.

"Everything's fine."

"Everything?"

"Everything."

"The family's good?"

"The family's good."

Jojo affectionately pats Pito on the shoulder and goes back to his occupations.

"The family's good," Pito mutters under his breath, half turning to the crowd. There's Heifara deep in conversation with a forty-something woman who is right now doing a forced smile.

"Pito, where are you, *copain?*" a colleague nudges. "You're not saying a word tonight."

"I don't feel like talking." To you lot, Pito means.

Okay, then, since Pito doesn't feel like talking, nobody is going to talk to him. Nearly every Friday there's a colleague who doesn't feel like talking, and tonight it is Pito's turn. When this happens, nobody asks questions, the person who doesn't feel like talking is left alone with his thoughts. The bar is often the place where men feel liberated to do a little *examen de la conscience,* to go deep down in their conscience and think about important things, like their relationships with their woman, children, siblings. Eyelids closed, they replay their lives, list their faults, the promises they haven't kept...

But Pito is not doing any self-analysis, he's just watching Heifara carry on with his seduction plan, which isn't going well, considering the bored expression on the woman's face. Perhaps Heifara is talking too much. Perhaps he's showing off and he's starting to get on the woman's nerves. Here she is, nodding, but her eyes are elsewhere. They are on the ceiling, they are on other men, they are here and there, and then they are on Pito.

They are on the ceiling again.

They are on Pito.

Here and there, and on Pito again.

Pito doesn't wink. He just looks at her with his beautiful sad eyes. She arches one of her eyebrows, meaning, Eh, you at the bar looking at me, why are you so sad? then smiles. Pito smiles back. She smiles again and runs her fingers through her hair. Pito notices her wedding ring. Ten minutes later, as she discreetly leaves the bar while Heifara is in the toilets, she gives Pito the look, the look that says — *Coucou,* look at me closely, I'm interested!

Pito quickly finishes his drink and follows the interested woman outside.

She is waiting for him behind a tree.

"Where's your husband?" he asks out of politeness.

"In New Zealand, get in the car."

Once in the car speeding away towards Tipaerui, Pito glances at his future lover from the corner of his eye, and he's feeling less and less interested. Why is that? Who knows! He's not interested because he's not interested, okay? There's nothing to explain. He changed his mind, that's all. That woman just doesn't look as appetizing as she did in the bar. And plus, she has smelly feet, she doesn't clean her feet properly. Materena scrubs her feet every day. With perfumed soap.

Also, what if that woman finds out who Pito is — Materena's husband — and what if she finds out who Materena is and starts blabbing about how she had sex with the husband of that woman with the popular radio show. People will laugh at Materena. They will say, "Ha! Maybe she has the most popular radio show in Tahiti but can she keep her husband's *moa* in his pants? Apparently not!"

Plus, it might be very flattering when a woman you don't know wants you, but the way Pito sees the situation, it's more flattering when it's a woman who knows you to your last pubic hair who wants you. Now that's something to brag about to your *copains*.

"I changed my mind," Pito says calmly after his analysis. "Can you drop me in Faa'a?"

"What!" the woman shrieks, angry. "We're nearly at my house! Do you take me for an idiot or what?"

Well, now Pito is *definitely* not interested. "Eh, stop the car." It's an order.

She stops the car in front of a house. All the lights inside are turned on.

"Who's in my house?" the woman asks her companion, as if he'd know.

Seconds later, the front door opens and out comes a man. Pito suspects it to be the husband, judging from how the woman shrieks and orders Pito to slide down the seat.

"*Chéri!*" she calls out, quickly getting out of the car. "I thought you were coming home tomorrow."

"I wanted to surprise you, Suzette," Pito hears the husband say. The husband doesn't even ask his wife where she's been.

"What a nice surprise!" The wife sounds like she really means it. "I'm so happy!"

Purée, Pito thinks. Women are actresses.

"Miss me?" the husband asks.

"Oh *oui,* I missed your company."

"Just my company? Nothing else?"

There's a cackle, and Pito suspects the husband has pinched his wife on the bottom, something like that. A little shout, and next thing the car starts to rock backwards and forwards. Pito suspects the married couple to be going at it on the hood of the car.

"Let's go in the house," Suzette says in a very sultry voice. "The neighbors might see us."

"I don't care, they can watch if they want to."

The car shakes again, and the husband sounds like he's having a really good time. Then it's all over.

"How are the children?" the husband asks, after a gap as they do themselves up.

"They're fine."

"And the grandchildren?"

The *grandchildren?* Pito shouts in his head. She's a grand-mother!

"Let's go in the house." This is Suzette's answer to her husband's question about the grandchildren. "I'm cold."

Okay, the coast is clear, but to make sure, Pito waits for a few minutes more, then sneaks out of the car and starts running. He stops a hundred feet further on for a few breaths and continues to run, stops again, runs, stops...until it's safe to walk. He walks his normal walk. He walks and thinks about this and that, his little escapade, and how Materena will be greeting him.

The light is on, and this means Materena is awake, but perhaps she left the light on out of consideration for Pito because she decided to be nice for a change.

Pito takes a deep breath. This is what he plans to do. Walk in the house a different man. Walk in and take Materena in his arms, kiss her tenderly, and hold her tight, and say, "Materena...you're the woman of my life, give me one more chance." Something like that.

Pito opens the door, walks in, and this is what he sees: Materena sitting on the sofa, crying her eyes out with a baby sound asleep in her arms. For a second Pito thinks that he's hallucinating. He widens his eyes, but Materena is still sitting on the sofa, crying her eyes out with a baby sound asleep in her arms.

"Who's that baby?"

Materena lifts her crying eyes to Pito and tenderly kisses the baby on the forehead.

"Our *mootua*."

Fa'amu — to Feed

Tiare, *alleged* baby daughter of Materena and Pito's eldest son, Tamatoa, is fast asleep in her *alleged* Auntie Leilani's bed, with pillows on both sides of her tiny body. Her name, Tiare, a flower name, the white, sweet-scented flower, is also the emblem of Tahiti.

Materena softly kisses the baby's head, wipes her eyes with the back of her hand, sighs, and, walking out of the room, gives Pito the let's-go signal. She stops by the door to have one more look at that baby who fell from the sky, closes the door halfway, and whispers, "Pito, I'm going to make us a coffee, we need to talk." Once in the kitchen she adds for good measure, "I know you don't like to talk about serious things but —"

"I'll make the coffee," Pito interrupts, which is as good as him saying, Stop talking *merde,* Materena, are you a mind reader or what? He fills the saucepan with water, puts it on the stove, grabs two cups, gets the Nescafé jar out of the *garde-manger,* all of this without a word. Meanwhile Materena, at the kitchen table, briefs him on the situation.

Only two hours ago, Materena was looking at photos in the family album after coming home from finishing her show, when somebody knocked on the front door. *Oui?* she called out, thinking, Who's that visiting me at this hour?

A woman called out, "It's me! Tiare's great-auntie! I can't talk for too long because my friend is waiting for me, and it's her car!"

Puzzled, Materena hurried to the door, opened it, and saw a woman of about fifty holding a sleeping baby in her arms.

"Are you Tamatoa Tehana's mother?" the woman asked.

"*Oui,*" Materena replied. "Why?" The woman passed the baby to Materena, and Materena, used to having babies passed to her, automatically took the baby. Tenderly, so as not to wake it up.

Now, about the situation, which the great-auntie was more than happy to explain to Materena, though she had to rush out of consideration for her friend waiting in the car. This baby belongs to her great-niece Miri Makemo and the baby's father is Tamatoa Tehana. Miri met him in Paris, she was there on a dancing tour, and, well, what do you want, these two young people instantly liked the look of each other, they started doing *parau-parau,* went to bed, and conceived the little one.

Miri came home from her dance tour five months pregnant, but her belly was very small, you wouldn't have guessed she was pregnant at all, and so she didn't tell anyone about it. When Miri started to wear loose dresses, the auntie didn't suspect anything. She just thought that Miri had decided not to dress like a *pute* anymore like her mother, skirts so short men didn't have to imagine, they could see what was underneath.

Then about three months ago, very early in the morning, about two o'clock, Miri woke up with a bellyache and she was yelling so much that the auntie got scared and ran to the doctor who lives a mile away. She yelled from the grilled gate, "Doctor! Quick! It's a matter of life or death!" By the time she finally got the doctor out of his bed, two hours had passed and there was a newborn baby in the house.

The auntie looked after the baby because her niece, who is too young to be a mother, barely eighteen, took off to New Caledonia with a boy (a Tahitian, but who was born and grew up there, his family owns an orange plantation) — but she has just too many babies to look after already, and she's not young anymore. That's why she brought the baby to her father's family, to see if they can help and everything. It's a good thing Miri told her the story of the baby's conception, otherwise the auntie would have been forced to give the baby to strangers.

Materena had no chance to ask any questions because the woman fled the house (her friend beeped the horn), but she gave Materena her address. They'll talk more later on.

That's the situation, from the beginning to the end.

"And you let that madwoman leave the baby with you?" Pito can't believe it! Had he been home, he would have told the woman to come back tomorrow when she'd have more time to talk. You don't just barge into people's houses and leave babies like that!

"She ran off!" Materena protests. "What did you want me to do, eh? Leave the baby on the road for the dogs? Until you came home from I don't know where?"

"Tamatoa has never spoken to me about a girl called Miri," Pito remarks, sitting at the kitchen table with the cups of coffee.

"And you? You told your mother about all the girls you slept with in France and Tahiti?" Materena fires. "The first time I met Mama Roti, she didn't know who I was and I'd known you more than two years. And plus, I was pregnant!"

"In France?" Pito asks, thinking, Why is Materena talking about France now? That was more than twenty-five years ago.

"Ah," Materena says, waving a hand in front of her face. "I don't want to talk about that, I want to talk about the baby."

"We can't keep that baby." This is an order from the man of the house. Pito has had his babies, the diapers, the bottles, the whining, the crying. It's not going to start all over again.

Shrugging, Materena tells Pito that she really doesn't understand why he's all stressed out, it's not as if he'll be the one looking after the baby, because she will. Just as she has looked after their three children.

"You're talking like that baby is really our granddaughter!"

"I prefer to believe that Tiare *is* my granddaughter and then find out that she isn't than the contrary, okay, Pito?" Materena takes a sip of her coffee. "But I feel a connection with that baby, here, in my *a'au.*"

"You're like that with all babies," Pito says. He's seen Materena in action with babies many times. Let's just say that whenever a baby appears, Materena melts. She wants to hold the baby, she wants to kiss the baby, and she wants to have another baby.

"My son only slept with that girl one time," Pito says. "Talk about bad luck."

"That's all it takes," Materena snaps. "One time, and there's a score...and *aue,* let's stop arguing, we're going nowhere, we should talk about what we're going to do."

By twenty past midnight, it is agreed that:

1. As soon as Tamatoa calls the family, hopefully soon, he will be asked if he knows of a girl by the name of Miri Makemo.
2. The Makemo family will be visited before Tamatoa calls the family (he usually rings collect whenever he feels

like it) but Materena will call Leilani to track Tamatoa down and get him to call home.

3. Should the baby be confirmed to be Tamatoa's, then Materena and Pito will look after the baby until Tamatoa comes home or until the mother decides to fulfill her duties. It will also be expected that Tamatoa recognizes his daughter. Tiare can't have Father Unknown written on her birth certificate if her father is known. Materena feels strongly about this. In the meantime, Materena and Pito will be the *fa'amu* parents.

Fa'amu, meaning "to feed," is the traditional adoption, to help the mother while she gets herself together. You feed the baby, put clothes on the back, give a roof over the head, and you love the baby too — but all with the understanding that it is not your baby. It belongs to the mother. The *fa'amu* parents are only passing through the child's life because the mother will come back and profoundly thank them for all their help. If the mother doesn't come back, then the baby will go to the father, but if the father is not interested, well, then the *fa'amu* parents might become the parents.

4. Now, should that baby not be baptized yet, then she will be as soon as possible. Should the baby be already baptized but not in the Catholic Church...*Aue,* let's just pray that Tiare is not baptized yet.

5. Materena must get some formula milk tomorrow morning for Tiare. The poor baby only came with a bottle and the clothes on her back, but luckily it so happens that Materena kept most of her children's clothes, including their quilts and cloth diapers, in cardboard boxes for her grandchildren. She is very glad she thought about that.

Many times Pito told Materena to get rid of all those clothes. She is very glad she didn't listen to him.

And with this verbal agreement Materena and Pito go to bed, she sighing worried sighs, he aged by fifty years.

At five thirty the following morning, the old man is woken up by a baby's cry. For a second Pito thinks he's gone back to the past and that the baby crying is one of his children. Then he remembers Tiare. Grumbling, he turns to the other side of the bed and notices that Materena is not in bed. Good, Pito tells himself. That baby is going to stop crying soon. But the crying gets louder and louder.

"Pito." Materena is at the door, the crying baby in her arms. "*Bébé* has done a *caca,* I'm going to wash her, you go to the Chinese store to get her formula milk, and a new bottle too, that one is dirty, I need to sterilize it in boiling water. I can't believe she slept all through the night, she must be so hungry now."

Pito half opens an eye.

"*Allez,* Pito," Materena commands.

Pito stays still. It's too early to be getting up, Materena can be in control like she was with her own children, Pito doesn't mind.

"Okay, I'm going to the Chinese store," Materena says, placing the smelly baby next to Pito. "You can wash Tiare."

Pito springs to his feet. There is absolutely no way he's going near that baby's *derrière.* He'd rather crawl to the Chinese store. So, muttering curses under his breath, he puts on his shorts, slips his feet in his thongs, grabs a banknote from Materena's purse, and he's out of the house in a flash, swearing.

"Pito!" Materena's Cousin Tapeta calls out from the other side of the road. "Is that you? What are you doing up at this hour? Is

Materena sick?" Pito waves a distant wave, meaning, why don't you say what you really want to say, you big-mouth?

Another relative-in-law, this time bigger-mouth Loma, stops Pito at the door of the Chinese store. "Pito?" Loma does her I'm-so-shocked-am-I-dreaming? look. Is this Pito I see in the flesh before my very eyes? "What are you doing here?" she asks.

"Same thing as you," Pito snaps as he darts up an aisle. He looks back and here's Loma still standing at the door watching him. If she sees him buy formula milk and a bottle, she'll...Pito carefully selects a can of peas and strolls back to the cash register.

There, it did the trick, Loma is gone. There's not much to say about a can of peas. Right, now Pito can go on with his mission, running up and down the aisle until finally, *bingo,* he finds the baby section with the diapers, the bottles, the baby-food jars, the whole lot. So, *tack, tack, tack,* Pito grabs what he needs and heads straight to the cash register.

"How old is your baby?" the young woman, whom Pito has never seen before, asks, a big friendly smile on her face.

Pito shrugs. He remembers Materena mentioning something about the baby's age, but the information has already gone out of his head. The young woman gives Pito a strange look, the look that says, You don't even know how old your baby is? You should be shot!

"Deux mille et six cent quatre-vingt francs." Pito doesn't get a smile anymore. He gets a cold look. Well, anyway, there's no time to dwell on this. There's a baby to feed. With the groceries in the bag, Pito runs back to the house.

Baby Tiare is nice and clean now, with her hair neatly combed to the side, and she's wearing one of her Auntie Leilani's pretty floral baby dresses. The dress is a bit big but it'll do for now.

"Here," Materena says, passing him the baby. "I'm going to make the bottle."

Minutes later...

"Here," Materena says, thrusting the bottle into Pito's hand. "She looks happy with you." Pito doesn't have the chance to complain. That bottle automatically goes from his hand into the hungry baby's mouth. Here is *bébé* Tiare sucking on her new bottle as if this was her last feed, her eyes staring into Pito's eyes. Very soon the bottle is empty but the baby is still sucking and checking out that grown man.

"What?" Pito asks, a half-smile forming. "You want my picture?"

The three-month-old baby spits the nipple out of her mouth and keeps on staring at that man for a few seconds before giving him her most beautiful I'm-shy smile.

And that is when Pito notices the dimple on the baby's left cheek. The dimple Materena has, and which she inherited from her French father.

Welcome to Our
Humble Neighborhood

Since the matter about that baby who fell from the sky last night must be resolved as soon as possible, Materena decides to visit the little one's maternal family now, today. And she's expecting Pito to go with her. Firstly, because he could be the grandfather, but also she needs a man in case... Well, in case the little one's maternal family is a bit *zeng-zeng*. Materena doesn't want to deal with crazy people on her own.

She also needs Pito so that he can hold the baby in the car. She sure doesn't want to leave the baby on the backseat. What if she has to suddenly hit the brakes, and the baby rolls off? *Non,* it's best for everyone that Pito goes too.

"I know that Saturday is your day," Materena says, "and that you do what you want to do, but —"

"I'll go and get changed." This is Pito telling Materena that she can count on him. This is also Pito telling Materena that as of now, every time she assumes something about him, he's going to prove her wrong. He sneaks to the car with Tiare hidden under a crib-size quilt that belonged to Tamatoa — you would think she was a celebrity baby! Materena, positioned behind the steering wheel, is ready to take off, and here they go — quick, before a relative sees what's going on! They are now on their way to Purai, there, up in the mountains.

"You know where the house is?" Pito asks, sitting in the backseat with the little one sound asleep in his arms.

Materena throws him a glance in the rear mirror. "It's a yellow house."

"A yellow house," Pito repeats. "I hope you have more information."

"There's a dog tied to a tree at the front of the house."

"And..." Pito is still hoping for more information.

"There's an old truck parked two houses away from the house."

"A truck?"

"A red truck."

"A red truck." Still no proper information.

"Don't worry, I'm going to find the house, I only have to ask."

"Ask who?"

"The people in the street..." After a bit more driving, "Ah...I think we've arrived...*Oui,* the nice houses...and here's the Chinese shop, bars on the windows...Keep going...*Oui,* garbage everywhere...and children too." Materena slows down, waves a friendly wave to the barefoot brown children playing on the road with sticks, marbles; some flying kites, others eating ripe mangoes. Pito looks at these children who stare suspiciously at the woman behind the steering wheel. He notices a child standing looking at him as if to say, And who are you? Get out of my neighborhood.

"*Ouh la la,*" Materena whispers, still driving very slowly. "These children look so serious."

"They don't know us, that's all," Pito says, eyeing the kids now lining up along the road to take a good look at that car they've never seen. He remembers doing the same thing when a car he didn't know would drive into his *quartier*. He stared at the people in the car with suspicious eyes too. Once, he even showed them his angry fist — he just felt that he had to. It was his way of telling these foreigners, "Don't even think about coming here to make trouble for us. I'm going to box your eyes."

His *quartier* was much cleaner than this *quartier* here, though. In fact, this *quartier* is disgusting. Look at the dogs knocking the garbage bins over and nobody cares. There are dirty disposable diapers lying everywhere, and rusty abandoned cars — that one looks like it has been set on fire. All around is filth. Pride does not live in this neighborhood.

But Pito won't get carried away being judgmental. His *quartier* doesn't have what you call postcard houses either. To a foreigner's eyes, Pito's place, filled with fibro shacks, could also seem like a ghetto where no-hopers live. It is only when you get to meet the people who live in those fibro shacks that you realize that these people, far from being losers, have a strong sense of right and wrong.

"What are you doing in our *quartier?*" one of the children yells, before hurling a mango at Materena's car. She hits the brakes as another child also lets go with his mango.

"But!" Materena shrieks. Another mango follows.

"*But!*" Materena shrieks again, this time louder. "They're going to put dents in my car! Pito, do something!"

He pokes his head out of the window and growls an angry growl. "Oi!"

That does the trick.

"Here's the yellow house!" Materena exclaims, relieved. "And the dog, and the red truck...We're here...and...Oh, look at the men drinking under the tree, they don't look very Catholic." She parks the car, and turns the engine off. "I'm glad you're with me, Pito. Imagine if I was by myself."

Pito gently taps Tiare's bottom and gets out of the car. He stands straight, tall and proud. True, he is a man carrying a baby, but it doesn't mean he's a *mahu*. He's a man capable of knocking all your teeth out with one punch, so keep your distance and don't judge him stupidly.

He nods a distant nod to the angry-looking men drinking under the tree. It is not a polite nod. It is not a please-be-kind-to-us-we've-come-in-peace nod. It is a nod pure and simple, a nod that says, I see you and so?

The angry-looking men nod back. Their nod is not a polite nod either. It is not a we-are-very-pleased-to-welcome-you-people-to-our-humble-neighborhood nod. It is a nod pure and simple, a nod that says, I see you too and so?

Materena is now by Pito's side, and these two are quite a sight this Saturday morning in the Makemo *quartier*. Pito has never heard of this family before. It could be that they're not even Tahitians.

Tahitians know the welcome-into-the-neighborhood protocol. These people are another kind altogether, or maybe they're just *niakue,* Tahitian people who don't have manners. There's no *Iaorana,* just stares. It doesn't seem to occur to any of these people to at least greet the baby who has lived in this neighborhood for the first few months of her life.

What kind of people are these people? Even the four women busy washing clothes in buckets outside look bizarre. And what about the babies crawling in the dirt? Where's the pandanus mat?

"What do we do?" Materena asks Pito discreetly, smiling a faint smile at the women, who don't smile back.

Just then a shriek pierces the air. It is a desperate shriek and it is coming from inside the house. It is the shriek of a woman in trouble. A man yells an angry yell, and it is also coming from inside the house. It is the yell of a man who is in control. The louder he yells, the more desperate the woman shrieks, and soon Pito understands that the woman is getting bashed and nobody is running to her rescue. A child starts crying, and soon a naked two-year-old boy comes outside, wiping his eyes. The yelling must have woken him up from his sleep. He sits by the door and sticks his fingers in his ears.

The man is still yelling. The woman is still shrieking. And the dog tied up to the tree howls. You can always rely on the dogs to howl when there's trouble in the neighborhood, they are the messengers when the human cries aren't loud enough. Although you wouldn't think that was the case today.

Good dog, Pito thinks, nodding to the dog howling louder. Pito is expecting this family's relatives to come sprawling out of their houses soon, with women yelling, "*E aha te ra!* What's this?" Ready to tear the basher to pieces, or at least do the pleas and threats until he stops.

This is rescue Tahitian-style, which Pito witnessed many times in his childhood. The women yell their heads off and a cranky great-auntie comes running and shouting, "When will I have some peace in this world, eh? Plus, my legs hurt when I run!" And to the basher, the old respected woman (she who makes beautiful quilts, rakes the leaves, and minds the grandchildren) will say, "You make me ashamed. You're making me want to curse you!"

But here, nobody comes and the colorful curtains are drawn closed. It's a case of what we don't see doesn't concern us.

Pito holds Tiare in his arms tighter. The woman stops shrieking and starts to cry, sobs of great anguish and pain. The man walks out of the house. He rubs his hands, spits on the ground, and joins his comrades drinking.

"Who are you?" he asks Pito, giving him the evil look. Then, recognizing the baby Pito is holding, he smiles. "Eh, that's

Miri's daughter, it's Tiare." He reaches out to the baby's head, but Pito's hand is much quicker, his grip firm and tight on the man's forearm.

The two men stare into each other's eyes. The comrades stand on their feet ready to strike. The women washing outside gather their flock and hurry inside the house, banging the door shut. Materena starts bawling her eyes out.

"Get in the car, woman." This is an order from Pito.

Materena scurries back to the car and takes her position behind the wheel as Pito slowly lets go of the man's arm. He turns around and walks to the car. He can hear each one of his footsteps. He can feel the eyes on his back. He knows that a man must never turn his back on his potential attackers, but sometimes a man simply cannot walk backwards. Pito opens the back door of the car.

"Pito," Materena tells him, "I can't put the key in, my hands are shaking."

"Get in the back," Pito orders, and Materena scrambles into the backseat with her bundle of her precious baby granddaughter still asleep. Pito makes himself comfortable behind the wheel, starts the engine, and puts his right foot on the accelerator, getting out of this neighborhood as fast as he can without looking like he's hurrying.

Driving confidently and slightly above the speed limit, Pito imagines himself growing up in this neighborhood. He wouldn't wish this on anyone, not even his worst enemy. His granddaughter? Don't even think about it.

The Man of the House Speaks

There's a baby in Materena's house — quick, let's go and see if it's true, maybe Loma made up the whole story to seem interesting...though Mama Teta also swore she saw Materena in her car holding a baby. Pito was driving, and it's not like Materena to let someone who doesn't have a driver's license drive her car, especially with her in it. Driving a car without a permit is against the law and Materena always keeps to the law. She must have been completely turned over by the baby she was holding. That baby must be a very important baby, eh? Not just any baby.

Who is that baby?

Within less than an hour a crowd of curious relatives (all women) has gathered in Materena's living room. As for the baby girl, she's sound asleep in Pito's arms, while Materena is busy getting some refreshments. Barging into a relative's house is not considered polite at all, and certainly doesn't justify freshly squeezed lemonade and Sao biscuits with jam; but then again, today is no ordinary day.

Today is the kind of day people will talk about for years and years and years, a tree might even be planted to mark the event. If refreshments are not served, you can be sure this will also be remembered, so here are your Saos, relatives. Materena has even had to use a few of the plastic cups from her wedding more than ten years ago.

Drinking and nibbling, the relatives are comfortable on the floor, facing Pito and the baby, along with Materena's mother, sitting on the sofa. They know the story about Tiare being the alleged daughter of Materena and Pito's eldest son — the unwanted baby given away by the auntie because the mother went walkabout and the auntie has enough babies to look after. This valuable information was passed on minutes ago.

"She looks a bit like us," Mama Teta ventures.

"Oh," Meme Agathe snorts, "it's best not to trust appearances. My brother Thomas, he's dead now, he had nine children but three of them aren't from him, they're from the man who used to sweep the church and —"

"We don't need to hear the whole story," Meme Rarahu steps in, "your story has got nothing to do with the story here, learn to listen. Sometimes I have the impression that your ears aren't attached to your head because —"

The baby stirs, whining a soft whine, and silence immediately falls in the room. A few women who have been fanning themselves stop in midaction.

"She has a dimple like me when she smiles," Materena says, carrying on the conversation.

"Lots of babies come to the world with dimples," her mother shrugs.

Heads nod. The matriarch has spoken. It is her duty after all to protect the inheritance of her present and future grandchildren, the true ones, the certified, the proved. A few relatives think it's a bit strange to hear Loana talk that way, though, she having been a denied child and everything. You would think she'd have a bit more compassion.

"This is the first baby with a dimple I've seen." There, Pito has just decided to voice his opinion. "In my life," he adds, to give his opinion more weight. The mother-in-law shoots him an irritated look. "In my *whole* life," Pito clarifies.

Heads nod. True, the relatives are saying, dimples are extremely rare, a bit like twins, or a particular dot on a particular spot. They're the rarest — particular dots on particular spots — they're almost sacred actually. God gives these dots, God places them where it counts, God decides our fate.

It's like when God gave Loana the face of her father, the face of the Mahi people, there was never any question about her roots. She belonged to the Mahi clan.

But a dimple, eh? It has to be worth nearly as much.

"When is Tamatoa going to call?" Meme Agathe asks, noisily fanning herself with a blank sheet of paper.

"He's going to call when he's going to call," Meme Rarahu fires back.

"I was only asking, I don't know why you always —"

The baby stirs again.

"Every time you open your big mouth," Meme Rarahu whispers, "you wake up the baby."

"It's you, you have the voice of a man."

"What!" Meme Rarahu shrieks aloud.

The baby opens her beautiful brown eyes, stares at the curious eyes staring back, gurgles, and smiles up at Pito. Then, her eyes rolling backwards, she falls back to sleep.

That did the trick.

"Oh," the relatives sigh, smiling.

Opinions have now shifted. Poor baby, the women say. Imagine not being wanted like that, and by your own mother! Very soon, a passionate discussion begins about all those unwanted babies growing up without love in their lives, what becomes of them? Eh, they turn into cranky people, cranky and sad too, because in all honesty, eh, speaking from the heart here, being unwanted would have to be the worst curse of all, worse than having no money, worse than having no roof over your head, because . . .

Pito decides to put the little one to bed. When he comes back to the living room, the discussion sounds a bit more fiery, voices have risen, and the two incorrigible old women, Meme Rarahu and Meme Agathe, are once more at each other's throats. These two shouldn't be sitting next to each other, Pito thinks. He'd like to send one to that corner and one to the other, but he's never done anything like that before. Separate old women.

The telephone rings, and everyone jumps.

"*Allo,*" Pito says, grabbing the phone before anyone else can. "*Oui, oui,*" he tells the telephone operator, accepting the reverse charges.

"Mamie?" Tamatoa sounds worried.

Pito understands that Leilani must have exaggerated the urgency for Tamatoa to call home. Well, with Tamatoa, one has to exaggerate a little to get some reaction.

"It's Papi," Pito says.

"Papi?" Tamatoa sounds even more worried now. "Everything's fine?"

"You know a girl called Miri?" Pito won't be going by four paths. It's straight to the point.

"Miri Makemo?"

That wasn't the answer Pito had hoped to hear.

"I can't say that I *know* her," Tamatoa continues, "but *oui,* a little bit, I guess, but" — Tamatoa's voice drops to a murmur. In polite sign language Pito asks his wife's relatives to please be quiet, but they just go on ignoring him, and now Pito can hardly hear a word his son is saying, especially with the cacophony in the background, the mother-in-law being the leader of the pack. The only quiet woman around here is Materena. As usual, she's the one to be polite, the one showing respect to people on the telephone.

"What did you say?" Pito asks his son. "Speak louder, I can't hear."

"I said, why are you asking if I know Miri?"

"Ah, I'm glad you're asking, do you know that —" Pito turns to his rude relatives-in-law. "Eh!" he shouts. "*Mamu!*"

Jaws drop, and eyes widen in stupefaction, meaning, did Pito *Tehana* just dare tell us Mahis to be quiet? Who does he think he is? This is not his house! The talking continues, louder, if only to put Pito back in his place.

So Pito tells his son to wait, and puts the telephone down. "*Allez!*" he shouts, louder. "*Rapae!* Outside!" He waves them away towards the door. "*Allez!*"

Bodies hesitantly stand up, and eyes appeal to the woman of the house for her to say something.

"I need to go to the toilet." That's all Materena is going to say for the moment.

Pito picks up the phone and goes on. "Miri had —" he begins, then stops to advise his mother-in-law that she can stay. Loana, a big grin on her face, hurries to take her place on the sofa. "Miri had a baby, it's a girl, and it's yours apparently —" Pito indicates to Mama Teta with a nod that she too can stay. He knows how much Materena loves her great-auntie Mama Teta, who, a big grin on her face, also hurries and takes her place on the floor.

By the time Materena is back in the living room, her relatives, all thirty-seven of them, are still where they were when she left, and they're quiet as mice, and looking at Pito with admiration.

"Oui, I hear you," Pito tells his son, defending his cause. He only slept with Miri once, well, three times, but it was all during one night, so technically it was only once, and so, technically, it's impossible that he's the father of that baby, it's not like he had a relationship with that girl...

On and on the young man presents his side of the story, talking fast, panicking almost, blaming that girl for being so irresponsible, because...

"What did I always tell you about your seeds?" Pito cuts in. Silence.

"I didn't tell you to be careful, eh? I didn't say, Plant your seeds into the wrong woman and your life, your whole life, is going to be ruined?"

Silence.

The baby wakes up, and Materena runs to the rescue.

"Plant your seeds in the wrong woman," Pito repeats, "and —"

Materena is back with the baby, now crying her eyes out, crying as if someone were twisting her arm.

"And your whole life is going to be ruined," Pito continues, raising his voice above the baby's cries. "What? Of course the baby is with us. Miri? She's in New Caledonia. Why is the baby crying? What do you think? She's in the *merde,* in the *caca.*" What Pito means by this is: the baby is in a very shitty situation with a mother who's run away, a father in denial, and an auntie who has too many babies to look after.

At this point, Materena nudges Pito and passes him the baby. She'd like to have a few words with her son. The baby settles down at once.

"Tamatoa?" Materena is ready to say her piece. Ah *oui,* she will talk, she will say what's on her mind. "Imagine if Tiare didn't have my dimple, eh? Tamatoa, you better recognize that baby. I'm not having my granddaughter with Father Unknown written on her birth certificate. You should have thought about all of this before! What? That girl tied you up to the bed? She forced you? She hypnotized you? Tamatoa...don't turn me against you. I'm warning you! As soon as you finish military service, you are coming home, understand?"

And Materena bangs the telephone down. This is as good as the woman of the house yelling, "I HAVE SPOKEN!" Indeed, the woman of the house *has* spoken. Her "unknown" French father went back to his country after military service, and her grandfather only acknowledged Loana as his daughter on his deathbed (because, so the relatives said, he wanted to die with a clear conscience, he was afraid to be in purgatory for too long. It's boiling hot in purgatory, all Catholics know this), but Tiare will have what is due to her. Now, today. That is why Materena banged the telephone down for the first time in her life — and what's more, on her son she loves so much.

The crowd in the living room is still silent from the shock.

Then a very serious voice, belonging to the baby's great-grandmother, once a woman of pleasure before falling passionately in love with God, mentions in passing that now that the baby's name has been cleared, her religious education should be taken care of.

Is the baby baptized at least?

The Godfather

Catholics take the soul of a child very seriously. *Enfin,* it is the case in the Mahi family of Faa'a. You will never see a baby who's not baptized in this hard-core old Tahitian Catholic family. Put it simply, a baby must be purified from the mortal sin his parents committed in order to give him life, and this as soon as possible. So there's the baptism at the church and then the party at the house, where the relatives sing, eat, and drink until they can't walk.

That is what you do. You make sure to mark the day a child becomes pure and innocent, and you fete the godparents. As for the parents, well, they've done their bit and have already been feted during the welcome-into-the-world rituals.

Anyway, there's an unpurified child in the house. This has been confirmed by the baby's maternal great-auntie herself, who dropped in an hour ago to bring Materena the baby's birth certificate dated three months ago. She also brought a letter written by her friend who owns the car, stating that she was giving the baby (conceived by Tamatoa Tehana) away for familial reasons.

The situation about Tiare's soul is about to be corrected. Not at the St. Joseph Church, though — Pito has just decided this.

"Not at the St. Joseph Church?" Materena repeats as if she didn't hear properly the first time. "Where, then?"

"At my church," Pito says, tapping his fingers on the kitchen table. "St. Etienne."

"At your church?" Things are still unclear for Materena.

"*Oui,* at my church," Pito maintains, explaining that he got married in Materena's church, their three children were baptized in Materena's church, and, well, for his granddaughter's baptism, he'd like to give his church a go for a change.

"But you haven't been at your church for years and years," Materena protests. "Pito, think a little, it's —"

"It's what? You're going to tell me that your church is better than my church?"

"Do you know who the priest is there at least?"

"Father Fabrice. He baptized me."

"And he's still there?"

"But *oui!*"

The mama sitting at the desk outside the priest's office is the same woman who used to give Pito cranky looks during his one-week stint as a choirboy — when he was a child and the mama wasn't a mama. She advises Pito and Materena that Father Fabrice passed away.

"*Eh-eh,*" Materena says, firing a cranky look at Pito, meaning, Your priest is dead and you didn't know about it! Do you realize how embarrassing it is for me to be asking to speak to a priest who's dead? "I'm so sorry."

"Oh, don't be sorry," the mama says, also firing a cranky look at Pito, a look that says, You would have known the sad news earlier had you made the effort to visit your church now and then. "He died twelve years ago," she sighs, gazing at the child happily gurgling in her grandfather's arms. "He passed away peacefully in his sleep."

"Who replaced him?" Pito asks, a bit sad about the news. He liked Father Fabrice, but there's no point crying now, the priest has been dead for a long time.

"Father Martin replaced Father Fabrice," the mama advises Pito.

"Well, can we see Father Martin?"

"Father Martin is no longer with us."

"He died too?" Pito asks.

"*Non,* he didn't die," the mama snaps, as if to say, You would have known the wonderful news earlier had you made the effort to make an appearance here where you belong. "He went back to France three years ago to look after his father."

"Oh, that's wonderful," Materena manages to utter.

"Who replaced Father Martin?" Pito asks.

"Father Fabien."

"Can we see Father Fabien?"

"*Non,* Father Fabien —"

"All right," Pito interrupts. He's starting to get *fiu* of this. "Who's the priest here these days?"

"Father Sebastian."

"Okay, can we see Father Sebastian?"

"*S'il te plaît,*" Materena adds with a smile, stamping discreetly on Pito's foot.

Father Sebastian, who has a long red beard and a smashed nose, is at present checking his diary and whistling an upbeat disco tune. Materena glances at Pito and widens her eyes. She's saying, This is your priest? He doesn't look like a priest at all, he looks more like someone who just got out of prison!

The priest frowns and says, "I'm afraid the earliest I can do it is in six weeks."

"Six weeks!" Materena shrieks softly. "Father," she pleads with her begging voice, "we were hoping for next week, we can't wait six weeks because —"

"Unfortunately, you'll have to," Father Sebastian shrugs.

"We want this child baptized on Sunday." There, Pito has said his piece.

"*This* Sunday?" The priest scoffs as if he has just heard the most ridiculous request in his entire career as a priest.

"*Et alors,*" Pito snaps, "we're bringing you another Catholic and you're going to put sticks in the wheels?"

Pito ignores his wife's hand on his knee, begging him to please be quiet and to let her do the talking, she has more experience dealing with priests than he has. "You baptize this child on Sunday or I'm going to the Protestants."

Materena's hand is now pinching Pito's knee, commanding him to shut up before he ruins everything. You don't bluff with priests. This is not a game of cards!

"I understand how busy you are, Father." This is Materena's attempt to pacify the priest. "We can wait a little, but we'd really appreciate from the bottom of our hearts if —"

"Are you threatening me?" The priest is not listening to Materena. His eyes are fixed on Pito.

"Eh," Pito fires back, "I'm telling you things as they are."

Who does he think he is? Pito tells himself. A king or something? He's just a priest. It's his job to baptize babies, marry people, and bury the dead. Pito has never raised his voice to a priest before — but then again, he's never had a one-on-one meeting with a priest. He's always left the one-on-one discussion up to Materena, but he's here today and so he will speak what's on his mind.

"What's the problem with getting this baby baptized on Sunday?" he asks. "What do you need to do?"

"I need to consult with the godparents." The priest's voice is cold. Still speaking with a cold voice, he adds that he's not trying to put sticks in anyone's wheels at all but he simply cannot baptize a child without consulting the godparents first.

"The godparents are right in front of your eyes." Pito has just decided this. He glances at Materena, who's nodding in agreement.

"You're the godparents?" The priest himself sounds very shocked. "I thought you were the parents."

"We're the grandparents," Materena says softly.

"And the godparents." Pito is still firm on this.

"Where are the parents?" the priest asks.

Ah, now the parents, Pito says in his head. What is the next question going to be? Where are the great-grandparents?

Materena hurries to inform the priest of the delicate situation. The baby's mother is in New Caledonia and the father is in France.

"Hum." The priest doesn't seem too impressed. "And they will be coming back?" he asks. "I presume soon, and together?"

"I'm not sure about the baby's mother," Materena softly says, worried now that the information she's just given the priest might jeopardize her granddaughter's baptism. "But our son is —"

"What is this salad?" the priest exclaims.

"What salad?" Pito snaps. "Where is the salad in the story?" He glances at his wife, dabbing her wet eyes. And plus, that *con* has made my wife cry! "What salad?" Pito asks again, ready to yell his head off at the priest for having made his wife cry.

But his granddaughter starts to cry too now, so, gently tapping the baby on the bottom, Pito, speaking softly (well, close enough) tells the priest that there's no salad in the story. Some children have parents and other children have grandparents. That's life. There's nothing to judge.

"And have you been godparents before?" the priest asks, ignoring Pito's let's-not-be-judgmental speech.

"Three times," Materena smiles.

"And you, Monsieur?"

Ah, Pito would love to be able to tell that priest, "What do you mean *have been?* I'm still a godfather. When you're a godparent it's until you die." But unfortunately, Pito has never been a godfather. Nobody has ever asked him to be one. Now Pito feels like he's losing face. *Merde.*

Pito can already predict the priest's next question: Oh, you've never been a godfather, and why not? Next question: Oh, nobody has ever asked you, and how come that is? And how would Pito know this, eh? How would he know why nobody has ever asked him to be a godfather? It's like he has DON'T ASK ME TO BE A GODFATHER tattooed on his forehead?

Not being a godfather has never bothered Pito (being a father was more than enough, thank you, even if he didn't do much), but today he wishes he had one godfather experience at least, if only to put this priest in his place.

"Monsieur?" The priest would like his answer. Here he is grinning, smelling victory in the air, and Pito could pop him in the head right now.

"I've raised three children."

The priest shrugs. "You still haven't answered my question."

"None of my kids has ever been to prison." As far as Pito is concerned, if the priest can't understand why this is such a big thing for a Tahitian father to say, then he shouldn't be a priest. Not in Tahiti anyway.

Unexpectedly, the priest smiles his first genuine smile, and getting the necessary papers from his top drawer, he advises

Pito that he's very much looking forward to Pito's journey as a godfather.

"I can be the godfather?" Pito asks, just to make sure he understood properly.

"Indeed you can."

"This Sunday?"

The priest gives Pito the oh-you're-pushy-aren't-you look.

Pito looks back with his well-you-know-it-is-the-squeaky-wheel-that-gets-things-done look. He's lived in Tahiti all his life. He knows the ritual.

"This Sunday," the priest confirms, chuckling.

Despite the very (*very*, VERY) short notice, the Tehana tribe have managed to pull magic tricks out of their pandanus hats. Today is no ordinary baptism, though. It isn't, for example, the baptism of a niece's ninth child. It is the baptism of Pito's FIRST grandchild; what's more, with Pito as the GODFATHER!

Oui, you can say that the last twenty-four hours have been very hectic in the Tehana *quartier*, women running all over the place like chickens without a head. This is a great day, with the pride of at last having a ceremony for Pito in their church. All of the other ceremonies related to Pito and his tribe took place in Faa'a but now, for once, the Mahi tribe will be the guests. They will be the ones feeling a bit embarrassed having second servings and relieving themselves on other people's toilets.

So there is a flurry of cooking, cleaning, and making the house pretty, because with that many guests expected, all bathrooms in the *quartier* will be visited. The only thing they didn't have to worry about is the cake.

And here they are, two large Tahitian families gathered in Punaauia for the baptism of Tiare Makemo, soon to be Tiare Tehana. Women from both clans are eyeing each other, smiling little forced polite smiles, uttering polite sentences. "It's a beautiful day to be baptized, eh, Mama Teta?" "That is a nice hat you're wearing, Loana." "You've lost a lot of weight, Rita." "Giselle! Is this a new haircut?"

And many relatives from both clans would like to hold the little one in her frilly white dress before she gets purified, but there is only one person the child wants and it's her soon-to-be godfather.

Even later on, with food and drinks galore and relatives by the hundreds, the godfather is still the only one who can hold the newly baptized child without making her cry. So far, one hundred and twenty relatives, the godmother, and Pito's three sisters-in-law included have tried to carry the baptized baby girl and share a moment, even a brief one, in her new journey as an innocent and pure child. But the child only wants the strong arms of her *parrain* who fought so hard to get her baptized today.

It is now time to cut the cake — there is no party without a cake — and here it is being carried out to the table of honor in the skinny arms of the baptized baby's Auntie Vahine. Everyone goes silent with fear that the woman with the so-thin arms might drop the cake.

The silence is also one of profound admiration before that beautiful cake, decorated with icing of Tiare Tahiti flowers all around the borders and with the name TIARE written in the middle. Everyone agrees that Moana's handwriting is the handwriting of someone who writes a lot. It is so elegant and confident.

The young woman carefully puts the cake on the table beside the magnificent bouquet of flowers with the banner that reads *WELCOME BÉBÉ TIARE! WITH ALL OUR LOVE, AUNTIE LEILANI AND PAPA,* although everyone knows that the baby's father, Tamatoa, had nothing to do with it. Leilani was the one who called the florist in Tahiti and paid for that bouquet with her credit card.

Vahine rubs her sore, skinny arms and exclaims aloud in her little-girl voice, "*Ouf!* I was so scared I'd drop the cake!" Laughter erupts in the crowd. She isn't the only one relieved that the cake is still in one piece.

"I'd like to say a few words before the godparents cut the cake," Vahine goes on, smiling to her father- and mother-in-law. They smile back — as far as they're concerned, Vahine will be part of their family forever, no matter what happens with their son. She flew from Bora-Bora especially to deliver the cake. That is worth more than words. It's a ticket for life into Moana's family.

"My fiancé, Moana, was up at three o'clock this morning to make this beautiful cake for our niece. He's sorry that he couldn't be with us on this very important day but he's catering for the mayor's daughter's wedding —" Vahine pauses for a moment while her fiancé's relatives nod and look at one another, meaning, The mayor's daughter's wedding? *Wow!* She continues, "But Moana is with us in spirit, and ... well, let's cut the cake."

But first there are many relatives, at least those in the proud possession of a camera, who would like to take a picture of that amazing cake.

So, *click, click, click* and *click;* meanwhile, Pito's guest of honor, Father Sebastian — squeezed between Mama Roti and Auntie Philomena — is flicking a peanut in the air and expertly catching it in his mouth.

This is a trick you learn in prison. Everyone knows that.

An All-Different Route

Most godfathers get to go home after the baptism of the baby and carry on with their lives until the next church ceremony, which is the Communion, when the eight-year-old child finally tastes the body of Christ he's heard so much about from his older cousins. But Pito is not just the godfather. He is also the grandfather. And the guardian. He has three responsibilities:

1. to ensure that his goddaughter fulfills her requirements as a Catholic
2. to cuddle his granddaughter and pass on stories about the old days
3. to feed the little one, put clothes on her back, give her a roof over her head, and all the rest of it

Any normal man would panic at having three responsibilities at once, not to mention ongoing from one day to the next! Pito is a normal man and he's panicking, don't you worry about that. Even more tonight, because Materena is off to work and he's expected to mind the baby, because, well, he's the godfather, he's the grandfather, and he's the guardian, and Materena didn't want to ask her mother for help. Apparently Loana is getting old, what's more, she is very busy with her prayer meetings. So Pito has to stay home. Materena didn't give him a choice, she didn't order him to stay home either. She just stated the facts — without her martyr face.

Pito doesn't mind it much tonight, he never does anything on Mondays except watch TV and recuperate from the week-end. But what about tomorrow? How is he going to attend his nocturnal meetings with his *copains?* What about Wednesday and Thursday, eh? And what about Friday! How is he going to get to the bar to celebrate payday and the end of the week with his colleagues? These meetings are the only pleasures Pito has in life, on top of fishing, promenading in his best friend's speedboat, and of course doing sexy loving with his wife. When she'll be in the mood — which is hopefully soon.

"I hope it's not going to be in the next century," Pito, sitting on the sofa watching TV, mutters as he gulps his beer. He glances at his granddaughter, comfortable next to him, and she gives him one of her irresistible smiles.

"You smile a lot, eh? You were born smiling or what?"

The baby girl kicks her legs to show the old man how thrilled she is to be with him.

"When do you sleep, eh?" Pito asks. "It's nearly nine o'clock."

Another sweet smile. You would think that with all that she's probably been through, she'd be doing her miserable face. Pito gently taps his granddaughter's feet to show her, well, that he's not cranky with her, since it's not her fault. She was just born to a woman who was too young to have children and a man who doesn't live in the country. What can a baby do about that, eh? *Rien.*

But how cute Tiare is, how could anyone resist this baby girl? She is...ah...she's something. She's definitely part of the family, there's no denying the resemblance with her grandmother Materena, she's a Mahi for sure, and a Tehana too, a little. Let's hope she doesn't inherit any of the Mahi women's craziness. Anyway, there's no more beer left, so Pito gets to his feet to get himself another one from the fridge. He hasn't even walked three steps when Tiare starts whimpering.

"I'm coming back," Pito says. "It's not like I'm going off to war."

Tiare is now wailing. It isn't a piercing wail, the wail that Pito's children used to drive Pito crazy, so crazy he'd put his hands on his ears and tell himself, "It's not my child who is wailing, it's the neighbors'." Tiare's wail is like a pleading wail, a lost little wail that says, Please don't leave me. Pito hurries to the fridge, cracks his beer open on the edge of the table, and is back on the sofa in record time.

"I'm here," he says.

Tiare, sniffing, gives the old man an accusing look.

"Ah, now I'm in trouble, eh?"

The baby looks away and sighs.

"I only disappeared for thirty seconds," Pito justifies himself, "less than a minute!" Pito is about to continue, when he remembers that he's talking to a baby. "Why am I talking to this baby like she can understand?" he says out loud. Shaking his head with his eyes back on the TV, Pito chuckles, "*Copain?* You're starting to act like a bloody woman."

Pito never understood women talking to babies as if they could understand, and Materena did this a lot, even when their babies were only a few days old. "Oh, I see that you're awake," she'd say. "Did you have a nice dream?" One day Pito, who was a bit confused with the whole talking-to-babies issue, asked his mother if she talked to him when he was a baby. "I only talk to people who understand what I'm saying" was Mama Roti's answer. "I don't talk to babies and I don't talk to dogs. I don't talk to statues either."

Pito cackles and throws a furtive glance at Tiare to see if she's asleep, but she's still awake, and sulking.

"You're practicing already for when you grow up?" Pito asks. He taps himself on the forehead and says, "Stop talking like she can understand!"

Minutes later. "You're still cranky with Papi?"

Minutes later. "Come here, you." And with this, Pito takes the baby into his arms and gently taps her on the bottom. She looks up to him with her big, sooky brown eyes and Pito goes warm inside. He can't remember melting that way with his own children. In fact, he can't remember holding them that way. When his children were babies, Materena was always in the whereabouts, and she'd give him the baby to hold only to take the baby back seconds later because . . . why? Well, maybe she didn't trust him. She thought he'd drop *her* precious baby on the ground; or maybe she just wanted to hold her babies herself.

Leaving him with a baby like that would never have happened twenty years ago. Materena would have organized her mother to come over to babysit, or she would have asked an auntie. Better yet, Materena would have gratefully accepted her cousin Rita's kind offer to look after Tiare while Materena was at work.

But although Materena is fine with Rita coming around during the day in her lunch break to hold the baby for a few moments — to help her conceive — she decided that tonight

Pito would be in charge. Plus, Materena walked out of the house, without even making a fuss or giving him one thousand recommendations. She just walked out smiling and said, "I'll see you two when I come back."

There was a day a long time ago, Tamatoa was about three years old, Leilani was just a baby, and Materena had to go somewhere for a few hours. That day, for some reason, Materena decided to let Pito mind the children but she gave him such a long list of things to do and things not to do (such as not feeding her beloved son chicken wings because he might choke) that Pito got very annoyed. He told Materena off, she did her long face, Pito yelled at her, she grabbed her children and fled to her mother's. Pito copped cranky looks from his mother-in-law for weeks.

But here he is fully in charge. He looks down at his granddaughter, and her big brown eyes are staring at him like he's the most important person in the whole universe.

"*Dodo* soon, okay?" he says, feeling pretty tired himself. Actually he might go to bed now. "Okay, *dodo.*" He carries Tiare to her auntie's bedroom. The mattress has been moved to the floor and is covered with fluffy teddy bears the baby's relatives from Faa'a and Punaauia gave her on her baptism. Pito brushes the fluffy things off the mattress with his hand. How many teddy bears can a baby play with? And what's with the teddy bears anyway? People didn't give babies teddy bears back in his day. But now it seems that the world has gone bear mad.

Pito gently places Tiare on the bed — faceup. That is the only recommendation Materena gave Pito: until the baby is six months old, it should always sleep faceup. She gave him that recommendation at the baptism and explained why. It made sense to Pito, and when things make sense to Pito, he follows through.

"*Allez,* princess; *dodo.*" He pulls her quilt over her body. "Sleep well, I see you tomorrow morning." He softly kisses her on the forehead, switches the light off, and walks out. She whimpers and Pito stops dead in his tracks and waits. She stops and so he takes another step, and she starts whimpering again. He stops walking — she stops whimpering. He takes another step and she starts up again and doesn't stop.

He's back in the room, she stops whimpering. Growling, Pito lies on the floor next to the mattress with his hand lovingly resting on the baby and counts one to ten to pass the time. Ten to twenty, twenty to thirty, thirty to forty...three hundred and seventy-five. Pito can stop counting. He can hear his granddaughter's regular breathing. She's asleep.

But just in case, Pito lies still and waits for a few more minutes.

Standing at the door, Materena looks at her husband fast asleep on the floor. "*Eh-eh,*" she whispers tenderly, a hand on her heart, with tears welling in her eyes. Many things in this world move Materena. Babies, children, love songs, love movies, sunsets, kindness, flowers, prayers...the list goes on. It isn't difficult to move a sensitive woman to tears. But a man sleeping on the floor, his hand lovingly resting on a baby, is guaranteed to give a sensitive woman like Materena more tears and emotions, especially when she loves that baby very much. And despite the real fact that only four weeks ago she was seriously thinking of divorcing that man there, now on the floor looking so adorable.

People might say that the way to a man's heart is through his stomach...or more likely, in Materena's experience, his *moa.* But the way to get to a woman's heart, and just as fast, is an all-different route.

Love Like When
You Can't Think Proper

The dream she had last night, Materena tells Mama Teta and the other six *memes* who are gathered today to work on a quilt with Tiare comfortable on a mat, is the same dream she had four weeks ago, but it's a bit different. She's in the ferry, okay, with Pito, and they're standing at the rail looking down to the dark blue sea, when Pito falls overboard. It's not clear how Pito falls, but one minute he's standing by the rail next to Materena, and the next minute he's yelling his head off and *plouf!* He disappears into the dark blue sea with Materena looking down thinking that it's so sad that she will never see her man again for her whole life.

The seven old women have stopped their work and are now sitting still, needle and thread in hand, eyes focused on the storyteller, waiting to see where the story is heading to.

So back to Materena's dream last night. Same thing: Pito falls overboard, yells his head off, disappears into the dark blue sea, but this time Materena gets into action, and in the background, the music from *The Pink Panther* movie is playing.

"Can we hear music in dreams?" Meme Agathe ventures.

"Of course! She heard it, didn't she?" Meme Rarahu replies. "Mamu, don't talk. Materena, continue your story."

Okay, so Materena jumps overboard.

"And?" Meme Agathe asks.

And? Well, that's the end of Materena's dream.

"That's it?" Meme Agathe looks disappointed. "That's the end of your story?"

"Meme Agathe!" Meme Rarahu scolds. "You don't understand, you never understand anything! There's a message. Before, Materena didn't jump from the ferry, but last night she jumped from the ferry. There's a message."

"True," Mama Teta agrees. "There's definitely a message."

All eyes are now on the storyteller. What is the message?

"*Bon,*" Materena cackles. "*Bon.*" She has a dreamy look on her face now. Last night after Materena woke Pito up tenderly and helped him to the marital bed, Pito was so sweet. He held Materena tight and whispered, "Materena, my *chérie,*" in her ears, over and over again. Materena expected Pito to jump on her at any moment, since they hadn't done sexy loving in almost a month, but he kept on holding her tight, whispering her name and caressing her hair.

It was a very magic moment for Materena. It was like she had just met Pito, and he was taking his time before jumping on her because she was so special and he was afraid that he'd do the wrong thing and she'd run away.

And then they talked for nearly an hour! It's years since they talked for that long. Actually, they have never talked like that. Usually one ends up saying something that annoys the other within three minutes.

Materena felt like she was with a really good friend (but a *really* good friend; a friend who was making her feel, let's be honest, a little bit...*en chaleur*). They talked about their children, their granddaughter, and how beautiful she is, but also very demanding when she wants. Pito held Materena tighter and said, "My *chérie*, I'm going to take my holidays as soon as I can to help you." *And then —*

"*Alors?*" The *memes* are getting impatient. "Your message? What is it?"

"It could be that I'm —"

"*Oui,* that's it," five *memes* hurry to agree. "You're in love, in love like when we can't think proper, that's the message, you're in love like when you first met Pito... It's the big love between you two." Two *memes* casually mention that, actually, they did notice something different about Materena today, there's a twinkle in her eye... But let's get something straight, would Materena really jump overboard for Pito in real life?

Materena thinks a little. Would she jump overboard in real life? Well *oui,* to save one of her kids, of course she would jump, one hundred percent absolutely. Although they swim far better than she does. And... *oui,* she'd jump to save Pito too.

"Probably," Materena adds.

"Eh," Meme Agathe cackles, "what is the craziest thing you've ever done for love?"

Again, Materena has to ponder for a few seconds. Hmm... "I sneaked out of the shutter at night to meet Pito." Materena adds that this was back in those days when he wasn't her official boyfriend.

"That's not crazy!" Meme Agathe shrieks. "We've all sneaked out of a shutter to go and meet some boy we like!" She glances at the other *memes* to back her up on that one, but she gets only stares, meaning, speak for yourself.

"Do you want to know about one of the crazy things I did for love?" Meme Agathe asks. And before anyone can tell her that *non,* they're not particularly interested, she fires away, "I dyed my hair blond!" Blank looks, meaning, That's it? And you call this crazy? Anyway, next!

Well, Meme Rarahu walked twelve miles to see a boy she liked. She walked in the dark, alone, which wasn't a small thing for her to do, since she was quite a *peureuse* in her younger days. She was mostly afraid of *tupapa'u,* the evil wandering spirits — petrified, as a matter of fact — but she wanted to see that boy so much she overcame her fear and walked the twelve miles, reciting prayers and looking behind her back every two seconds. She walked fast, of course. Actually, if she remembers correctly, she ran, mixing her prayers and thinking about scary stories nonstop, like the story of that three-month-old baby possessed by the devil. Then when Rarahu finally arrived at that boy's house, he was busy with another girl! So Rarahu retraced her steps (same thing, praying and running) and she never saw that boy again. That was the first and the last crazy thing Rarahu ever did for love.

For Mama Teta, the craziest thing she's ever done for love, love for a man, she stresses, was promising her dying husband to remain faithful to him until her death. She was thirty-two years old, twelve weeks pregnant with Johno and the mother of three boys under the age of ten, with a husband she loved to distraction, even when he was alive.

Her dying husband said, drawing his last breath, "*Aita,* Teta, don't talk like that." But Mama Teta repeated her promise. "There's only one like you, how can I replace you?" And these were the last words Mama Teta's husband ever heard on this earth. Nor did she fail her words. Oh, Mama Teta isn't saying that she was a saint, *non,* she went out dancing in nightclubs to forget about her smelly boys for a while and be reminded that she was still a woman. She danced, flirted, played around. But she never fell in love again. She remained faithful to her husband in her heart. That is Mama Teta's story (the edited version) — followed by another story and another. Everyone gets a turn to speak out.

Now in the Radio Tefana studio Materena, greatly inspired, appeals to her listeners for their stories. Their stories of doing crazy things for love when they couldn't think proper. Women jump on the telephone to share their stories with Materena and the whole island.

Such as:

Lying to the judge with her hand on the Bible to give her boyfriend an alibi. Yes, I swear on the Bible and on the head of my ancestors that on the night of the fourteenth of April my boyfriend was in my bed. So it is quite impossible that he was involved in the theft of ten hi-fis from Sony music shop in Papeete.

Lending money to a boyfriend for him to invest, and then they would buy a block of land. But after she gave him the money sealed in an envelope, she never saw the boyfriend again. The last she heard about him, he was in Rapa Nui, growing flowers.

Giving up sewing, which she loved but the boyfriend was feeling left out. Often, he would say, "You love your sewing machine more than you love me." The woman gave up sewing for ten months, then she had to sew like crazy for about a year to catch up on the lost time after she chucked her boyfriend out.

Giving away her chickens because her boyfriend couldn't stand the noise they made in the morning. She didn't even stop to think how special her chickens were — they weren't just any chickens; they were the grandchildren of her grandmother's chickens. And she loved her grandmother. By the time the woman realized her foolishness, all the chickens she'd given away had been killed and eaten. She yelled at her boyfriend for having forced her to give away her chickens. She punched him too. He packed his bags and left.

There are still no stories from the men's front, but the women keep on calling.

Swimming across a shark-infested channel. Waxing. Tattooing his initials on the lower back. (Materena knows about that one, her own daughter having done this. Not on her lower back, though, on her hand for the whole population to admire.) Borrowing the ute — without permission — from one of the uncles to drive — without a driver's license — the boyfriend home...

Wait a second, there's a man on the line, the two assistants exclaim through the intercom. A man! Quick, connect him through. His name is Hotu.

"*Iaorana,* Hotu!" Materena cheers, but carefully. She doesn't want to frighten the first male listener ever to call her program.

"*Iaorana,* Materena, *e aha te huru ite poipoi?*"

"*Maitai.*" Materena finds the young man's sweet voice familiar to her ears, even though she hasn't seen the Hotu she knows for a long while. "*Alors?* What is your story about doing crazy things for love when you couldn't think proper? Tell us."

"I'm packing my suitcase to catch a plane to France tomorrow morning," the young man says. He wouldn't call this crazy, though, he insists, he'd call this natural. *Not* catching that plane would be the crazy thing to do.

"Who are you catching that plane for?" Materena asks, though she knows. She's now sure the man on the other line is the sexy dentist Hotu, her daughter's ex-boyfriend.

"The love of my life."

Ohhh, Materena is so moved. Here she is, placing a hand on her heart. Her two assistants are doing the same.

"When did you decide to catch that plane?"

"This afternoon."

"And what made you make that decision?"

"My heart... longing for her so bad."

Materena is going to cry in a minute. In fact, tears are already plopping out of her eyes.

She's so glad Hotu isn't ruining this magical moment with a comment like "And my other parts are longing for her too, *he-he-he.*"

"The love of your life, she knows you're on your way?"

"*Non.*"

Eh hia, now this whole thing is starting to sound dangerous. It reminds Materena of Meme Rarahu's story of walking twelve miles in the dark. Materena knows there's nobody on Leilani's horizon at the moment. Or at least, Leilani hasn't *mentioned* there was somebody, but it doesn't mean that there's actually nobody. Leilani could be keeping her news a secret, and...

And not counting the fact that Leilani might want to get herself emotionally ready for this big reunion, wash her hair and everything. So, without sounding like she's trying to pour cold water on Hotu's romantic plan, Materena tells him that he might consider giving the love of his life some hints that he's on his way.

But Hotu maintains that he'd rather throw himself overboard and see what happens. He will only be in Paris for six days because that's all he has, that's all he can give. At the moment anyway.

"Good luck, then," Materena says.

"Could I say something off the air? Off the record?"

"Hold on, it's time to play a song anyway." And seeing the special occasion, she requests a song that has been covered by many Tahitian bands, a song that is always played at weddings, a song that makes women want to hold their men. So please, "Guantanamera" for the ladies, and the gentleman.

Off the air . . .

"It's me," the young man says.

"The Hotu I think it is?" Materena asks just to make sure. "Leilani's Hotu?"

"*Oui, c'est moi. Eh . . .*" Casually, Hotu asks Materena if the love of his life is seeing anyone.

"There's only one boy in her head, and it's you," Materena says. She gives the young man her blessings but still wishes him good luck.

Waiting for the song to finish, Materena ponders if she should call her daughter to advise her of Hotu's arrival so that Leilani can do her things — shave her legs, pluck her eyebrows, buy a beautiful dress, things like that. But then it would ruin Hotu's surprise, and anyway, he's already seen his girlfriend in a ripped, oversize T-shirt with her hair all over the place and hairy legs.

No, no need to call, Materena decides, Hotu's so hooked on Leilani he's not going to care about what she looks like when she opens the door.

"Girl?" Materena smiles tenderly, eyeing Pito doing up his tennis-shoe laces. "Hotu is on his way to see you. He's already on the plane."

"*AHHHHHHH!*" A shriek of delight. "But I haven't shaved for weeks!" Panic sets in. "I haven't plucked my eyebrows either! What am I going to wear? I've got to get ready! Okay, *nana* Mamie!"

This is the shortest phone conversation Materena has ever had with her daughter. Not even thirty seconds.

Magnet for Pulling Women

His tennis shoes tied, his granddaughter safely tucked in his arms, Pito is on his way to do a bit of walking around the neighborhood, a bit of exercise. They might even go as far as the international airport. When you have a hot woman, you've got to keep fit.

"Be careful of the dogs!" Materena calls out to Pito as he steps out of the house.

But it isn't the dogs that Materena should be worried about, it is the women! For Pito is about to find out that a man with a baby in his arms is Prince Charming as far as women are concerned, even if he isn't, well ... very appealing to the eye.

But being Prince Charming isn't the reason why Pito is taking his granddaughter along on his new journey to be fit, the reason is much simpler. He just feels like taking this baby out of the house a bit, to give her some fresh air, change her ideas and everything. And there's also the desire to appear normal.

The way Pito sees the situation, a man walking around on his own attracts suspicion. People will say, "What is that man doing walking on his own around here, eh?" People will think that he's plotting to steal their TVs, worse, harm their children. A baby, so Pito believes, will camouflage him, and make him walk past unnoticed. But first, a quick *Iaorana* to Mori sitting under the mango tree at the petrol station as usual.

"*Eh, Iaorana.*" Mori stands up. "And how's the queen today?" he asks, kissing Tiare's feet. The queen giggles. She loves her great-uncle Mori.

"So?" Pito says. "What's the latest news on the coconut radio?" Although Pito already knows the news on the coconut radio, since Mori has told him the news yesterday and the day before, it doesn't hurt to be told again how wonderful you are.

"They say you're wonderful."

"*Ah bon?*" Pito feigns surprise.

"*Ah oui,*" Mori confirms. "You're wonderful, you're a champion, you're number one."

"Hmm." Pito stands up proud and tall. "So they're not backstabbing anymore, eh?"

"*Non,* Cousin, women adore you." The women in question, of course, are the in-laws who have never thought highly of Pito until recently when he became Mr. Mama, looking after his granddaughter while Materena is at work.

When the news that Materena had nominated Pito to be in charge of Tiare got on the coconut radio, the relatives were deeply concerned. What is our cousin doing? they asked. Trusting a man who can't be trusted when there are so many women in the family available to help.

But now it is a known fact that Pito can change diapers, make bottles, massage the baby's belly to ease gas pains — he can do the whole lot, and without any supervision. And plus, he's taking his holidays next month to help Materena with the baby! Talk about a miracle! *Bon ben,* since the news is still the same, Pito better go and start his exercise program. Off he goes, walking fast steps and feeling a bit healthier already.

"Pito!" Mama Teta and her gang of six respectable-looking *memes*, all wearing missionary dresses (also known as mama *ruau*, old-woman dress), running shoes, and pandanus hats, spot Pito and hurry over.

"*Eh mea ma!*" Pito calls out, thinking, Great, they're going to talk to me for days, and then I'm never going to do my exercise. Simultaneously and with astonishing speed, the women fish out their handkerchiefs from inside their bras to wipe their faces. Nobody wants to kiss sweaty people.

Pito greets the venerated Mama Teta with two kisses on her cheeks. He also kisses her companions because, speaking from experience, *memes* like to be kissed. You kiss one, you kiss the whole lot or they get sad. So, *bisous-bisous* multiplied by seven.

"Where are you off to?" Pito asks.

But nobody cares about Pito anymore, he's already an old story. The baby in his arms is much more interesting.

"*Aue!* She's so tiny, she's so beautiful, she looks like a doll, can I hold her for a little while?"

But the baby hides her head in her grandfather's shirt.

"She's hiding, the little *coquine*, come on, *mistinguette*, give your old Mama Teta a little smile." After a bit more persuasion, Mama Teta finally gets her much-sought-after smile. "*He-he!*" she brags, "she gave me a smile, it's because she knows I'm her blood, I'm family."

The other *memes* push Mama Teta out of the way, they want to be blessed with a baby's smile too. They coo and coo, whisper tender words, beg with their hands joined in prayers, tickle the baby's feet, and very soon there are about thirty relatives trying to get close to baby Tiare. Cars driving past slow down, and heads, the drivers' included, turn to the crowd to see what's going on. Is it a politician mixing with the people to get some votes? A celebrity who had hoped to pass incognito? *Eh non,* it's just a man with a baby in his arms, keep driving.

But it is not just a man with a baby in his arms. It is, according to the crowd of women present, a man going through the next stage of his life, the stage of enlightenment and maturity.

"Ah," sighs one of Mama Teta's companions, "I've seen this lots of times in my life. When men are young they make babies as if they were free, but they don't care, they want to *stay* free. Then they get old and you see them walking around with a baby in their arms, and they're even changing diapers... Ah, *maitai,* it's good."

"True," another of Mama Teta's companions agrees. "I think men should only become fathers when they're mature in the head. There are too many irresponsible young fathers around, they understand nothing, not even themselves."

"It should be the law that our men can't become fathers until they're at least thirty years old."

"Eh, forty is better."

On and on and Pito is getting *fiu* of all of this, not counting that the way a few of his in-laws are staring at him is making him quite uncomfortable. Here, Loma for instance, she's staring at Pito like she wants to jump on him. Lily too... Lily, who's never given Pito a second glance before because he's married to her cousin and he's not her type, but this morning for some reason she's openly admiring Pito like he's a hero, a fireman with a medal for bravery or something. She gazes at the baby in his arms with longing and smiles at Pito.

Pito smiles back, turns his head to one of Mama Teta's companions, the eldest one, she must be close to being eighty years old, and she's also looking at Pito like she wants to jump on him.

With brief excuses, Pito escapes his fans, walking as fast as he can past the Chinese store, the fibro shacks, and making a right turn towards the international airport. *Voilà*, at last, nobody knows him here. Pito's plan is to walk around the carpark ten times, twenty times if Tiare doesn't whine, thirty if he's up to it. Okay, then, let's go for the first lap with fast steps to make the heart beat faster. Go, go, go — *allons-y!*

"Oh, the beautiful baby!" a pretty young woman exclaims, getting out of her car. "How old is he?"

"Four months," Pito replies, looking straight ahead. He's not going to bother rectifying that woman's mistake about the baby's gender. He's seen many women get all upset when people misjudge their baby's sex — It's a girl! or It's a boy! — but who cares about things like that? Pito tells himself. It's not the end of the world if people think your baby is a boy when it's a girl, and vice versa. They are only strangers. They don't count.

And now, let's have a little tour at the airport, let's count the tourists, eh? There are three young women, tanned with sun-bleached hair, slouched on the benches with surfboards and backpacks at their feet. They give Pito the biggest, friendliest smile, as if they know him well. He gives them a friendly smile too. Further away, two thirty-something black women dressed in jeans, white tops, and high-heel shoes openly admire Pito and the baby in his arms. They are so beautiful that Pito's eyes pop out of his head. They ask, in sign language, if they could touch the baby. "Absolutely!" Pito replies in sign language. "Touch the baby for as long as you want."

The black women go ahead, caressing the baby's arm very softly, talking to the baby in their language, smiling at the baby smiling at them, breathing their mint-scented breath all over Pito, making his head spin with their heavy perfume.

Pito is in paradise. These women, top models for sure, would never in a million years have given Pito a second glance without this baby in his arms. Actually, they wouldn't have given him a *first* glance. Ah, if only Pito had known this earlier, he would have taken his children for lots of walks when they were babies. He would have been more popular, instead of pretty-boy Ati getting all the attention.

But the beautiful black women have to go now and, adopting a sad face, they blow the beautiful baby a kiss, and another. The grandfather too gets a kiss blown his way, and he's still smiling minutes later, long after the angels have gone.

When he comes out of his reverie, he's in front of the airport café, and who does he see sitting right out the back? Ati — on his own.

That's strange, Pito tells himself. Ati usually has company, and plus, he's looking quite gloomy today. It's a change from smiling-with-all-his-teeth Ati. Smiling-with-all-his-teeth (because he has the apartment in town, the flashy car, the speedboat, the women, the whole lot) Ati has occasionally gotten on Pito's nerves. It's nice to see Ati looking a bit normal. But still, Pito hopes his best friend isn't going through a depression.

"*Copain?*" Pito gently taps Ati on the shoulder, counting the empty coffee cups on the table. Eight.

"*Eh copain!*" Ati exclaims, smiling, but by the time Pito is sitting with his granddaughter on his lap, Ati's face is long again.

"You're fine?" Pito asks.

"I have nothing." There, Ati has spoken.

"You have nothing?"

"Nothing, *copain;* no wife, no family, no nothing." Ati goes on about how he used to look at men with children and think, I'm glad I'm not him. But these days he thinks, I wish I was him. Here, what about his sister's husband with his tribe of eight children? One day, only last year, Ati's brother-in-law came home from work while Ati was visiting his sister, and the eight children ran out to their father and jumped on him, and Ati thought, I'm so glad I'm not him. Imagine being attacked like that every day. But yesterday, Ati's heart was full of envy for his brother-in-law. He thought, Imagine being greeted that way every day. When Ati walks into his empty apartment, all he gets is a look of reproach from his dying plants.

"Look at what you've got, Pito," Ati says with his sad voice. "A beautiful wife, three fantastic kids, and now this little princess. Look at me, I'm going to be a lonely old man who scares children."

"Ati, you've been drinking too much coffee."

No response from Ati.

Pito has never seen Ati like this, but he will be the first to admit that Ati is reaping what he sowed. Pito can't count on his fingers the women his best friend has brought to tears. Hundreds? There were quite a few nice women willing to devote their whole life to Ati, but *non,* Ati had to see if the next catch was better. And pretty-boy Ati is not getting any younger, though sometimes he believes he is, chasing younger and younger women. Some of them a bit *too* young — green, far from being ripe — because, as Ati has said, "A man is only as old as the women he's sleeping with."

"I tell you, *copain,*" Ati declares with seriousness. "The next woman I meet is going to be my wife."

"*Ah oui?*"

"*Oui,* this is my promise to you."

"You don't have to promise me anything, it's your life."

"The next woman I meet," Ati repeats, "is going to be Madame Ramatui."

"What about one of Materena's cousins?" Pito says for a laugh. "That way we're going to be in-laws."

"Who do you have in mind?" Ati sounds interested.

"Loma?" Pito is still joking.

"Loma! Are you crazy?"

Pito cackles and thinks about Rita. If she weren't with Coco, Pito would recommend (and highly) that Ati tries his luck with her. Pito has always liked Rita. She has her feet on the ground, she's a very nice person, and lately very pretty too. Rita has lost even more weight in her quest of falling pregnant, something like sixty pounds! Coco must be dreading the day Rita finally falls pregnant and starts eating for two again.

"Well, what about Lily?" Pito remembers that there was a time Ati liked Lily but was too intimidated to approach her. Ati claimed at the time that Lily was out of his league, and plus, she only liked men in uniforms with medals. Ati was still tempted to try his luck, with a bit of encouragement from Pito, but then he heard that Lily was a heartbreaker. And that was it, since Ati is also a heartbreaker. You can't have two heartbreakers breaking each other's hearts.

Well, maybe Lily has changed, just as Ati has.

"Lily..." Ati looks up, pondering. "*Oui,* I could try my luck with her...but she doesn't look like a woman who wants a family."

"See if you can get into her pants first," Pito says, shrugging, "then ask her nicely."

"Can you organize something, then?" Ati asks, interested. This is Ati saying, *Oui,* I will try my hardest to get into Lily's pants and then I will ask her very nicely to give me children.

Pito nods. He doesn't mind playing Cupid. "We'll eat at the house next week, I'll get Materena to invite Lily...leave it to me."

Her New Man

Looking after a baby during your holidays can't really be called a holiday, but it doesn't mean that Pito is not enjoying the first day of his well-deserved break from work, even if it involves changing diapers and making bottles.

It's nice for a change to be the person who counts the most. Now, Pito isn't saying that Tiare ignores her grandmother and he's not comparing at all, there's no comparison to be made, but let's just say that Pito has the magic touch with Tiare at the moment. Whenever Tiare is in her bizarre mood, crying for no reason and fidgeting, Materena automatically passes the baby to Pito. Luckily, so far, anyway, Tiare only does her theatrics when her grandfather is around. Time will tell how long Pito's magic touch will last.

Right now, Tiare is on her grandfather's belly. Every now and then Pito swells his belly and baby goes up and laughs. Materena, nearby, working on a crib-size quilt for her granddaughter, cackles. "Pito, eh, you are a clown, you know."

Pito winks at his wife, finding her very beautiful this morning. She used to make him shit bubbles on Saturday mornings. He'd be on the sofa, trying to recuperate from a hangover, and she'd decide to do a huge cleaning, drag furniture around, sweep like a madwoman. But here she is now, quietly embroidering her granddaughter's name on a quilt, a serene look on her face and a bit of rouge on her cheeks.

They had a joke earlier on about names on crib quilts. Most Tahitians have a crib-size quilt with their name embroidered on it. Pito has, so does Materena, and each of their three children. And now Tiare. When they get old, Materena cackled, walking around in circles at the nursing home with their quilt on their shoulders and forgetting their own name, they will ask someone, "Pardon, do you know my name?" The person will take a quick look at the name on the quilt and say, "Well, if this is your quilt, your name is..."

Ah, Pito is enjoying the new Materena. It's fun when a man can share a joke with his woman without her getting all defensive because she thinks he's criticizing her.

Pito is now thinking about that night she didn't spend in the marital bed...Where did she go? And with whom? They haven't had the chance to talk about that since Tiare came into their lives, and perhaps they haven't wanted to either. Pito hasn't asked questions, and Materena hasn't confessed. He knows there's a confession. He knows his wife didn't spend the night with her invented girlfriend Tareva. He knows because he asked her a few nights ago, and very casually, "How's Tareva?" and Materena replied, "Who?" Well, all right, Materena was half asleep but still... you would remember a friend you stayed out with all night.

Materena catches her husband checking her out. "What?" she asks.

"I'm just looking at you," Pito says, giving his wife the hum-not-bad look.

"Papa, eh...," Materena cackles.

She used to have a girlie cackle when she was young, but the high-pitched cackle (the *hi-hi-hi*) has been replaced by a deep cackle (the *he-he-he*), the cackle of a mama. Not that Pito minds, the cackle of a mama is nice to listen to, it tells many stories. Unlike the croaky cackle of a *meme,* which can be a bit freaky.

Pito was so afraid that Materena would turn into a *meme* overnight after finding out that she was a grandmother. Pito has witnessed this strange phenomenon in his own family. Lots of his aunties transformed themselves into *memes* overnight.

One minute they were cackling the sexy mama cackle and doing the sexy mama walk, the walk that says, I may be past forty but I've still got it in me, and next minute they were doing the freaky *meme* cackle and doing the slow walk with the dragging sound of thongs, accompanied by the long and exhausted sighs. The walk that says I'm a *grandmère* now, don't even think about getting ideas.

Luckily for Pito, Materena stayed a sexy mama. She kept on doing her fast walk, the walk that says, I may be past forty, but I've still got it in me: the sexy loving, the energy, the enthusiasm — the package!

But it's so nice when she's sitting still instead. A man can look at his wife properly when she's sitting still, like Pito is doing right now. He's really happy that his wife didn't lose those fine ankles. Pito loves fine ankles. He loves Materena's wrists too, they're so small, you wouldn't believe they belong to a strong sexy mama. As for Materena's body, well, it is a bit larger than when he first met her, there's a bit more flesh around the waist, but she's still a sexy mama.

Pito feels very grateful his wife looked after herself. Many of his cousins were very cute when they were young but as soon as they popped that first baby out, they started to eat like crazy.

Every dish had to be drowning in coconut milk, and every serving had to be multiplied by two, sometimes three. But Materena...

"Eh, Pito," sexy mama cackles. "Stop looking at me like you've never seen me before."

"You know when I was in France for military service," he says. For some reason Pito feels these two missing years must be clarified today.

"And I was crying on my pillow for you and you didn't even send me a postcard, and you had six girlfriends, *oui,* I know." Materena's voice is not angry. She has resigned herself to the fact that it was a long time ago and she wasn't really Pito's official girlfriend.

"I didn't know you were waiting for me," Pito says.

"I told you that I was going to wait for you."

"Well, I didn't know you were serious."

"Pito, you knew I was crazy about you," Materena says.

"I didn't know you were serious," Pito repeats. "I thought to myself, Ah, she's with someone else now, she's not going to wait for me for two years without playing around, she's a pretty girl."

"I didn't look at any boys. The only boy in my head was you." Materena puts her quilt down for a few seconds to sigh with nostalgia, and confesses that she knew, she just knew in her heart, that it was her destiny to be with that boy Pito Tehana, it was her destiny to have his children.

"I'm still the only boy in your head now?" Pito asks, taken by surprise by his wife's confession. He knew she liked the things he did to her under the frangipani tree behind the bank, but he had no idea that she was fantasizing about having his children.

Materena gives him a long look, a look that says, You ask a silly question. Ah, Pito loves those big brown eyes, especially when they're not cranky. Pito looks down to Tiare, staring at him with her big, beautiful brown eyes, the eyes of her grandmother.

"Tiare has your beautiful eyes," he says.

"Beautiful eyes?" Materena smiles. "You've never told me that my eyes were beautiful."

Ah, and when she smiles, she has that cute dimple on her left cheek. Pito looks down to Tiare again, still staring at him. He smiles and she automatically smiles back. "And she's got your cute dimple too."

"Cute dimple? You've never told me that my dimple was cute."

"*Bon ben,* today must be your day for compliments."

"I accept them, *Maururu roa.*"

Pito waits for Materena to say something nice about him too, but she's busy stitching. "What about me? You're going to give me some compliments too?" he asks. "That way we're equal."

Materena scrutinizes Pito. He's now doing his not-bad-for-my-age-eh? expression. And-plus-I'm-exercising-these-days. Half a minute passes and Materena is still scrutinizing Pito.

"*Allo?*" Pito says, half serious, sucking his belly in. "You're sure taking your time with my compliments."

"Pito... when I look at you I see..." It seems Materena isn't sure if she should tell her husband what she sees or not.

"What do you see?" Pito is now worried. He knows that he's not as handsome as he used to be, like his mother has been so fond of telling him. *Oui,* the gut is a bit *tautau,* and the hair a bit gray, well, what do you want? People can't look like they're eighteen years old all their life. "*Alors?* What do you see?"

"I see a friend." There, Materena has spoken.

"A friend!" Pito was hoping for a compliment. "Is that all you see? What about my body, hum? You think I need to walk further?"

"You're fine as you are in my eyes."

"*Ah bon?* You don't want a man with more muscles?"

Materena informs her husband that she's never been interested in muscles, so why should she be now? When she met him he didn't have any muscles. Pito informs his wife that, *excuse-moi,* he did have muscles when they met. *Non,* Materena insists, he was skinny like a nail when he used to come for his sandwich at the snack where she worked. Pito denies this, and why on earth did she like him anyway if he was skinny like a nail?

"There was something about you... And then when you kissed me, I was gone."

Pito smirks. "How did I kiss you?"

"Like you kiss me now."

"And —" Pito is really enjoying this conversation.

"Well you kiss me good, your lips are very soft."

"My lips are soft, eh?" Pito is really, *really* enjoying this conversation. "What else did you like about me?"

"The same things I like now."

"And... tell me —"

"Well, I like the way you —"

"You... come on... spill the bucket."

Materena cackles her sexy mama cackle and shakes her head. "I don't need to do you a drawing Pito, you know what I mean. But you're becoming like a friend to me because —"

"So my lips are very soft," Pito interrupts. He's not interested in the friend story. He doesn't want to be his wife's friend. He has enough friends as it is. He wants Materena to talk about his lips and everything.

"I don't think I loved you before like I love you now, Pito."

"Eh?" Pito is suddenly confused.

"Well, *oui,* I loved you, but not like I love you now, you know what I mean?"

Non, Pito has no idea what Materena is going on about!

She explains what she's going on about, and it's fairly simple. Before, when their children were little, she was adamant about not letting the father of her children escape, she wanted a father at the kitchen table, a father in her children's lives, she was prepared to keep him no matter what. No matter how insensitive he was, if he forgot her birthday, preferred his *copains* to her; but now the children are big and —

"You can chuck me out," Pito cackles. "And go with your Chinese boyfriend."

"What Chinese boyfriend?"

"The boyfriend you met at Kikiriri."

"Pito." Materena bursts out laughing. "I was with Cousin Lily."

"The whole night?"

"*Oui,* the whole night, we slept at the hotel." Materena is still laughing.

"Why didn't you tell me that you were with your cousin instead of lying about that girlfriend?"

Materena puts the quilt down to look Pito in the eye. "Pito...do you know how angry with you I was? I was so angry I wanted to divorce you."

"Eh?" The room becomes black for a quick second, and baby Tiare, sensing her grandfather's shock, begins to cry. "*Non, non,*" Pito hurries to say, lovingly tapping the baby's bottom. "Don't cry, *chérie* —" And giving Materena the questioning look, he says, "Divorce me?"

"Divorce you," Materena confirms. "Pack your bags, send you back to your mama, and never speak to you again."

"Why? What did I do?"

"It's not what you did, it's what you said."

Pito is even more confused now. "What did I say?"

"You don't remember?"

Pito searches his memory. He remembers Materena not talking to him for six days because, so he concluded, she was just *fiu* of seeing his face, as it happens with couples. And then she acted like she hated him for all that time but...

"What did I say?"

"When I told you that I wanted to look for my father, you said —"

"You want to look for your father?" This is the first time Pito hears about it.

"You said," Materena continues, "'you think he's going to want to know you?'"

Pito widens his eyes with stupefaction and again baby Tiare starts to cry. Pito sits up and holds baby on his knees. He needs some fresh air. His head is spinning a little. *Non,* he did not tell Materena these words, no way. "Did I really —"

Materena sadly nods.

"I was *taero?*" Pito asks, although he already knows the answer.

Another sad nod.

Pito is flushed with shame. "Forgive me, *chérie,* I was —"

"I have already forgiven you," Materena smiles. "Otherwise you wouldn't be here today, you'd be at your mother's house going *taravana.*"

"But...Materena, your father is going to be so proud to know you!" Pito exclaims, dumbfounded at how close he came to being ejected — and over something he had no idea about. "He's going to think you are amazing!"

Materena shyly lowers her eyes and cackles. "I think you've given me enough compliments for today."

"It's not compliments, it's the truth. I can help you look for your father."

Materena picks up her quilt and shrugs. "I've got too much in my head at the moment. Work, the children...Our *mootua* who doesn't have her mother and her father."

"*Chérie,* as soon as Tamatoa is home," Pito says, thinking, That boy *will be* coming home, "we can start the search for your father together."

Smiling, Materena continues stitching. "Eh, Pito...one thing at a time."

She'd like to enjoy her new man for a while first.

The Golden Boy

After Tiare arrived, Pito was the man in Materena's eyes for two blissful years. But there's a new man in the house now — Materena's golden boy, her firstborn, her adored eldest son, Tamatoa.

Since he's been home, thanks to his father paying the fare on his *carte bleu,* Tamatoa goes out dancing and drinking with his *copains* and cousins, and then he comes home and expects a feed waiting for him at the kitchen table. He does the clown and makes his mother and daughter laugh with those stupid dance moves he's learned God knows where. Here, his last trick is to dance, pull out his comb from the back pocket of his jeans, and comb his hair — still dancing.

After eating, he lies on the sofa in front of the TV like a corpse...for hours! Either that or he goes out for the whole night to the nightclub to dance his stupid disco moves, comes home in the early hours of the morning, and doesn't get out of bed until the afternoon.

This situation is making Pito lose his screws. He had a word about this to Materena tonight before she went to work, and she said, "*Aue,* Pito, our son has just come home. Don't worry, he's going to be all right, at least he's home every night to eat. He doesn't go to other people's houses, and he doesn't drink on the road. Give Tamatoa time to play a little."

Time to play? He's been playing all over Europe for months since his military service ended. And anyway, Pito didn't have time to play when he became a father. He walked straight from the delivery room into a job, so to speak. Ah, true, the day his precious son came into the world, Pito became serious. He wasn't dancing in nightclubs. He was slaving away at the factory for eight hours a day!

Pito should have known better than complain to Materena about Tamatoa. As far as she's concerned, he's a very good son, bless the day he was born, et cetera. After two years of listening to her tell him off on the phone (and to his photo in the living room, the one of him in his military clothes) for taking so long to come home to meet his daughter, Tamatoa has turned into a saint in his mother's eyes because he's here now. What's more, he came home before Mother's Day.

If only Materena could see her golden boy now, Pito thinks. They are in Papeete with Ati and his son to buy Mother's Day gifts.

Pito glances to his two-year-old granddaughter fifteen feet away, wearing her brand-new red tennis shoes that match her red dress and the red ribbons in her pigtails. Presently, she's standing still next to her father, who came into her life less than a week ago, her father who is too busy checking out the girls walking past to notice her brand-new shoes.

Her little voice says, "Eh, Papi, look at my shoes." But the young man hears nothing, being now fascinated by a pack of schoolgirls strolling by, firmly holding on to their precious textbooks. He whistles and calls out sweet words. "Eh, bella! Bellissima!" The schoolgirls turn around and giggle, and next thing, the fit and handsome twenty-three-year-old young man wearing nothing but a pair of faded jeans rolled at the bottom follows them, doing his robot walk. The schoolgirls turn around to look at him and giggle some more.

"Tamatoa!" Pito calls out, thinking, Great, you send your son to military service so that he becomes a man, and they send you back a clown. "Be careful of *bébé!*"

The father (too young to know better) walks back to his daughter, dragging his feet along, and doing his long face. For a moment, he looks like he's about to call something out to his father, something like what he told him last night and the night before and the night before, and on the telephone many times.

"I didn't ask for a child. Children should be with their mother. Miri is a bitch for abandoning her daughter like that. It's not enough to send toys and photos of herself with her Godzilla French boyfriend... He really doesn't look Catholic, that one. She should take her daughter to live with her in France. You and Mamie shouldn't have legally adopted Tiare. Now Miri thinks she doesn't have responsibilities." But one look at his father grinding his teeth and Tamatoa understands that it's not the time to make a scene.

"*Merde!*" Ati is losing his cool. Right in front of a pizzeria, and plus, it's so hot today! Sweat is pouring off his forehead.

"*Copain, haere maru, haere papu;* go slow, go right." This is Pito talking with his calm voice. How hard can it be to put a carriage together? But we're not talking about a cheap carriage that unfolds easily here, we're talking about a science-fiction gadget, the top-of-the-line carriage, imported from the USA. It cost Ati the eyes in his head. And today, one day before Mother's Day, Ati will be getting the mother of his child, Lily, something even better. As soon as he gets that *putain* carriage up.

Ati's beautiful baby boy was conceived the very night his parents were guests at Materena and Pito's table (where Ati greatly impressed Lily with his historical knowledge) and made his entrance into the world eight months ago at the private clinic.

On that day, which Ati solemnly proclaimed to be the best day of his entire life, he had a serious talk with Lily. "Look," he said, "even if it didn't work between us two, let's agree to do the best by our son. He needs to grow up with both his parents."

She replied, "Okay, good. You can have your son three days a week, and I'll have him for four."

"What?" Ati had expected something a bit more full-time. "Are you serious?"

"Better not to complain," Lily said sweetly. "Maybe you will only be having my son for two days."

Pito told Ati not to worry too much, it's not the best time to negotiate with a woman when she's just given birth — of course, Lily would soon realize that it is much more practical to raise a child when both parents are living under the same roof. But Pito underestimated Lily's top organizational skills. Within a week of Rautini's birth, his mother's very unusual arrangement with his father was proving to be quite successful.

"*Merde!*" The carriage is tipped over, and two pairs of mystified eyes scan the bolts and the knobs, *purée de bonsoir,* who invented this stupid thing?

"Look at my shoes," a little voice says again, trying to attract her papa's attention.

But Tamatoa doesn't care about that little girl's shoes. He cares more about the brown girls walking by. Ah, he missed those brown girls. French girls are beautiful but Tahitian girls are better. He'd forgotten. Tahitian girls don't get cranky if you mess up their hair. When he met Miri Makemo, he was in all honesty very taken by her, but it was the costume she was wearing — the traditional grass skirt and the bra made out of coconut shells. She was like a fantasy in that gloomy street of Paris. He was walking by, and she was in the street, smoking a cigarette after the show. And she called out, "Eh? You're Tahitian?"

If she had been wearing normal clothes, jeans and a shirt, for example, Tamatoa wouldn't have looked at her twice. But he did, and now he's getting punished for it. After the wild and passionate night they had together, she asked him where he was from, and he, *stupido,* gave her his address in Tahiti.

When Pito looks up, there's no sign of his son, and Tiare is showing off her new shoes to an old French man smoking a pipe, shirt unbuttoned, and looking extremely interested in this little girl and her brand-new shoes.

"Tiare!" Pito's booming voice is enough to wake up the dead.

The little girl immediately looks up at her grandfather. He gives her a nod his way, meaning, *haere mai,* come here right now, and the little girl, not one to disobey her grandfather when he's cranky, hurries over to him.

"Go and wait in the car," he says, giving the old Frenchman the look that fires bullets straight to the heart. The Frenchman takes on a defensive expression as if to say, "But Monsieur, my intentions were honorable." But you don't argue with an overprotective grandfather.

Now: back to that STUPID carriage.

"Why not just carry *bébé?*" Pito asks Ati.

"Lily wants —"

"Okay," Pito interrupts. He's not in the mood to hear about Lily's instructions. These days whenever Ati expresses an opinion, it is linked to Lily's instructions. Let's just say that becoming a father has done something to Ati's head. He will do everything the mother of his son says. Her wish is his command. She says, "When you take *bébé* out, make sure he's in the carriage, you might carry him the wrong way and damage his spinal cord," then so be it.

OUI! Finally! The carriage unfolds, and a burst of applause congratulates the two men, who did not realize they had been entertaining pizza eaters. "Bravo!" the crowd cheers.

All right, let's go shopping for the mamas. Ati pushing the carriage with his son still sound asleep, his precious head and tiny body protected from the sun by a net, Pito holding his granddaughter's hand. A little voice says, "Grandpère, look at my shoes." And Pito says, "They're very beautiful shoes."

They walk into a shop that sells very reasonably priced gifts, cheap, actually. Pito's Mother's Day gift for his mama is a pandanus bag. Ati's choice is also a pandanus bag, but he hasn't found Lily's gift yet, he says.

"Lily isn't your mother," Pito reminds Ati.

"I just want to get Lily something small," Ati says, walking towards a jewelry shop. "Something to show my gratitude for having given me a son."

"What if she had given you a daughter?" Pito asks, remembering how he felt when his first child was born and it was a boy. Ah, he was so proud. Perhaps Ati feels the same way.

But Ati informs his best friend that had Lily given him a daughter instead of this beautiful healthy golden baby boy he so adores, he would still be — forever, he insists — grateful, because a child is a child. Lily had to carry it, and push it out, ruining her body. That's a big sacrifice, Ati explains, for a woman to ruin her body like that. *Ah oui,* many men who have known Lily in her pre-baby days are mourning her statuesque body. It's gone, they say... for eternity.

Well, Lily still looks good because she's been addicted to the gym for years and years, and has already gone back to training. It's not the same, say the men, it's not the same. But Pito would be the first to tell you that since giving birth, Lily has never looked better. There's a bit more flesh, Pito approves; she doesn't look like Mr. Muscles anymore. He follows Ati into the jeweler's shop.

"*Bonjour.*" The middle-aged woman behind the glass counter immediately smells a buyer. "We have beautiful gold necklaces on special. A great Mother's Day gift for less than fifty thousand francs."

"It's not for my mother," says Ati. "It's for my wife."

Pito raises an eyebrow.

"Oh." The saleswoman's smile is even bigger now. "Well, we have some beautiful pearl necklaces over there —" She leads Ati to another section of the shop, to a locked cabinet, making sure to notice the sweet baby sleeping in the carriage he's pushing, and completely ignoring Tiare and her brand-new shoes. "A girl? A boy?" she asks, like she really cares.

"A boy."

"Oh, he's very handsome, how old is he?"

"Eight months."

"Oh, he looks very alert."

Sleeping babies don't look alert, Pito thinks. They just look like sleeping babies!

But Ati, grinning with pride, confirms the saleswoman's statement. *Oui,* his son is very alert for his age, even his doctor says so.

"And what would your budget be?" the saleswoman lowers her voice.

"How much for that one?" Ati has already made up his mind. His eyes are set on a black pearl necklace.

The saleswoman hurries to open the cabinet. She'd like Ati to feel the pearls first, their smoothness. "It's like touching silk," she smiles.

Ati does what he's told with Pito looking on and feeling a twinge of envy. Ha, he would have loved to give his wife (who *is* his wife) a necklace like that to...to thank her for having given him three children. A smart daughter studying medicine in Paris, a son destined to be the greatest chef Tahiti has ever produced, and a son Pito used to adore.

Tamatoa is so...what would the correct word to use here be? Yes — *irresponsible.* For Tamatoa, life is about being a clown. For Pito, it's about getting a job and fulfilling his duties as a father.

Now Ati would like to get a card because a pearl necklace by itself means nothing. He wants to write a few words of gratitude to Lily for the golden boy she gave him. Pito nods, thinking, Maybe today your son is a golden boy, but let's see in twenty-three years. And speaking of which, here's Tamatoa appearing out of nowhere.

"Where were you all?" he shouts, waving his arms in the air. "I've been looking for you all over the place!"

They sit on the bench and wait for Ati.

"Papi?" Tamatoa asks with a sweet voice. "Can I have some money for ice cream? For me and Tiare?"

Pito looks down at Tiare. "You want ice cream?"

Tiare nods, her eyes twinkling with delight, and so Pito gets his wallet out. "And I want the change, you hear?" he tells his son.

"You want an ice cream too, Papi?" Tamatoa asks.

Pito shakes his head *non,* he doesn't want an ice cream, but it's nice of Tamatoa to ask, even if he's not paying, that's thoughtful.

Minutes later, waiting for Ati, who can't make up his mind about that card, Pito hears his granddaughter giggle and looks down to see what's going on. Here she is, rubbing her chin on her vanilla ice cream like her father is doing so that she can have a beard too, and those two are showing off their beards to each other, laughing their heads off. Pito cracks up laughing too.

"Eh, Papi," Tamatoa asks, "you got Mamie something? For Mother's Day?"

"Your mother is not my mother," Pito snaps, "she's your mother. Are you getting your mother something?"

"Of course!" Seconds later, "Papi, can I have some money? I'm going to get Mamie a *cadeau*."

Nodding in agreement, Pito gets his wallet out, and, pulling out the last banknote he has, says, "Spend the whole lot on your mother."

"The whole five thousand francs?" Tamatoa asks, just to make sure.

"Buy something nice."

"And my maman?" a small voice says. "She doesn't have a *cadeau*."

"Your *maman*," Tamatoa snaps, but one look from his father and he understands that he better shut it about Miri. "Come with Papa," he says, giving his hand to the little one, but the obedient granddaughter looks to her grandfather first to see if it's fine. With a smile, Pito gives Tiare his permission.

Discipline 1, 2, 3

For Mother's Day, Tamatoa composed a special dance show for his mother, which she absolutely loved. He also bought her (but there was no mention about his using his father's money) a child's jewelry box, with a ballerina who starts dancing every time you open the lid. It is the same jewelry box, so Materena swore, that she used to have as a child, but one of her mother's lovers' children stole it. That jewelry box truly overshadowed the Mother's Day gifts Materena received from her other two children: a journal from Leilani and a bouquet of flowers from Moana.

But the real reason why Materena burst into tears when she unwrapped the newspapers from Tamatoa's gift was that she had told Tamatoa about that box when he was eight years old and he remembered. "*Aue!*" she cried, when she saw the gift. "You haven't forgotten!" Next minute Materena was sobbing over her precious jewelry box and going on about how she couldn't believe that Tamatoa remembered the story. Meanwhile, Tamatoa was standing straight, and looking very proud of himself. "Everything you tell me, Mamie," he said, glancing at his father with triumph, "stays in my head."

Even Pito was moved. But looking at his son now, on the sofa (where else?), sucking on his near-empty bottle of beer, is making Pito want to shake him. Pito takes another sip of Hinano to relax and keeps his eyes fixed on the TV screen instead. If he were alone, he would be enjoying tonight's movie about the kung fu master Bruce Lee, the man himself. But Pito's heart is too much in turmoil, and so he gets up.

"Papi," Tamatoa says. "Can you get me another beer?"

"Get your own *putain* beer." This is Pito's answer in his head. But out loud he just grunts as he goes into the kitchen. Come on, Pito, he tells himself, don't be like that, he's your son, he's your flesh and bones, he's your blood. He's only just come home, and he makes his daughter laugh. It's better than nothing. Stop comparing yourself to him. Sighing, Pito opens the fridge and cracks open a beer for his son.

"Here."

"*Merci,* Papi."

"Hum." Pito goes back to the kitchen. He sits at the kitchen table, thinking maybe he should go and see his *copains.* He hasn't seen them for a long time. Tonight could be the perfect opportunity to say, "*Eh, copains!* Long time no see, so what's the news?" But Pito doesn't trust Tamatoa to stay home and look after Tiare. One of *his* drinking friends might come to the house and invite Tamatoa out for a few drinks; or one of his dancing friends might call to go out dancing and Tamatoa will be up in a flash, leaving his daughter behind because he's a coconut head, and then the house might catch on fire and then...

Eh, Pito is going to listen to Materena's program for something to do. He's listened to it a few times before and got quickly bored or annoyed, but perhaps there's something interesting tonight.

"Listen, Materena," a woman is saying, "I hope you don't mind me digressing from the subject, but I'd like to make a few points."

"That's all right, go ahead," comes Materena's warm, lovely voice.

"What I'd like to say is that in the old days, the very old days, men were the providers. They hunted fish to feed their women and children. They hunted wild pigs, they climbed up coconut trees, it was the survival of the fittest. Then things started to change. The bomb made an apparition in French Polynesia, I'm talking about the nuclear testing in Moruroa. Legionnaires came by the thousands, it meant more shops, more restaurants, more hotels, more jobs, and women got out of their houses to work." The woman draws in a quick breath. "I'm not saying that this was bad, *non,* it's very important for women to be financially independent, but men lost their place in the society. They were no longer the providers. They lost their power, they lost their voice, and that is why men are so hopeless today. These days men are most likely to be the ones who are unemployed, so the statistics say. They sit by the side of road drinking beer with their so-called friends and wait for jobs to fall out of the sky."

The caller, whom Pito is finding very interesting, goes on about how these men are draining their family's resources because, unlike in France, there's no *chomage* in Tahiti. There's no money coming from the government for food, but these men have still got to eat and who is going to feed them? Their woman, their mother, their father, their sisters... Well, says the caller, this must stop. "Our society is going backwards."

Pito rubs his chin, thinking, Hmm, very interesting. What is the next caller going to say?

"*Aue,* too much blah-blah!" That's what the next caller has to say. "Discipline is the key, 1, 2, 3! Let's get our boys into sports, because sports are the best way to learn discipline, discipline is the key, 1, 2, 3!" She insists that she doesn't just mean sports like soccer or boxing, but all kinds of activities, you could even include playing music or dancing as long as there's some training or practicing involved. But on the other hand, she says, having a job is really how we can get our boys to move forward and be responsible. "When you don't work for too long, you become a slob."

Pito agrees with this one hundred percent. It happened to him. When you do nothing for too long, you wake up later and later in the morning, and everything, getting out of bed included, becomes a chore.

Ah oui, Pito remembers those distant days when he'd sleep until midday because he had nothing to get up for. He had just come home from military service in France, where everything was organized, scheduled here, scheduled there, the adjutant yelling his head off for no reason. Then Pito came home to a mother who was so relieved to see him alive and in good health that she spoiled him rotten, cooking him his favorite dishes and slipping coins into his hand for beer. Pito was basking in this special treatment.

But it wasn't long until his mother started to get agitated. "Get a job," she'd say. "Get out of bed. Do something with your life, I beg you, Pito." But Pito was quite comfortable doing nothing. The more he slept, the more he felt like sleeping. He had *zéro* energy. Even taking the garbage out for his mother was too much effort. When he was awake, it was to drink, and when he wasn't drinking, he wanted to sleep. In between playing with that girl from Faa'a, Materena Mahi.

But then Pito became a father and things changed like *that*, from one day to the next. One of his uncles came by and told him that he was now a man. "A boy doesn't become a man when he's circumcised," the uncle said. "A boy becomes a man when he becomes a father." The uncle ordered Pito to get out of bed, have a shower, and get dressed as if he were off to work. Pito's mother hurried to iron her son's wedding-and-funeral suit, but the uncle said that he meant working clothes — clothes you don't mind getting dirty.

By the following day, thanks to that uncle's connections, Pito had a job. He's still in that same job today.

"I must get my boy a job!" says Pito to himself. These aren't just words in the wind. This is a committed Pito speaking.

The following morning, a job falls from the sky, and right where Pito works! Heifara quit, he's gone walkabout with his new woman and her three children, back to her island, Huahine. The colleagues are shocked, considering all the crying Heifara has been doing lately.

His ex-wife has been found to have a lover, but Heifara cared more about his wife making it hard for him to see his daughters. He couldn't keep up with her rules. "You can have the children this weekend but only if you promise not to feed them junk... You can have the children this weekend but only if you promise to take them swimming... You can have the children only if you promise not to let them watch TV all day." Et cetera et cetera, and now Heifara is going off to be a full-time father to another man's children. What a shock!

Well, Pito admits that it is sad for Heifara's daughters, but what's more on Pito's mind right now is that there's a job here ready to be taken by the first person who asks. Pito wonders if he should go straight to the boss instead of talking to the boss's secretary — there's a saying, if you want to ask something, go straight to God, don't bother going through the angels — but sometimes it's okay to see the receptionist.

So here is Pito in the front office, a smile on his face, and feeling quite nervous.

"*Oui,* Pito," Josephine, the receptionist, says, looking surprised to see him. Today isn't payday.

Pito wishes he had spoken to Josephine a bit more over the years instead of just the usual hello–good-bye he does when picking up his pay. He wishes he had asked her a little bit about her family and everything; that way, Josephine would be like a friend today and Pito would feel a bit more comfortable with his request. He knows nothing about Josephine, except that she has a husband, a son, and an answering machine.

"Pito?" Josephine asks again. "What is it? I've got work to do."

Pito can't ask her about her family today, it's too late, so he throws himself into the water. "Are you going to put Heifara's job in the newspapers?"

"At this stage, it hasn't been decided."

"Ah."

"Why?"

"It's just that my eldest son is — "

"Tamatoa?"

"You know my son?" Pito is pleasantly surprised.

"When Materena used to pick up your pay, we always talked about our children." Then sighing, she adds, "I wish she was still picking up your pay, I miss Materena...*Enfin,* you want the job for your son?"

"Well, if — "

Josephine doesn't let Pito finish his sentence about if it's all right with the company, if she wouldn't mind, if it's possible she could do something . . . She's telling him that she'll see what she can do. "He's got a CV?" she asks.

"A what?"

"A curriculum vitae." Josephine explains that it's the done thing these days for potential employees to drop off a curriculum vitae. "It's like a story about the jobs a person has had, his experiences, his strengths, his knowledge . . . it's a new thing."

Pito doesn't know if his son has one of these but he'll make sure that he gets one, and Tamatoa will drop it off at the office, let's say tomorrow?

"Okay, but it must be typed. The boss doesn't like handwritten CVs."

"Typed? Like on a typing machine?" asks Pito, slightly dumbfounded.

"*Oui,*" Josephine nods.

Pito doesn't know anyone who has a typing machine. "I can't just bring my son in for him to talk to the boss and see how he is and everything and — "

"The boss wants a CV, I'm sorry, Pito." Josephine grabs files from her desk. She's terminating the conversation. "You need something else?" Something else like an advance.

"*Non,* it's okay. *Maururu* for your help."

What help? Pito asks himself once outside the office. How is Tamatoa going to get a typed CV by tomorrow? And what the hell is his son going to put on his CV? What experiences? What knowledge? There will only be two lines. One line: military service. One line: dancing stupid disco moves in nightclubs in Paris. Who is going to hire someone like that?

Pito could ask his brother Frank. Frank has a lot of connections. But Pito isn't really enchanted by the idea of his son mixing with Frank's connections.

Aue...eh, maybe Materena should be the one using her connections, she knows more people than Pito does. Or perhaps Pito is going to ask his friend Ati for help. Ati knows a lot of people too.

There, it's decided. Pito takes his place back behind the cutting machine. One thing is for sure — his son will be in a job by the end of the month. Spit, swear, thank you, Jesus Christ.

Pito steps off the truck at the petrol station after a hard day at work and gives a slow nod to one of his relatives-in-law walking by to the Chinese store, meaning, *Iaorana,* how are you? The woman gives him a frantic friendly wave and a smile. He shakes Mori's hand on his way past the mango tree, has a few words about this, that, the weather, and then keeps on walking.

And there is his beautiful little princess, sitting outside the house on a mat, waiting for her grandfather to come home from work.

"Grandpère!" Tiare runs out to her grandfather with open arms.

"Eh, princess, *e aha te huru?*"

"*Maitai.*"

A big hug, a big squeeze, and Tiare hops on her grandfather's back.

"Papa is at the house?" he asks.

"*Oui.*"

"He's sleeping?"

"*Aita.*"

"What is he doing?"

"He's with Grandmère."

"What are they doing?"

"*Parau-parau.*"

"*E aha te parau-parau?*"

"I don't know."

Pito walks into the house and heads straight to the kitchen. Here's Tamatoa and here's Materena, both sitting at the kitchen table, with an unopened bottle of champagne and four glasses, one already filled with water.

"Ah, you're here!" Materena exclaims, kissing her husband on the cheeks. "Our son has some wonderful news for us," she says, with her see-I-told-you-not-to-stress-about-this voice.

"What's the wonderful news?" Pito asks.

"First, let me pop the champagne," Tamatoa says.

"Come on, then, pop your champagne" — that your mother paid for, Pito adds in his head.

And *pop!* Tamatoa fills his father's glass, his mother's glass, his glass, and pretends to fill his daughter's glass. Let's all raise our glasses together, please. Let's all have a toast. As for the news, here it is: *Mesdames et messieurs,* let me present to you the new member of the dancing group at Club 707.

"Eh!" Champagne flies out of Pito's mouth. "What?"

Materena's eyes are also popping out of her head. "Don't you have to be a *raerae* to dance there?" she asks.

Her cousin-in-law Georgette is a dancer at Club 707 and she's a *raerae,* she dances her sexy moves three nights a week for an audience made up mostly of women. And lonely old men sitting in the dark.

"People are going to think you're a *raerae*," Pito says. He wouldn't like this to happen to him. People mistaking him for a *raerae.* Can you imagine?

"Well, *I* know I'm not a *raerae*," Tamatoa laughs. "*I* know that I love women." Then, shaking his hips, he shouts, "All I care about is dancing!"

Third Time Lucky

The first time Materena went to a nightclub, it was to the Zizou Bar with Cousin Mori. The second time she went to a nightclub, it was to the Kikiriri with Cousin Lily. Tonight, Materena's third experience in a nightclub will be at the Club 707 to watch her son dance, and she's asking Pito to come along because Tamatoa is also his son, not counting that Tamatoa has personally invited both his parents.

"We're going to have lots of fun, *chéri*." Materena has already asked her mother to babysit Tiare, and she has bought herself a very pretty red dress for the special occasion. "*Hein, chéri?* We've never gone to a nightclub together...*Allez*."

Okay *oui,* but Pito is not particularly interested in watching his son disguised as a *raerae*. Fathers don't really want to watch their sons doing their show on the dance floor dressed as a woman. In fact, fathers don't want to watch their son doing their show on the dance floor full stop. They want to watch their son score the winning goal at a soccer match (actually, any goal will do), things like that.

But it would be nice to go out with his wife — she's so excited by the whole thing. She's excited because her son is excited. Dancing is apparently in his blood, he said. Materena is also excited to be a VIP guest and going out — for the first time ever — on the arm of her handsome husband.

"Ah, all right, then." How could Pito resist? And he's glad he is going now; looking at his wife in that red dress with thin straps which sits dangerously just above her knees, and her loose hair carelessly falling on her back, Pito is finding her very spicy and very brown too.

"You've been sunbaking?" he asks.

"Sunbaking?" Materena giggles, applying a coat of red lipstick.

"It's just that you're really brown," Pito says.

"Pito, this is my natural color. I'm a brown woman." Winking, Materena whispers, "All over."

Pito chuckles and grabs his wife on the waist, but she playfully slaps his hands. Her mother is in the kitchen studying the Bible, so no funny business, please.

Allez, time to go! Good-bye, Mamie, and thanks again. Loana lowers her reading glasses on her nose and wishes the middle-aged couple a pleasant evening, along with one thousand recommendations. "Materena, don't you dare drive *taero,* if you ever kill an innocent, I swear to you I'm never going to look at your face again. And you, Pito, don't do the idiot, men want to dance with your wife, *aita pea pea,* no problems, remember, it's you who's going to go home with my daughter. Hold yourself good, count your drinks, and watch your mouth. There's a time and a place for talking *merde,* and it's not in front of people. And give my grandson my blessings for his new job." Loana doesn't know about her grandson dancing dressed as a woman. All she knows is that he's working behind the bar, which even then she wasn't too happy about but it's a job, a place to start.

"*Au revoir,* Mamie," says Materena and gives her mother another kiss and a quick one to Tiare sound asleep, her hand clutching her favorite quilt that used to belong to her father when he was a baby. Then it's off to Papeete, to Club 707.

When they arrive, the queue is already long. Pito is annoyed. He hates queues of any kind, even if it consists of a queue made of women wearing their best dresses and looking very appetizing. He glances around, stopping here and there to admire (very quickly) a pair of *titis* spilling out of a tight outfit. Ah, he's just spotted another man. Good. Pito would hate to be the only real man in that club. There's another man over there too, but he's old and falling apart.

Pito turns his head the other way and meets the disapproving eyes of a woman walking by. Since Club 707 opened its doors, the island has been divided. The first group believes *raeraes* are harmless and fun, great at making women feel special — and they are deep too, a bit like philosophers. The other group believes that *raeraes* are bizarre and unnatural, the shame of their religious country.

What does Pito think about that? Nothing, don't ask him. All he cares about is to pass incognito. So he buries his head in between his shoulders and keeps his eyes firmly on his going-to-church shoes.

At the door Pito hears Materena tell the bouncer (and not with a little voice), "We are guests of our son Tamatoa, he's dancing tonight. Our names are Materena and Pito Tehana."

The bouncer — more Mr. Hulk than him and you would die — checks the situation, calling out over the jazz music to someone in the club, "Materena and Pito Tehana!"

"*Oui!* Let them in!"

Once inside, the VIP guests are ushered to a table near the dance floor by another hulk, who pulls a chair for Madame. Pito pulls his own chair out, but Hulk II stops him in time. Here the VIP guests are kings. They don't have to pull out their own chairs, and they don't have to queue at the bar with the soon-to-be-hysterical women either, because here's a bottle of some fine red wine.

Hulk II half fills Pito's glass.

Pito sniffs the drink as he's seen it done on TV, then gives it a nod.

"Monsieur, Madame. Enjoy the wine, and enjoy the show."

By the time the show is about to start, there is no more wine in the bottle. Materena is a bit tipsy, and Pito, well, he's less embarrassed to be here. Just as he's about to go to the bar, another bottle of wine appears, still with the compliments of the house. Talk about special treatment! It's like there's a conspiracy to get Pito and Materena off their faces. Maybe it's to minimize the shock, because they're about to see their son wearing a nurse's uniform.

The jazz music dies down and is replaced by the pulsing of drums as the lights are dimmed, and a roar of clapping and women yelling fills the club. Startled, Pito turns to look at the hundreds of crazy women. My God, he's never seen women acting that way. It's like the Pope is about to make an entrance, or someone equally famous, like... well, like Pito's son.

Here he is, wearing nothing but a loincloth hiding his private parts, standing still like a coconut tree for the audience to admire his oily, tanned, and fit body. The crowd goes wilder, and Materena is not far behind, frantically clapping her hands.

"Oro," a smooth voice comes out of the speakers, "Oro, god of war, is bored..."

The drums come back and the lights are now on Materena's cousin Georgette, dressed as an Indian princess but wearing high-heel shoes and fake plaits. The crowd goes even wilder as

Georgette dances her famous sexy moves, rolling her belly, shaking her shoulders at Oro, god of war, kissing his feet, throwing her body this way, that way. But Oro pushes away the Indian woman, who then crumples on the floor.

Drums stop.

"But Oro, god of war, pushes his first wife out of the sky, and he's still bored."

The drums are back, and this time the crowd has the pleasure of watching a cancan dancer complete with fishnet stockings — before she too is pushed off the sky.

Third wife: Cleopatra. She gets pushed out of the sky.

Fourth wife: a nymphomaniac nurse. Pushed off the sky.

Fifth wife: a ballerina, same fate.

That Oro is very hard to please, but Pito wonders if his son is going to do some action, or if he's going to stand there all night long pushing wives around.

"Oro looks like he's on the hunt again," the suave voice continues. "Oro... can you see anyone in the crowd worthy of your attention?" Oro looks around, now flashing his white teeth, and the crowd of drunken women goes ballistic. *"Moi! Moi!"*

Pito puts his hands on his ears, he's about to go deaf, but this is only the beginning. The crowd is about to spin out of control because the god of war will soon be showing them real dancing.

Drums roll louder and louder, and this is what Oro means by real dancing. He means energy, choreographed steps, leaping in the air, jumping on tables, sweat, rhythm, and flirting with the audience. He unzips a woman's dress and she shrieks with delight, so honored to have been noticed by the god of war. A kiss here, a wink there, a gentle caress, more gymnastics and jumping around.

Pito had no idea his son was such a dancing machine. He wonders how long Tamatoa will keep up with the dancing, the drums, the hysterical groupies who let him do anything he likes, since they're taking him for a *raerae,* a harmless man. Well, Tamatoa will be doing this until Oro finds his next wife. So, who is going to be the lucky goddess tonight?

"You." Oro is on his knees before Materena.

"*Moi? Non.*" Materena waves her son away. But he insists. "Tamatoa," Materena says in between clenched teeth. "I drank."

"*Allez.*" Pito nudges his wife to get up.

The crowd is also demanding that Oro's sixth wife get up. "*Debout! Debout!*" they chant. All eyes are now on Materena, dancing shy and hesitant moves. But she's not Tahitian for nothing. The drums, she knows about that. Rhythm too. It's in her blood, part of her upbringing, years as a child shaking her waist from left to right to the rhythm of Tahitian songs sung by the great-aunties. Materena's dancing in a nightclub might be very limited but her dancing in her mother's and aunties' kitchens is extensive.

Very soon, Materena is kicking her comfortable shoes off to the side of the dance floor, closing her eyes, and raising her arms. You haven't seen anything yet, you people, she thinks. And off she goes, dancing like a woman who's spent her whole life on the dance floor.

To say that Pito is captivated is an understatement. He will never let his wife go out alone ever again, he might not be so lucky the third time. *Ah oui,* as of now, when Materena goes out dancing, he's going too.

Roars and clapping thank Materena as she returns to her seat, laughing with her head thrown back. But here's Pito (to his son's greatest surprise) getting to his feet.

"Mademoiselle," he says, winking and taking Materena's hand in his, the other around her waist. At that moment the music changes and a crowd of women storms onto the dance floor to Abba's "Dancing Queen" blaring from the speakers. But not to be discouraged, Pito repeats, "Mademoiselle, are you ready to do the samba?"

"Madame," she smiles, and places her other hand on her husband's shoulder. Around them much younger dancers are madly gesticulating and jumping around in their high heels as the middle-aged couple, their bodies pressed close together, begin to dance.

Hours later, a very elated middle-aged Tahitian couple in love is walking hand in hand in a dimmed street of Papeete after a night flirting (with each other), dancing (also with each other, plus six songs with their son), and drinking (together). And there's no taxi in sight.

Luckily, there's a hotel not far away. There's always a hotel when there's a nightclub in the whereabouts — lovers who have a bit of money never have to do romance in the streets. The hotel is seedy, but they all are in this part of town. Nobody has died in this hotel, though, so that's good.

"That would be one room or two?" the wide-awake and smiling hotel receptionist politely asks. In this business, it's best never to assume anything.

Precious Seeds

If Pito and Materena collapsed on their hotel bed (after a quick romance, walking up the stairs), Tamatoa spent hours and hours romancing. And the girl must have been greatly impressed with her lover's performance, because she invited him to the restaurant tonight.

Presently, Mr. Lover Boy is busy dabbing cologne on the back of his neck. His father, drinking at the kitchen table, looks on.

"You've got money?" his mother asks, digging into her purse, since she already knows the answer.

"She's paying," Tamatoa says with a smirk.

"You told her that you've got a kid?" asks Materena.

"Mamie!" Meaning, Why would I tell her that I've got a kid, eh? She doesn't need to know my life. Tamatoa joins his father at the table, but he's not drinking. Tamatoa never drinks before a romantic rendezvous. That's the rule and the regulation, which so far has proved to be a recipe for success.

"You're careful with your seeds?" This time it is the father asking questions.

"What do you mean?"

"I mean, You're careful with your seeds. I'm not talking Morse code to you. You're careful with your seeds?"

Tamatoa shrugs. He won't be answering that question.

"I don't want a girl knocking at the door, looking for you in nine months," says Pito. "And she's like that." In sign language, Pito shows a swollen belly. "*Alors?* You're careful with your seeds?"

"*Oui!*" Tamatoa snaps, jumping to his feet. "*Oui,* I'm careful, okay?"

"Eh," Pito snaps back. "You make kids, you look after them, this house is not a *garderie.*" Commanding his son to sit, he adds that he loves his granddaughter, Tiare, adores her, she's a ray of sunshine and everything, but it doesn't mean he wants a repeat. "You get me?" Pito asks. "You get another girl pregnant, the baby is your affair, understand?"

Materena decides to cut in. "I really think you should tell her about *bébé.* What is that girl's name?"

"She's just a girl!" Tamatoa is clearly exasperated now. "We're going to eat and then we're going to have a bit of fun, that's all."

"But you're going to talk at the restaurant," Materena insists. "People always talk at the restaurant, they don't just eat." She puts a hand on her son's hand as if to say, Look, I'm not trying to tell you how to live your life, but listen to my opinion, I'm speaking with all honesty, my son. "This girl might get cranky if she finds out about Tiare in two weeks, and not tonight."

"Who said I'm still going to be with her in two weeks?" Tamatoa gets up.

"But what if — "

"She's married." There, that does the trick. It shuts both his parents up. "She has a wedding band on her finger, she has a rope around her neck, she's a bored housewife, and there's no restaurant. I'm going to her house and it's not to talk."

"Ah," Pito says, hugely relieved. A bored married woman looking for a bit of fun is safer than an unattached woman searching for a husband, the father of her future children. "Well, have a good night."

"*Merci,* Papi."

Father and son give each other a firm handshake.

"I'll see you tomorrow morning," Tamatoa sings, stepping out of the house. "Early."

Tamatoa does come home in the morning, early — but three days later.

"She has a blind husband or what?" Pito, at the kitchen table, buttering his granddaughter's bread, asks.

"What are you doing up so early?" Tamatoa looks like he can't believe his father is up at five forty-five. "You fell out of bed?"

"Some of us have to get Tiare breakfast and go to work five days a week," Pito snorts. "You're going to say *Iaorana* to your daughter? It's not like she's invisible."

Tamatoa smiles at his daughter, who is dipping her buttered jam bread into her Milo, and plants a quick kiss on the little one's forehead. He's come home to get some clothes, he says, and will be away for another five days. "Don't worry," he hurries to answer his father's questioning look. "I know my duties, she's going to drive me to work." And to make things clearer, Tamatoa explains the situation, which is quite simple really. The husband is away with the children for a week.

"And *bébé?*" Pito asks. "She's in your plan too? I didn't pay for your plane ticket for you to play Romeo."

"*Eh hia.*" Tamatoa dismisses his father with the back of his hand, drinks a glass of water at the sink, and heads to his bedroom to pack.

"Stay at the table, *chérie,*" Pito tells Tiare as he gets up. "I'll come back."

In his son's bedroom now, with the door closed, "Tamatoa," Pito begins, speaking with his let's-be-allies voice, "I just want to open your eyes a little."

"What?" Tamatoa, shoving clothes in a bag, is immediately on the defensive. "You're not going to tell me about the plane ticket again, are you? I'm going to pay you back."

"I asked for my money?" says Pito, his voice rising up.

"I'm still going to pay you back."

"Spend a bit more time with your daughter, it's for you."

"I'm just doing what you used to do." Walking past his stunned father, Tamatoa elaborates. "You were never at the house."

He opens the door. He's gone. And Pito, standing still like a coconut tree, pale and mute, hears his son tell his daughter, in a father's voice, mind you, "Don't put your elbows on the table, it's not polite."

Later that night, in the dark, in the bedroom on this humid night, with gentle rain splattering on the tin roof . . .

"Materena?"

"*Oui.*"

"Was I a good father?"

"What do you mean *was?* You're still a father, a good father."

"I was hardly at the house like I am now."

"True, but the kids still knew who you were."

And to refresh Pito's memory, Materena takes her husband's hand in hers and talks about the day their eldest son found out the truth about prisons.

A gendarme parks his car in front of the house and Materena, hanging clothes on the line, asks herself, "What is this gendarme doing at my house?" When Tamatoa gets out of the car, Materena shouts in her head, "But! What is my son doing in a gendarme's car!" She forgets all about the clothes and rushes to the gendarme holding her son by the arm.

"Good morning, Monsieur." Materena looks at her son staring at his feet. The gendarme eyes the pegs clipped to Materena's oversize T-shirt.

"Are you the mother of this young boy?" he asks.

"*Oui,* Monsieur." Materena is full of respect and anxiety. Gendarmes don't give lifts because they feel sorry for you walking. You must do something for a gendarme to give you a lift, something against the law. The thought that comes into Materena's mind is that Tamatoa has been shoplifting. She hopes it wasn't at the Chinese store where she does her shopping.

"Your son was caught stealing," the gendarme says, looking into Materena's eyes with that air of superiority.

"What did he steal?" Materena's voice is shaking a little. "Lollies?"

The gendarme gives Materena that cold stare gendarmes give when they think people are playing smart, and Tamatoa's giggle only makes it worse. He yells, "Do not make me regret my leniency, Madame!"

Materena jumps with fright and profusely apologizes and thanks the gendarme for his leniency, although she's not quite sure what that word means. The gendarme calms down a little and informs the mother why this young thief is here today.

It seems Tamatoa and another friend were having a little promenade at the airport, next to the jetty where people park their speedboats. And their canoes. Most canoes are chained to a pole, but one wasn't, so what did Tamatoa and his friend do? They pushed the canoe into the water. And since there were paddles in this particular canoe, they started to paddle away. So here were the young boys paddling, and meanwhile, the owner of that canoe arrived to go fishing and found out that his canoe had been stolen. He contacted the *gendarmerie,* and this gendarme was sent out to write a full report. But on his way to the airport, he spotted two young boys pushing a canoe into the sand.

The gendarme ordered the two young boys to carry the canoe back to where they had found it and introduced them to the owner of the canoe, who fortunately did not press charges.

Materena glances at her son, still staring at his feet, and she really wants to smack him on the head, but she'll do this later. Until then, she just gives him a very cranky look.

To Leilani and Moana, peeping from behind the curtains, she gives a very cranky look too.

The gendarme, now addressing himself solely to Tamatoa, says, "I will not be lenient next time, young boy. Do you understand me?"

Tamatoa nods and Materena wishes he would look up.

"Next time," the gendarme continues, "there will be fingerprints."

And with this, he excuses himself and leaves.

Materena waits until the car is fully out of sight to start giving Tamatoa his punishment, but he's disappeared.

"Tamatoa!" She's even crankier now. "Come here right now!"

"I wasn't going to steal that old rotten canoe anyway!" Tamatoa's voice is coming from inside the house. "It was only to borrow!"

"When you borrow from people you don't know, it's called stealing!" Materena marches to the house. "Tamatoa?"

"*Ouais,* what?" He's in the kitchen, spreading butter on a piece of bread. He looks at his mother like, Can't you see I'm busy?

Ouh...Materena is going to get the wooden spoon and give that boy a lesson! But she can't find that wooden spoon, and she wants that wooden spoon. The frying pan goes flying, plates are smashed, where is that spoon!

Tamatoa is now spreading a thick layer of peanut butter on his bread. Materena picks up her frying pan, and the light flickering in her eyes cannot be mistaken for a light of joy. Tamatoa, firmly holding on to his sandwich, rushes out of the kitchen in a flash. His mother chases him, brandishing that frying pan, and threatening to hit him with it.

The chase continues through the living room. Materena now has two helpers, the treacherous brother and sister, but Tamatoa moves here, moves there, jumps over the sofa, under the table. Three times Leilani nearly catches him. Materena wants to laugh now because it is so funny, all of them running around in the living room, but she reminds herself of the serious situation. She just won't have any of her children coming home in the gendarme's car!

Moana gets hold of his brother's leg. "I've got him, Mamie!" But Tamatoa shakes his leg and thumps Moana on the shoulders and now Moana is crying. Tamatoa bends over to see if his brother is okay but here comes Mamie with that frying pan.

He flies out the shutter, he's now climbing up the breadfruit tree like a monkey. Materena can't believe Tamatoa's audacity...and what agility! She didn't know he was such a good climber. She throws the frying pan away and climbs up the tree too, muttering, "You wait until I get you!"

But she's getting a bit worried now. Tamatoa is still climbing, and what if he falls?

"Tamatoa!" she calls out with her normal voice, not wanting to frighten him more. "When I tell Papi, he's going to get his belt and give you some."

She doesn't have to say more than that. Tamatoa stops and turns to his mother. "Are you going to tell Papi?"

"Well, I'm going to have to," Materena replies.

"*Non,* please don't tell Papi." Tamatoa is pleading with all his heart and soul.

Ah...Materena wished she had the power Pito has over the kids. All Pito ever needs to do to get some respect and obedience is cough. Or yell for one second. She can yell for hours and still nothing will happen. Especially when she's yelling at Tamatoa.

"Did you get him, Mamie?" Leilani and Moana call out from the shutter.

"*Oui,*" Materena calls back. "You two go eat some chocolate cookies."

"*Chocolate* cookies?" the children say with delight.

To Tamatoa, Materena says that he doesn't deserve the chocolate cookies and to her other children she reveals the hiding place.

"Now," Materena says to Tamatoa. "We talk a little." She makes herself comfortable on a branch, checking first that it is thick enough to support her weight.

Speaking very seriously, Materena tells her son that when the police have your fingerprints, it means you have a police record, and when you have a police record, it means you are a criminal, and when you are a criminal, it means you can go to prison.

She goes on about the inconvenience of having a police record: whenever there's a break-and-enter or a fight, the first people the gendarmes suspect are people with a police record, and this has happened to her cousin Mori quite a few times. That's why Mori always has to make sure that he's never alone, so that he always has witnesses to testify to his whereabouts, and when he's alone drinking, for instance, he can only drink under a tree by the side of the road for everybody to see.

"Your uncle Mori," Materena says, looking up to her son, sitting two branches higher, "is condemned to live in the public eye."

Another inconvenience of having a police record, Materena continues, is that you can't get a job, because no boss wants an employee who has a police record working in the company. You can do a super interview and the boss can tell you, "You've got the job, welcome aboard!" but when he finds out about your police record, he'll send you a letter instead to tell you that you didn't get the job. This has happened to Mori. Mori has tried to get a job seventeen times (Materena exaggerates here a little), and seventeen times a boss has said to him, "Welcome aboard!" but three days later he's gotten a rejection letter because of his police record and his visits to Nuutania Prison.

Tamatoa eagerly nods and Materena knows he's only doing this so that she won't tell his father about the canoe story. But perhaps he's listening too.

Materena goes on with her talk about prisons and how, according to her cousin Mori, who's been there quite a few times, it is a horrible place to be. The food is horrible, the toilets are horrible, and the beds are not comfortable at all. The beds in prisons are special beds, made for discomfort to punish the prisoners. The prison, even if we Tahitians call it a five-star hotel, is definitely *not* a hotel.

"But Mamie," Tamatoa says. "It was only a canoe, and it was rotten. We nearly sank, that's why we stopped paddling."

Ah hia hia, Materena is so annoyed. Her son didn't get the message at all. "Eh," she says angrily. "Have you heard of that saying, *Qui vole un oeuf vole un boeuf?*"

"*Qui vole un oeuf vole un boeuf?*" Tamatoa obviously hasn't.

"You understand that wise saying?"

Tamatoa shakes his head. No, that saying means nothing to him at all.

"Today you steal an egg," Materena says. "And tomorrow you steal a cow. Today you steal a canoe, tomorrow you steal a hi-fi system."

"But I didn't steal anything!"

Ouh, Materena is beginning to lose her patience and she's about to growl something, when out of nowhere, Pito appears. He's standing by the tree, eating a Delta Cream cookie and looking up to Tamatoa. "The whole neighborhood is talking about how you came home in a gendarme's car," he says. "What's the story?"

"Pito," Materena hurries to say, cursing her big-mouth relatives. "I already smacked Tamatoa with the frying pan and I'm just —"

"I'm talking to my boy, Materena. What's the story?"

Tamatoa tells his father the story, and by the end of it he sounds like he's going to burst into tears.

"You got caught!" Pito says. "That was pretty stupid."

"Luckily for Tamatoa, the gendarme didn't take his fingerprints." Materena is a bit put off by Pito's slack comment. Let's not move away from the seriousness of the situation. "When there's fingerprints, there's a police record, and then there's the prison."

"You know what happens in prison?" Pito asks Tamatoa.

"You eat horrible food?" Tamatoa replies.

"Food!" Pito exclaims, stuffing the last piece of cookie in his mouth. "Prisoners don't care about food. You know what they really care about?"

"*Non,* Papi, I don't know."

Pito swallows his Delta Cream and informs his son that what prisoners really care about the most is to keep their virginity, because in prison there are no women, and when there are no women, some men have to become the women. Sometimes willingly, more often not. Nonchalantly, Pito speaks of young men caught stealing TVs by the gendarmes, sent to prison, and ending up at the prison hospital to have their bum stitched up. "You understand what I'm saying, Tamatoa?"

Tamatoa nods; he is very pale and so is Materena.

Later, she asks Pito if he thinks this has happened to her cousin Mori. But all Pito will say is how gendarmes must have nothing else to do if they have to start the siren because a rotten canoe has been borrowed. What about catching the real criminals for a change?

Well anyway, this is the story that Materena felt like telling Pito to reassure him and show him what a great father he was. Pito is reassured a little, but he cares more about the thought that has just popped into his mind.

"Materena?"

"Pito...I'm trying to sleep now." To prove her point, Materena yawns a very tired yawn.

"Was it hard for you without a father around?" Pito respects other people's desire for sleep, but he'd like to know.

"Oh, I had my uncles and my godfather too."

"I really think you should look for your father."

"I'm not ready yet."

"You're never going to be ready."

A long silence.

"Materena?"

Either she's fast asleep or she doesn't want to talk about that subject tonight. Pito takes his wife into his arms and starts to think about two of his cousins, born from unknown fathers. They've never felt that they were less than the children who knew their fathers. It's not a big thing in Tahiti to have Father Unknown written on your birth certificate; you're not pushed aside. Some children know who their father is and others don't, it's simple. Sometimes the father is truly unknown, as is the case with one of the cousins, and other times the father is known but he can't recognize the child because he's married, as is the case with Pito's other cousin.

Both cousins are fine today, they have husbands, children, jobs — no problems. But it's also true, Pito thinks, that when they get together and have a bit too much to drink, they talk about their fathers and how those men abandoned them.

At the post office the next afternoon, Pito has a notebook in his pocket, a pen behind his ear, and six thick telephone books from France sprawled across the floor.

"D-a," he mutters, under his breath so that nobody can hear him, as he flicks the thin white pages. "D-a-c...D-a-d... D-a-v...D-e-b...Delors!"

Old Story Disturbed

How strange, thinks Materena, that she dreamed about her father last night. Actually, it was this morning, because when Materena opened her eyes, it was light. In the dream, she was about nine years old and standing by the rail on a ferry, holding the hand of a very tall man. Perhaps she was nine in the dream because she was nine when she first read her birth certificate with the phrase Father Unknown written on it.

Materena, presently ironing one of her darling husband's good shirts he wears at mass and other important events like baptisms, thinks back to that day she read her birth certificate for the first time. She remembers telling her mother, "You don't know who my father is?"

Loana got cranky. "Eh! What? Do you think I'd open my legs for men I don't know? Of course I know the man who planted you inside me."

"Who is he?" Materena asked.

But all her mother was prepared to reveal was the man's nationality. "He's French, that's all you need to know for the moment."

Why should Materena dream about her father this morning? She's never dreamed about him before, although she's thought about him, quite a lot. What could this mean, Materena asks herself, lovingly hanging up the crisply ironed shirt. Is it a sign?

In the dream, her father was wearing a long coat and he looked really sad. "Eh, Papa, eh," Materena whispers, tears in her eyes. "I hope you're fine." She starts thinking that she should really search for her father as soon as possible. If she waits any longer, he might be dead by the time she finds him. *Eh hia*... the regrets will haunt her until *she* dies. Materena visualizes herself at her father's grave. She's on her knees, reading the writing on the cross. *Tom Delors... Born... Died.* Materena unplugs the iron and chases the negative image out of her head. It's not wise, negative thoughts; they might come true. Materena hurries to picture her father playing golf.

Later, on the way to the Chinese store to get a few bits and pieces, Materena stops as usual by the mango tree next to the petrol station for a quick hello to Cousin Mori with his eternal accordion (presently resting on the ground; Mori must be having a musical break).

"*Iaorana*, Cousin."

The cousins proceed to kiss each other on the cheeks, and Materena immediately senses that something is bothering Cousin Mori today. He looks a bit bizarre. "Cousin? You're fine?"

Mori shakes his dreadlocks. "Can we talk a little?" He gets up and shows the rock he's been sitting on, meaning, please take a seat. Materena sits on the rock, and Mori sits on the concrete, his legs crossed, facing his cousin.

"I want to find my father," he says at last.

"Really!" Materena exclaims, thinking, What's going on in the universe today?

With a sad voice, Mori explains that his life would have been different today had he known his father. He wouldn't be a good-for-nothing for a start.

"Mori…" Materena takes her cousin's hand to squeeze it a little. "You're not a good-for-nothing. You're my nicest cousin, and you're always helping people out. That doesn't sound like being a good-for-nothing to me."

"*Maururu,* Cousin. I can always count on you to say nice words about me."

"I'm only saying the truth, Cousin."

"I really want to find my father," Mori continues, "but Mama refuses to tell me his name and you can't look for somebody who hasn't got a name."

Materena confirms the fact.

"When I ask Mama for the name of my father, she tells me, 'Ah, leave me alone with this old story. I don't know the name of your father' and 'Your father is me.'" Mori looks into Materena's eyes. "Cousin, you know how I'm very good with playing the accordion?"

"You're wonderful with that accordion, Mori, you play like a professional."

Mori giggles and does his I'm-shy expression. "I don't mean to show off to you but you know about my musical ear —"

"You have a wonderful musical ear," Materena agrees. "You only have to hear a song once to play it right. Pito used to say how he wished he had a musical ear like yours."

"*Ah oui.*" Mori nods several times. "You can still play without a musical ear but it's better to have a musical ear and —" Mori pauses for a moment. "You know I've never had music lessons. No one has ever taught me to play the accordion. One day I found the accordion and the next day I was playing like I'd had an accordion for years. You don't think it's bizarre?"

"*Oui,*" Materena admits. "It is a little bit bizarre."

"It's bizarre because I was born with a musical ear."

"*Oui,* it could be."

"And I was born an accordionist."

Materena looks at Mori, then at his accordion, and says nothing.

"I was born an accordionist," continues Mori, "because my father, he is an accordionist, and I think he's from Jamaica."

"Why do you think this?"

"Because of my hair, Cousin! Tahitians don't have dreadlocks!"

Materena is about to comment but here is Mori calling out to Loana, who is on the other side of the road.

"Auntie Loana!" Mori is frantically waving. "Can you come a little? I need to ask you something!"

She crosses the road and after kissing her nephew and her daughter she asks, "What's going on?"

Materena gets up, and Mori shows his auntie the rock, meaning, please take a seat.

"I'm not sitting on that bloody rock," Loana says. "And I'm in a hurry, Mori. What is it you want to ask me?"

Mori tells his auntie about his bizarre musical ear.

"Eh, Mori," Loana says, "you went to mass with your mama every Sunday from the time you were three days old right till when you were fifteen. When you listen to the choir every Sunday, of course you're going to develop a musical ear!"

Mori goes on about his bizarre gift with the accordion.

"Mori, you've been playing that accordion every day for over twenty years. When you do something for that long, of course you're going to be good at it!"

"Auntie," Mori pleads, "the story with the accordion is that one day I found an accordion and the next day I was playing it like I'd played an accordion for years!"

Loana laughs. "Not in my memory, you weren't. The first few months of you playing that thing sounded like a horrible noise. You can't remember your mama threatening to chuck that accordion in the bin?"

Materena keeps her eyes focused on the concrete floor.

"Well, I think my father is an accordionist," Mori says.

"Ah, you know, he could be anything."

"And he's from Jamaica."

"Ah, you know, he could be from anywhere."

"I want to look for him but Mama doesn't want to tell me his name. She says she doesn't know it."

"Maybe it's true that your mama doesn't know the name of your father."

"How can a woman not know the name of the man she's making a baby with?"

"Mori, dear," Loana says, "and you? When you take a woman back to your mama's house or when you go to the woman's house, do you always know that woman's name?" Loana is now squinting at Mori.

"That's the first thing I ask!" Mori looks mortified. "When I see a woman my eyes like, I go to her and I say, '*Iaorana*, my name is Mori and what is your name, beautiful princess?'"

This time Materena can't stop the laughter and soon Mori is joining her, but Loana doesn't think Mori's introduction line is funny. "There's a reason why your mama refuses to tell you the name of your father. Maybe she doesn't want an old story disturbed, but she might decide to reveal the whole story on her deathbed. You just have to be patient."

"Ah, because there's a story?" Mori asks, surprised.

Loana half smiles. "Mori, my nephew, there's always a story with conceptions."

And with that remark, Loana goes on with her mission to the shop, with Materena following. She'd love to talk to Mori for a little bit longer but Pito and Tiare will be home soon. They've gone to visit Mama Roti, and Materena promised them a surprise on their return. A surprise like a banana cake — Pito and Tiare's favorite cake.

And in the Chinese store, right out the back, behind the tower of toilet paper rolls, Loana tells Materena the story of Mori's conception. It is understood that Materena will be taking that story to her grave.

Here it is . . .

When Reva, Mori's mama, was seventeen, she was madly in love with a boy, and he was in love with her too. Emmanuel was the boy's name. He had a Vespa and he always put Pento cream in his frizzy hair to make it straighter and easy to comb.

One night Emmanuel arranged a rendezvous at the Hotel Tahiti with Reva, and Reva walked the three miles there. When she got to the hotel, there was a band playing and there was free punch being served. Reva stood in the corner next to a potted plant, listening to the music, her eyes looking around for Emmanuel and for any relatives she might have to hide from.

A whole hour passed, and Reva started to suspect that her lover had forgotten all about their rendezvous. She helped herself to a glass of punch and scurried back to her post. She waited, drank, and went back for another glass of punch. She waited again and tears started to fall out of her eyes. The music suddenly sounded very sad.

She drank another glass of punch and another, until the need to relieve herself came to her. She went to the toilet but there was a long queue of well-dressed women who looked her up and down, so she ran into the garden and relieved herself behind a tree. Then she burst into tears. A minute later she heard steps, she smelled Pento, and she said, dressing up as quickly as she could, "Emmanuel, is that you?"

The response was a whisper. *"Oui,* it's me, *chérie."* Reva was so happy her lover had come that she jumped on him, kissed him passionately, and professed her love for him. Within minutes they were on the grass doing the sexy loving with Reva giving herself to her lover with all her heart and soul. After the sexy loving, Reva held on to her lover and tenderly whispered his name in his ear.

A voice said, "I lied. I'm not who you think I am." Then the man jumped to his feet and ran away.

This is the story of Mori's conception, and Materena says that the man was Emmanuel for sure but he lied because... because... Materena searches for a plausible reason. Because...

"Emmanuel died on his way to the hotel," Loana says. "A truck ran his Vespa over."

The only person not crying at Mori's farewell concert is his mother. As far as Reva is concerned, God has finally answered her prayers. But for the relatives gathered here today, it will be so strange not seeing Mori play his eternal accordion under the mango tree near the petrol station anymore, even more so for Materena, who lives right behind the petrol station. But she's very happy Cousin Mori has decided to do something constructive with his life. Playing an accordion under a tree is fine when you're a kid, but when you're close to being thirty-five, it can look a bit sad.

Mori's age isn't the reason he's saying good-bye to his daily music and drinking routine, though, he's never cared about his age. Let's just say that after he's spent years harassing his mother to give him the name of his father, she finally cracked under the pressure and told him the whole bizarre story of his conception.

Mori, understandably, cried his eyes out, then he went to the grave of the man who would have been (without a doubt) his father. There he felt an instant connection with Emmanuel Mori Manutahia, abruptly taken away from us. The way Mori explained his tricky situation to the dead man, he was conceived with him in Reva's mind, body, and soul, and therefore he was his son, no question about it. Mori remained at his father's grave for a while. He gave him a glimpse into his life and left with the promise to change.

It means that as of today, Mori will no longer be playing his accordion under the mango tree near the petrol station, because a promise to the dead is sacred.

Two Ways to Plant a Seed

At the kitchen table, where many important issues are discussed in Tahitian households, Materena asks her husband to close his eyes for a moment.

Okay, done.

Now, Pito has to pretend that he gets a call from France, from a woman he doesn't know, and she tells him that she is his daughter. He fathered her during his two-year military service.

How would he feel? Would he be disappointed if his daughter was, let's say, a professional cleaner? And would he be proud if his daughter had, let's say, her own radio program? Anyway, what would Pito's reaction be?

Materena dips her buttered bread in her bowl of coffee, smiles at her husband now giving her the you-and-your-ideas-sometimes look, takes a bite of her bread, and waits for an answer.

"Just imagine," Materena says.

"And you? What would you do?"

"I'm going to invite your daughter to come and visit us!" Materena didn't even have to ponder. "But, I'm asking you."

"I'm asking you!" Tiare exclaims, waving her piece of bread. The grandparents jump and crack up laughing. They had forgotten that the little one was at the table too.

So, speaking rapidly, Pito tells Materena that it is impossible for him to have fathered a child in France, because he was always very careful. The last thing he wanted was to get a girl pregnant and be stuck in France for life. In fact, so Pito clarifies, he was very paranoid about his precious seeds with both French and Tahitian girls. He was one hundred percent careful.

Materena's eyes are popping out of her head. Pito *careful?* She had no idea he knew about this method of contraception. He certainly never applied it with her when they were meeting under a tree, on a quilt, in the dark. They were not even official boyfriend and girlfriend then. She was just this girl he knew, this girl who was crazy about him. Under that tree, on that quilt, and in the dark, Pito got Materena pregnant with Tamatoa.

"You, careful?" Materena cackles. "You've never been careful with me."

Smirking, Pito tells Materena that maybe he didn't want to be careful with her, has she ever thought about that, eh?

"What are you telling me? That you got me —" Materena glances at her granddaughter presently ripping tiny pieces of bread and dropping them in her bowl of Milo. Materena mimes the word *pregnant* and carries on, "under a tree on purpose?"

Pito shrugs. "Maybe, maybe not."

"Pito —" Materena can't believe Pito's almost-confession. It's like Pito was so afraid of losing her to another man, he got her pregnant to mark his territory. "Pito —" But Pito has got to get ready for work. Still, he gracefully accepts passionate kisses from his wife on his mouth, his cheeks, his head. "Somebody loves me," he cackles. And to his granddaughter, now collecting her soggy pieces of bread with a spoon, Pito adds, "*Parahi bébé.*"

She looks up and throws her arms around her grandfather's neck, with Materena thinking.

Later in the day, Materena visits her mother.

Mother and daughter embrace each other as if they haven't seen each other for weeks. The last time they were together was only yesterday at the mango tree near the petrol station for Mori's last concert. Tiare gets her kiss from great-grandmother and hurries out the back to get her watering can. That is the ritual. When she's here, she waters great-grandmother's flowers. She knows where her watering can is and she knows where the tap is too. But most of all, Tiare knows which flowers she's allowed to water.

"How's the health, Mamie?" Materena asks sweetly.

"Oh, my legs are a bit stiff when I get out of bed in the morning, but other than that all is fine, girl."

"Ah, better the legs be stiff than something else more serious."

Cackling, Loana agrees.

"Your garden is so beautiful, Mamie." Materena is still talking with sugar in her voice.

"*Oui,* I love my garden, it's —" She stops to call out to the little one getting carried away with her watering. "*Faaoti,* Tiare! Go and water the orchids now, my love."

A bright smile on her face, Tiare looks up and calls out, "I help Grandmère Loana! I'm nice!" And off she hurries to fill her watering can.

"She reminds me so much of you," Loana says. "So much . . . you were like that at her age, always smiling, always willing to help."

A silence follows, with Materena eyeing her mother from the corner of her eye and taking big, deep breaths.

"What is it?" Loana asks. "There's something in your head."

"Mamie, I need to ask your permission."

Loana turns to Materena. "My permission!" she laughs. "You haven't asked my permission for anything for years!" Loana reminds her daughter that she certainly didn't ask for her permission when she used to sneak out the shutter in the dark to meet her Romeo waiting under a tree. She didn't ask for her permission when she fell pregnant, got married, et cetera, et cetera. "And now you need my permission?"

Then, in a very serious and worried voice, Loana asks Materena if her permission has something to do with changing religion, or worse, selling land.

"Mamie," Materena laughs. "Where did you get these crazy ideas from? I'm happy as a Catholic, and I'm not the kind to sell my land."

"Ah." Loana sounds very relieved. "Well, you've got my permission."

"I haven't even told you what it is for yet."

"It's not about religion, it's not about selling land, you've got my permission."

"So it's okay with you if I go looking for my father?" says Materena, then quickly adding how she's wanted to do this for years but never had the confidence. "You must see that I'm more confident now, Mamie," Materena says.

"That is true, and I'm very happy for you. It's a good thing to be confident when you're a woman, but —" Loana seems lost for words. It's like she really wants to say something but doesn't know how to put the words together.

"Mamie," says Materena taking her mother's hand in hers. "I'm going to respect your decision. I understand if you don't want me to go looking for my father. You're the one who put food in my stomach and everything, and perhaps you want me to wait until you're dead, but what if he's —"

"Don't expect anything, girl." There, Loana has spoken. "When you're young, you think you're so in love, but then you grow old and realize that it was only a bit of sport." In Loana's opinion, Tom Delors is very likely to say, "Loana? Loana who?"

"He wasn't careful with you, Mamie," Materena says lightly. "It's almost like he didn't mind you falling pregnant because you were so special for him."

"Special," Loana repeats, cackling. "Girl, you're here today because your mother never asked your father to stop!" And sighing, Loana starts talking about that French man who was so funny, and so full of life, and how she really wishes she had met him elsewhere than at the Zizou Bar.

Meeting someone in a bar sounds so bad — not serious, not *joli* to hear. When you tell people, "Oh, we met in a bar," they automatically think, In a bar! No wonder she has a child with Father Unknown written on her birth certificate! What was she doing in a bar? You don't meet husbands in bars!

But where else was Loana Mahi supposed to meet Tom Delors? He didn't go to church, he didn't know anyone she knew, she didn't know anyone he knew, the bar was the only place for the French boy and the Tahitian girl to bump into each other.

Well anyway, it's the past, and if Materena wants to search for her father, she can, her mother is giving her permission. But it's best Materena expects nothing and tells nobody about her search (not even her husband) just in case Tom isn't interested to know his daughter. The last thing Loana wants is for Materena's story to turn into politics. There are enough stories about arrogant French people going around the neighborhood, Tahiti, French Polynesia... the whole world.

"Don't expect anything, girl," Loana repeats, to make sure this advice is imprinted into her daughter's head. "If your father wants to know you, it's wonderful. If he doesn't, well, I'm warning you now...you will be hurt." Sighing, Loana adds, "You know my story with my father, how much I suffered."

Oh *oui*, Materena knows. She knows the whole story about her grandfather, Apoto, leaving his pregnant wife, Kika, and five-year-old daughter for another woman (who couldn't cook), but not before advising the whole village that the child in his wife's belly wasn't his, the Chinese man had planted it.

When the child came into the world with her father's face, still it wasn't a proof for Apoto. As far as he was concerned, he only had one daughter, and he stole her from Kika (using the law) not long after his desertion, to raise her with his infertile teacher mistress. As for that newborn baby girl, he spat — she was Kika's, keep her. Which was exactly what Kika did.

When Kika died — in Tahiti, far from her own island — Loana was fourteen years old. Shy, speaking acceptable French (but very little compared with her sister), lost without her mother. And Apoto still didn't acknowledge that child who had come from his seeds, leaving it up to his relatives to take over instead.

The child became a cleaner, then a single mother of two, drifting from relative to relative, from lover to lover, long resigned to not ever being good enough for her father — the owner of a petrol station, the offspring of a chief, a man with hectares of land to his name.

But on his deathbed, Apoto requested to speak to her. "Loana," he moaned, "Loana, my child. Forgive me."

She did. In that instant, there was no hesitation. "I forgive you, Papa," she cried, fervently kissing his hand. "Go on, die in peace."

Without that child who loved him so much, Apoto Mahi would be choking in weeds today.

From Tahiti to France

Okay, Materena is ready to call. She's got her list of fifty-two numbers from the telephone books at the post office, and she's decided her system: she's going to start by dialing the very last number and work her way up. There, it's decided.

She's ready, emotionally, that is. The way Materena sees the situation, she has nothing to lose. If her father says, "Of course I want to meet you," then wonderful. If her father says, "So what if you're my daughter?" then he can choke on weeds.

It is about eight o'clock in the morning, meaning it's about eight o'clock at night over there, but Materena might just wait for another half hour in case people are still eating. She sits on the floor and waits, rehearsing her introduction line in her head over and over again, taking deep breaths, her hands shaking. "Good evening, Monsieur," she will say (if he's a man; Madame if she's a woman), "my name is Materena and I'm calling from Tahiti. I'm looking for Tom Delors who did his military service in Tahiti forty-two years ago —" The rest of the introduction line will depend on how the person on the other end responds.

She's terrified. Terrified, petrified, ready to start crying, wishing she could have shared her anxiety with Pito, but it's best he knows nothing. Five more minutes to go — deep breath, Materena, and breathe slowly. Relax, it's only a phone call. But now she's thinking that perhaps she should have hired that detective she's heard about from one of her listeners, to get a bit of information about Tom Delors first: what he does for a job and everything, if he's mean, if he has children.

Two more minutes...come on, Materena, pull yourself together, no more procrastinating. Tiare is with her great-grandmother Loana and it's not often you have the whole house to yourself for a few hours.

Thirty seconds...one second, you're on, Materena! Good luck, girl!

And Materena grabs the phone and starts to dial, yelling in her head, *"En avant!"*

A woman picks up the telephone after the first ring. *"Allo oui?"* She sounds very excited that somebody is calling her.

Materena, who had expected the phone to ring at least three times is caught totally unprepared. After the *euh* and the *ah* embarrassed people do, Materena finally manages to spill her introduction line. "Good evening, Madame, my name is Materena and I'm calling from Tahiti and —"

"Tahiti!" The woman doesn't let Materena finish. "I've been to Tahiti, dear. It was a long time ago, now...let me think. I was seventeen years old...I'm eighty-six years old now." The woman, whom Materena didn't expect to be so old, goes on about her holidays in Tahiti, traveling with her parents. She loved every minute, every second of her Tahitian adventure. She remembers the red hibiscus hedges, chickens in trees, young girls walking, some holding breadsticks, others babies; barefoot children, women gathered outside the shop to talk and laugh. She remembers meeting so many people and how friendly they were! Always smiling.

"Do people still smile as much in Tahiti?" the woman asks.

"*Oui,* Madame, when they're happy."

"Oh that's very good." And off the old woman goes again, reminiscing about the only holiday she's ever had in her life. She got married not long after her expedition to Tahiti, she explains. She became a wife, and then she became a mother... there was the war of course, and then she became a grandmother, and now she's a great-grandmother. She's lived in the same town, the same street, and the same house for over sixty-five years.

Now she'd like Materena to tell her something.

"I'm listening, Madame," says Materena.

First of all the old woman reminds Materena of the custom back then for people leaving Tahiti to throw a flower wreath in the sea. "Is this still a custom?" she asks.

Materena confirms that it is, when the people leave on a ship. "And what did your wreath do?"

"It drifted back to shore, dear."

"It means that you will come back, Madame."

"Do you really believe it? But when will that be? I'm eighty-six years old, dear."

Materena tells the dear old woman that in fact she's never left Tahiti since she still remembers Tahiti and the people and there's no doubt in Materena's mind that the Tahitian people she met still remember her too.

"You know, Madame," Materena says, "Tahitians never forget nice people like you. I'm sure the people you've met talked about you to their children and their children talked about you to their children, and on and on. So in a way you're still with us."

"Oh, you're such a treasure, dear." The old woman continues her Tahitian tales, this time giving Materena little details, like how on a rainy day a very nice young man cut off a banana leaf for her to use as an umbrella. She talks and talks, and Materena, smiling, is now looking at the clock going *ticktock, ticktock.* But an old woman reminiscing cannot be interrupted. It's rude, and plus, Materena is feeling so sorry for the old woman. Poor her, she thinks, that old woman must not talk to a lot of people.

A whole hour passes before the old woman runs out of stories to share, and she's now ready to ask Materena why she called her.

Materena jumps on the occasion to explain her delicate situation.

"Tom Delors," the old woman whispers. "Let me think, dear...*Non,* I don't know of a Tom Delors, I'm Tess Delors, but I was born Tess Many. Sorry, dear. The Delors are a big family, it is quite possible he's a cousin of my late husband, but I've never had much to do with the Delors family, dear, I stuck with my own family, let me think —"

Fifteen minutes later Tess Delors is sorry to say that she's never heard of a Tom Delors, but she wishes Materena all the best, thanks her for her call, and invites Materena to visit her when she's in France next time.

The next person Materena speaks to, a man, says he's also never heard of a Tom Delors but he would like to grab the wonderful opportunity of having a Tahitian on the other end of the line to discuss the nuclear experiments in Moruroa. He's writing a paper on this issue. Unfortunately Materena can't help him on this crucial subject, but wishes him good luck.

The next person who picks up the phone is a child who tells Materena that she's not allowed to speak to strangers when her mother is not home, the same as she's not allowed to open the front door.

Now Materena is speaking to a woman who accuses her of being her husband's Tahitian mistress. "How dare you call my husband on this number," she yells into her telephone.

Materena's denial, "I'm not your husband's Tahitian mistress, I don't even know your husband!" only makes the wife yell louder.

"I recognize your uneducated accent, you bitch!" In the end Materena has to hang up on the wronged wife, all the while apologizing because she's never hung up on anyone in her whole life (except on Tamatoa once). But she's also never been insulted that way.

Shaken, Materena decides to continue her calls next week. Actually, she might wait for another two weeks. It is emotionally draining to make calls like that, when you don't know who is going to answer — a stranger, your father's wife, your father's other daughter.

Or even your father himself, and if he's going to say something like, "Yes, I know your father really well, why don't you call him at this number," and he gives you the phone number of the local dump. This is what happened to one of Materena's listeners, who swore that subsequently her thirst to know her father has been quenched for life.

How Friendship Strikes

Staring at the list of fifty-two phone numbers (one of these being Tom Delors' number, let's hope), Pito asks himself if he truly was a good father, as Materena so kindly implied.

He was hardly home. A good father is a father who wants to be with his family, *n'est-ce pas?* A good father doesn't disappear three nights a week with his drinking *copains,* and he stays home during the weekend to spend time with the children he hardly saw during the week.

Pito did the contrary. It's like he was running away.

He can't even blame the wife, it's not like she was a dragon or anything, she didn't scream at him as soon as he came home from work. Materena's famous cranky eyes were reserved for when Pito came home drunk, noisy, and empty-handed after a supposed weekend fishing expedition. Other than that, Pito always got the welcome-home-from-work face, apart of course from when Materena was *fiu* of him for some reason, but those days were extremely rare.

Talk about luck, eh? Pito knows many men who come home from work to a bitch woman, a woman with her hands on her hips and cranky words flying out of her cranky mouth like diarrhea. His two brothers Tama and Viri, for example.

Pito carefully puts the piece of paper away again next to the phone. And now, flicking through the photo album, he is hoping to catch glimpses of himself with his children, but all he sees is photo after photo after photo of Materena with her tribe.

Here she is pregnant with Moana, hugging Leilani in her arms and with Tamatoa holding tight onto her sarong. Smiling like she's having the best day of her life.

In the next photo, the strain is showing on her face. It's not easy to have three children demanding your attention before mass... Ah, here's a photo of Pito smiling with all his teeth, thumb up. He's with Ati, the fishing gear is in the background, and they're off their faces. It was back in those days when Ati was normal — before he signed the blue cross and made the sacred promise to God to stop drinking.

Here's Materena again, posing in her mother's garden, hair plaited, a red hibiscus flower behind her right ear, and her three nicely combed children gathered close... Pito and Ati, smiling and off their faces... Pito and Ati (not off their faces) posing in front of the church for Leilani's baptism, with Godfather Ati smiling with pride and Pito looking a bit bored.

Pito looks up at his granddaughter playing nearby with a pen, flying it as if it were a plane, making *broom, broom* sounds, and happiness shoots through his veins straight to his heart.

Back to the photo album. More pictures of Pito looking like he'd rather be somewhere else. What's with the miserable face? Pito says to his younger self. Wake up, you idiot! He snaps the album shut and gets the pink album from the shelf, the one of Tiare. Ah, that's much better. At least now Pito is showing his teeth a bit more, he's snapped that bored look off, he's the picture of a man content with his lot. *Oui,* Pito nods to himself, that's right.

He's not saying that in his younger days he *wasn't* content with his lot, *non,* but...eh, maybe I was young, that's all. Pito puts the pink album away, stands silent for a while watching his granddaughter, still playing with her airplane pen. Tiare looks up and starts running towards him, flying her plane.

"Don't run with the pen," Pito says. "You're going to hurt yourself." The child throws her arms around her grandfather's leg, squeezes it tight for a moment, and goes back to her playing.

Pito opens another family album, though he knows that this will only make him more miserable. *Oui,* more photos of him looking bored, more photos of him not being in the photos...and photo after photo of his youngest son looking so close to crying.

Here he is, quivering lips and sooky eyes looking up to his father (oh miracle, Pito is in the photo!) looking down at him with disapproving eyes. For being a sook, no doubt. Pito was often telling his youngest son off for being a sook. "Stop being a girl!"

He was prouder of Tamatoa. Tamatoa was tough, he never cried, he was already a man at eight years old. Or anyway, Pito mutters, as much of a man as he is now. *Conneries!* Why do we want our kids to grow up so quickly?

Next minute, Pito is dialing Moana's telephone number. He just feels like talking to his youngest son, and why not? Fathers don't need a reason to talk to their children. It's Saturday morning, and Pito is not at work. That's a good enough reason.

Moana picks up the phone after the fifth ring. "*Oui?*"

"Moana, it's Papi."

"Papi!" Moana sounds very surprised. Then worried. "Is Mamie all right?"

"*Oui, oui,* she's with your grandmother Loana . . . I'm calling to see how you are and everything."

A moment of hesitation. "*Euh,* I'm good."

"Ah, that's good." What else can I say? Pito thinks. Eh, he's going to ask how Moana's girlfriend is. Pito never acknowledges that girl. When Moana and Vahine became a couple, Pito was shocked. He remembers telling Moana, "There are so many girls out there, why her? Your older brother's ex-girlfriend? It's like eating leftovers! Plus, she's so skinny!" But since the cake episode, Pito is now very fond of his daughter-in-law. Maybe it's about time he shows it. "And how's Vahine?" Pito asks.

Another moment of hesitation. "She's good."

"Ah, that's good —" Pito's voice breaks a little. "I'm very happy for you two."

"And Tiare?" It's Moana's turn to ask questions. "She's fine?"

"Oh, she's a numero uno, that one," Pito cackles and tells Moana about Tiare looking so cute when she puts her handkerchief over her mouth to cough. She coughed all day yesterday just so that she could use the handkerchief her great-grandmother Loana bought her, but she's over that game now, she's into flying pens.

Father and son cackle aloud, forcing themselves a little until the cackle gradually dies down and it's time to end the conversation. Pito has run out of stories to say and Moana isn't asking questions, he'll get the whole information from his mother later, when they will talk for half an hour at least. You can't call your son for the first time and expect him to open up just because you're ready.

"*Allez,*" Pito says casually, though he's shaking inside. "I'll leave you."

"Thank you for calling, Papi." Moana himself sounds emotional.

"Ah," Pito dismisses his sooky son with the back of his hand. "Okay, return to your oven." Then he sits on the sofa, his head in his hands.

When the telephone rings, Pito immediately picks it up, thinking it is Moana calling back to say something else. "*Allo?*"

"Pito, *e aha te huru?*" says Ati.

"*Eh, copain!*" Pito exclaims, thinking, how strange for Ati to call him on a Saturday. Ati never calls when he has his son with him, and it's understood that Pito leaves Ati alone to be a papa.

"What are you doing?" Ati asks.

"I'm with Tiare, Materena is at her mother's, they're doing the genealogy tree, something like that."

"You want to come for a walk on the quay?"

"A walk?"

"*Oui*...with the kids. And Tamatoa? He's home too?"

"That one?" Pito snorts, cranky. "His head is between his legs. He's gone until Tuesday — another married woman."

"Ah, married women," Ati sighs with nostalgia.

Ati gets his son out of the car and carries him — the Tahitian way, meaning like a pack of taro but with a bit more sensitivity, the sensitivity often found in grandfathers. Well, Ati could pass for a grandfather. He's quite old, by Tahitian standards anyway, to be a first-time father.

"What about the carriage?" Pito asks. "Lily isn't going to —"

"Lily does her things her way," Ati snaps, "and I do my things my way."

Oh, Pito tells himself, I smell roses...

"She's a *conne*," Ati explains, although he didn't have to. Pito understood.

The childhood friends walk on, mingling with the tourists strolling by, admiring the yachts anchored to the quay along with the *paquebots.*

"Tonton," a little voice says, "look at my shoes."

"They're beautiful shoes, *chérie,*" Tonton Ati says.

"I like my shoes. They're RED!"

Pito tenderly squeezes his granddaughter's tiny hand, and looks at his friend, this man he's known for more than thirty-seven years, who's more like a brother to him than a friend.

They met at school — where else would two boys not related to each other and not living in the same *quartier* meet? — they were seven years old. Ati was the new kid at school, fresh from the outer islands and, would you believe it, very shy. Within two days, he was the victim of bullies, until Pito, the kid with the three big brothers, stepped in and saved Ati's face.

From that day on, Pito Tehana and Ati Ramatui became an item, chasing girls in the schoolground, stealing lollies at the Chinese store, rolling lumpy cigarettes, losing their fathers in the same year, then their virginity, finding themselves tied to each other by hundreds and hundreds of sweet and sad memories. Friends for life.

"You're all right, Ati?" Pito asks, sensing trouble in the air.

"I need to see my son more than three days a week." Ati softly kisses the top of his son's head. "If Lily wanted a father for her child only three days a week, she should have gotten herself a sailor . . . or a married man."

Ati continues on about his battle, his fierce battle, to be part of his son's life seven days a week. He doesn't want to be a part-time father, he says. According to Ati, there's no point having children if you're only going to pop in and out of their lives Wednesday, Thursday, Friday, and every second Saturday.

"It's better than nothing, *copain,*" Pito says.

"*Non,* it's frustrating, Lily can get *enculée.*"

"*Eh, copain,*" Pito says, tapping his friend on the shoulder, "don't talk about the mother of your son like that."

"I really want to be a good father, Pito," Ati says.

"You're a better father than I was." Admitting this is killing Pito, but sometimes you've got to be honest. Then, cackling, he adds without bitterness, "Since your son is born, I rarely see you. I should —"

"Eh, Pito," Ati whispers, nodding towards two old men sitting on the bench talking about... Well, seeing their enthusiastic gestures, they could be talking about the size of a very big fish or the width of a very big house, or perhaps the size of a very big woman's arse. "That's us in thirty years."

What Pito meant to say before Ati interrupted him was this: I should have been like you when my kids came.

But he won't say a word about this now, he'll just take a moment to wipe away that tear that has sprung out of his left eye.

Leilani's Diagnosis

The promenade with Ati has made Pito feel very bizarre. Perhaps he's just tired. He's never walked for that long before, forty-five minutes. He might have a nap, like Tiare. On second thought, he might call his daughter.

A young man answers the telephone.

"Can I speak to my daughter?" Pito asks, thinking, Who the hell are you?

"Eh, Pito!" It is Hotu, the boyfriend. *"E aha te huru?"*

"Eh, Hotu, *maitai*," says Pito, then in his head: You're there again? Weren't you there only two months ago?

"Leilani!" Pito hears Hotu call out.

"Oui, chéri!" Pito hears his daughter call back.

"Your papa is on the telephone!"

"I'm coming, *chéri!*"

"Would you like a coffee, *chérie?*"

"Oui, thanks, *chéri."*

Chéri this, *chérie* that, and Pito is thinking, Why don't you two live together?

"Papi?" This is a grown-up independent clever woman

speaking, the first future Tahitian woman doctor, but she still sounds like a little girl to her father.

"*Oui.*" That is all Pito can physically say for the moment. *Merde,* what is the matter with him?

"You're fine?" says Leilani; then to her boyfriend bringing her a coffee, "*Merci, chéri.*" She takes a sip. "Papi?"

"*Oui.*" That is still all Pito can physically say for the moment.

"Papi, are you sure you're okay?"

"Well, if you need to know," Pito admits, forcing a chuckle, "your old man is feeling a bit bizarre today."

"What do you mean by bizarre?"

What does Pito mean by bizarre? What's this bizarre question his daughter is asking? He's feeling bizarre, that's all. You can't explain bizarre. Bizarre means what it means, doesn't it? It means bizarre.

"Are you having mood swings?" Leilani asks.

"Eh?"

"Are you feeling happy one minute and then sad the next?"

Pito hesitates for a few seconds. "Today, *oui.*"

"Are you also tired a lot these days?" Leilani continues her questions.

"Today, *oui,* I'm tired."

"Are you losing your hair?" she goes on.

Pito proudly rubs his mop of mixed black and gray hair. "*Non,* I'm not losing my hair."

"Papi, I'm going to ask you a question, but please, don't be offended. I'm not speaking as your daughter here, okay? I'm speaking as a medical student...Now, are you experiencing a decline in your sex drive?"

"What?" *But!* The questions that girl asks! Pito shrieks to himself. He didn't call his daughter to be interrogated...and about that subject! It's not a subject to talk about with your daughter, not even your friends, not even your doctor! And he only called to say *Iaorana*. "So all is fine?" he asks.

"All is fine." The daughter senses she's offended her father, so she quickly changes the subject. "And how is my adorable niece?"

"She's a numero uno, that one," Pito chuckles and goes on about Tiare's new saying. Well, when the mademoiselle gets up (from the sofa, chair, table, the floor), she says, "*Parahi,*" meaning stay seated. This is the Tahitian way to say good-bye, more Tahitian than the word *nana* everyone uses.

Leilani chuckles along. "Soon Tiare will be teaching me to speak Tahitian!"

"It's her acquaintances, I tell you, the old women from Mama Teta's nursing home."

"Her great-great-aunties, we can call them like that."

"We can," Pito agrees. "How long is Hotu staying with you?"

"Ten days."

"Ah, that's good, it's better than the last time, what was it, only five days?"

"Papi, you are going through andropause," Leilani cuts in, speaking fast, without giving her father the chance to protest. "It's like the female menopause, and it's because there's a drop in your hormone levels. It's normal, millions of men in the world go through this stage —"

Pito is speechless, so Leilani goes on, and urges her father not to panic. He must remain calm, okay? He must not hurry to do irrational things like leave her mother for a younger woman. It's normal, she insists, for her father to feel lost and believe that he hasn't accomplished much in his life, but this is simply not true. He may not earn a lot of money but he's a wonderful, wonderful person. True, he may have faults. Many faults...but who is perfect?

A younger woman is not the cure, gambling neither, nor

breeding fighting roosters, whatever. And it's no use tormenting himself with the past, all the things he didn't do and should have done. It's the past, done, out of the way, swept away. Only tomorrow counts. The other advice Leilani offers her stunned patient is for him to increase his physical activity. This means less sitting on the sofa and maybe some more walking. Serious walking, not promenades. "Walk to work, Papi," Leilani says, after a big breath.

"Walk to work?"

"*Oui,* and why not? It's only six miles. Get up earlier and walk instead of catching the truck. We don't walk enough in Tahiti. We go from A to B but only if it is less than seventy-five feet, when we should really walk at least two miles a day. It's good for the heart and for the head too. Papi, please promise me that you will do some exercise... And try to drink less too."

Here we go again, Pito thinks. It's very easy for Leilani and Hotu to ask drinkers to drink less. Those two are allergic to alcohol. Normal people aren't that lucky.

"I'm not asking you to stop completely," the daughter goes on, "but try to drink less, that's all. Drink two glasses of water for each glass of beer... Papi?"

"Hmm."

"You can't die before I have children."

And Pito, a hand on his heart, smiles.

I'm going to start my exercising program. Pito is not being Monsieur Monday here, so many people make new resolutions to start on Monday, but the problem is that when Monday comes, the new resolution evaporates until the following Monday. But Pito is being serious.

Monday I'm going to walk to work, I'm going to be in shape! I'm going to lose my gut. Pito chants his new hymn over and over again. He gulps two glasses of water, punches a fist of victory, and rewards himself with a few sips of his beer, which by now is warm. That's the problem when you don't drink your beer in one go, it goes warm, especially on a hot day like today.

He starts to jump around, one foot up on the sofa... now the other, alternate, keep jumping... breathe, well, try to...

Purée, it's hot today, sweat is rolling profusely down Pito's temples. He sits on the sofa to recover a little, take a few proper breaths, and stop the panting.

The front door swings opens. It is Tamatoa, covered in sweat and red in the face, his bag slung over his shoulder.

"Eh?" Pito is pleasantly surprised. "I thought you said that you were coming home on Tuesday."

"Her husband is a gendarme, I'm not playing with a gendarme's wife, *non merci.* As soon as I found out, I ran home." Then, noticing his father panting, he asks, "What's with you?"

Pito spreads his arms across the sofa. "Your sister says I have to start exercising, I'm trying, *copain,* I'm trying. I'm walking to work on Monday."

"Walking?" Tamatoa grins. His father has never called him *mate.* "Running is better."

"For young people, *oui,* but for us old men —" Pito shrugs and cackles.

"You're not old, Papi." Tamatoa sits next to his father. "I can run with you... if you want."

Pito considers the offer. "I'm not going to shame you? I'm warning you, I don't run like the wind."

"Eh," Tamatoa says, giving his father a man's tap on the leg. "As long as you don't crawl, *c'est le principal.*"

A Chance from the Sky

There are many things a father can learn when running with his son. Well, first, he learns *how* to run: how to pace himself, breathe right, how to hold his arms up so that they don't dangle and take up energy. But most important, he learns to trust his son.

Pito really thought that Tamatoa was going to dump him halfway through the run, seeing that Tamatoa could run twice as fast, if not three times. But Tamatoa remained by his father's side, circling him and all the while giving him words of encouragement like, "Just imagine you're representing Tahiti at the Olympic Games!" Pito had to stop a few times to laugh and catch his breath.

Still, he had not expected Tamatoa to run home with him later in the day after work as Tamatoa had promised him to. When Pito saw his son at the gate, he thought, *"Eishh!"* He had hoped to catch the truck and stop it about three hundred feet away from home, and then run. But deep down, Pito was really proud Tamatoa had lived up to his promise. Maybe his son is turning at last into someone you can rely on.

So that is why, a week later, Pito is proposing to his beautiful wife lying by his side to go camping for a night.

Materena ponders for a while before accepting the unusual invitation. I've never been camping in all my life, she thinks. Well, why not try something new?

Materena doesn't even bother asking Pito information regarding the camping equipment, doesn't fire one thousand questions about where he is going to get the tent et cetera. She just kisses him on the mouth, saying how romantic it will be, and how she can already visualize the three of them sitting around a campfire, with Pito telling stories to their granddaughter and...

Pito hurries to mention that the little one will be staying at home with her father.

"Eh?" Materena stops kissing Pito. "Leave Tiare with Tamatoa?" Her smiling face drops. "Pito, are you serious?" She goes on about her son's inability to look after himself, let alone a child. "He can't even cook rice!"

"So what if he can't cook rice, it's not the end of the world."

"Pito... what if Tamatoa leaves *bébé* at the house and goes out dancing... and then something happens —"

"He's not going to do that! Trust him."

"Pito!" Materena is now cranky. She gets out of bed and declares that he can go camping if he wants to but she's not going.

"Materena —"

"My answer is *non.*" Materena is adamant about this. "You go camping, I'm staying right where I am, we can have romance here, we don't need to go camping, and plus, I don't like camping."

"How do you know?" Pito asks. "You've never been camping in your whole life."

"I know. I saw it in a movie once, and it doesn't look comfortable."

"We can stay in a *pension* if it's more comfortable for you."

"*Non,* I prefer my own house." With this firm statement, Materena fluffs her pillow, she's going to sleep.

"Materena, listen to me, okay? Listen."

"I'm listening."

And so Pito fires away. He doesn't care if he never gets to go camping with Materena, he says, because, true, you don't need to go camping to have romance. You can have romance in the marital bed. You can have romance in the kitchen, bathroom, anywhere, because it's all in the mind.

The real reason behind his idea to go away for one whole day and a whole night is to give their son a chance to be with his daughter, alone.

"I —"

"Materena, let me talk, I haven't finished." As he was saying, he'd like to give Tamatoa the chance to be with his daughter, alone, the chance to see what he can do. Pito didn't get his chance to realize what he was capable of until two years ago, when his granddaughter came into his life and Materena gave him her trust. It was very difficult for Pito to adapt to his new role as a grandfather, guardian, and godfather, but he learned quickly and everybody survived.

The way Pito sees his situation, he was never given the chance to prove himself, women always took over. For example, when Pito was a young boy, his mother would always serve him his dinner so that he wouldn't spill rice everywhere — but maybe she should have let him serve himself, she should have let him spill a few grains of rice on the floor.

Then later, Materena would always get out of bed for a crying baby — but maybe she should have pretended to be fast asleep. Pito would have eventually gotten up because the sound of a crying baby would have gotten on his nerves. But *non,* the years passed and Pito stayed a little boy in his head.

Well, says Pito, this is not going to happen to his son, *non,* no way — but Tamatoa is sure to be making the same mistakes as his father did if something isn't done about it now.

"You women," says Pito, "you do your complaining because men don't help with the children, and at the same time, you don't give us men the chance to see that looking after children isn't voodoo! You make us believe that children need magic, special touch, and everything, because they're so delicate, they're like porcelain dolls. All of this is *conneries.* Wake up, you women!"

What women should do, well, according to Pito anyway, is to go away for a whole weekend now and then. Go, leave the children with their father, disappear, but don't tell the father what to do, what not to do. Just walk out of the house and close the door. Like Materena did with Pito, like Lily is doing with Ati.

Materena had no idea Pito felt that way. She takes his hand in hers and squeezes it tight. "All right, then," she says. "We can go camping."

"This weekend?" Tamatoa, sweating from his dance rehearsal, doesn't look too happy about this. But at least Pito is pleased that it isn't looking after Tiare that is making his son unhappy, it is the fact that he's expected to do it *this* weekend. Pito had expected to have to give his son a long sermon on fatherhood.

"I can't, Papi, not this Saturday."

"Why? What's happening this Saturday?"

"I'm meeting this girl."

"You like her?"

Tamatoa shrugs. "She has a sexy belly button."

"She can't wait until next Saturday, her and her belly button?" Before Tamatoa gives his father his answer, Pito tells him that his mother had to wait for more than twenty-five years to have a romantic night with her husband. Surely, whoever that girl is, seven more days isn't going to kill her.

Tamatoa chuckles. "You're right, Papi."

Pito is so tempted to go ahead and give his son a sermon on fatherhood, like how it doesn't mean leaving a child at home on her own, it doesn't mean not feeding her for a whole day and a whole night... But sometimes a father must trust his son.

And now, Saturday morning, close to seven thirty, the grandparents are saying their good-byes, glad to see that Tiare is taking the good-byes so well, but then again, she's very interested in what her father is mixing in the bowl.

"*E aha te ra?*"

"Pancake."

"Pancake? *E aha te ra?*"

"It's good."

"It's good? *Mona, mona?*"

Tamatoa smiles. "She speaks Tahitian a lot." He turns to his daughter. "*Oui,* it's *mona, mona.*"

Ah, it's good to see, and Materena reminds her son to make sure he turns off the gas bottle at night because...

"*Allez,* Mama," Pito interrupts, "let's go before we miss the ferry."

The car, loaded with camping equipment which Pito borrowed from Ati, is ready to go on a little adventure all the way to Moorea, one hour by ferry from Tahiti.

"*Eh hia,*" Materena sighs, turning the engine on, "I hope that —"

"Everything is going to be all right." Pito interrupts Materena before she winds herself up with worries. But it seems that it is a woman's second nature to worry, because that's all Materena does. About this, about that, if Tamatoa will remember to close the gas bottle, if Tamatoa will remember that Tiare doesn't like her rice soggy, if this, if that. The worrying pours out of Materena's mouth nonstop driving to Papeete, during the ferry ride, standing at the rails and holding on to Pito tight like she's scared he'll fall into the deep blue sea or something.

Materena only starts to relax at Temae Beach, the chosen camping site, the only beach without a TABOO sign nailed to a tree. She even manages to laugh her head off helping Pito set up the tent.

"I'm so relaxed!" she says as they go for a walk, picking up shells and funny-shaped rocks, and later on as they frolic in the sea.

Materena also feels very relaxed after the passionate sexy loving in the tent (her first ever sexy loving experience in a tent, and how wonderful it was except perhaps a bit hard on the back) as they get the fire ready, barbecue their breadfruit, and heat up their corned beef to celebrate their first Saturday away as a couple.

Night falls, stars appear, and there, right in front of the lovers, far away in the distance, is the magnificent island of Tahiti, all lit up like a Christmas tree. Thousands of lights, this way, that way, up high in the mountains, on the shore. It makes you think about things…

Like those expensive calls to France leading nowhere. So far, Materena has called twenty-one people of her list of fifty-two phone numbers, and nobody knows Tom Delors who did military service in Tahiti. But one woman did point out to Materena that the name *Delors* was very common in France.

"I'm so relaxed!" Materena forces the exclamation.

"Me too!" Pito doesn't sound too convincing either.

If a stranger were to walk past and glance at this couple sitting by the fire, he would think it odd that they look so gloomy on such a romantic night. Why the funeral face? It's bizarre. The stranger would probably put this down to a lover's spat, but then he would tell himself that it couldn't be, since these two people sitting by the fire don't look angry. They just look...sad, really. A bit flat. An amicable separation, maybe? The last night before the end...*Ah oui,* how tragic.

"I'm worried." There, Materena has decided to speak the truth.

"Okay, me too."

Just then, a shooting star flashes by, heading towards the ocean, traveling very fast, giving people who believe that a shooting star is a chance from the sky merely two to four seconds to come up with a wish from their heart. People are often caught unprepared and panic, coming up with a wish only after the shooting star has disappeared. In this case, the wish doesn't count, since you've got to make it there and then, on the spot. Since Materena and Pito have been wishing nearly all day, they have no trouble coming up with a wish within one second.

Meanwhile, back in Faa'a, a young father is putting his daughter to bed, realizing how little she is, how fragile she looks, defenseless. At the door, his new friends look on.

"Tamatoa, *mon bijou,*" Brigitte says with her much-practiced femme-fatale voice, "you're the man — you make sure your daughter grows up safe. The world is a dangerous place." This *raerae extraordinaire* knows what she's talking about. Born a boy, the last child of the family, and raised as a girl by the mother, Brigitte has seen all kinds of colors as a woman.

"Look after her, Tamatoa," she says. "Don't fail your daughter's trust in you."

Raising Daughters

When his daughter grows up, Tamatoa tells his father — actually, as soon as she's six years old, perhaps even sooner — he will get her into kung fu classes. Father and son are sharing a beer at the kitchen table, in between drinking their required glasses of water.

"Kung fu?" Pito cackles. "Why? You want your daughter to be the next Bruce Lee?"

"Heh, and why not, eh?" Tamatoa sees no reason to set limits on his little girl; but for now, *non,* Tamatoa has no intention for Tiare to be a martial arts expert. He just wants her to be able to defend herself against idiots. This is worrying him a bit, he admits, having a daughter, a pretty daughter, so it's best she knows a few self-defense tricks. "There are too many idiots running around who are after only one thing," he says.

"Like you?" Pito teases.

"I never forced a girl," Tamatoa says seriously, to show his father the kind of man he is. "If a girl is not interested, it's not the end of the world for me."

"That's good."

"But I get girls easily." Tamatoa is not showing off here, he's just stating the truth. He's got the eyes girls (and women) love looking into, the body girls (and women) can't have enough of, and a smooth tongue that can whip out a charming conversation.

"What about boys who can't get girls easily?" Tamatoa goes on. "They're the boys I'm worried about, they don't always take no, those animals. If one of them hurts my daughter, I tell you, Papi, I'm going to slice his throat. I'm going to *taparahi* him until he dies, until he chokes on his blood and vomit —"

Pito takes a sip of water.

"My daughter isn't going to be a victim," Tamatoa says. "She's not going to be a statistic, because she's going to know how to defend herself." His daughter won't need to call out for help, Tamatoa continues, she won't need to pray either, she won't panic or cry for mercy, *non*.

She will surprise her assailant with a powerful punch in his gut and a sharp kick in his *couilles,* and then she will run and not look over her shoulder. Her assailant will run after her, cursing his head off, but he will not catch up to her because she will run like the wind.

Oui, that's why Tiare will be joining an athletics club as soon as she's five. Tamatoa has just decided this. His daughter will be a Tahitian gazelle, and she will have iron fists too. Nobody will be pushing her around, *ah-ha* no way.

"I remember a girl," Tamatoa says, "she was about nine and I was ten, it was at school, she had a packet of Twisties in her hand, and I told her, 'Give me the Twisties or I'm going to *taparahi* you.' She started to cry and gave me her Twisties. This is not going to happen to my daughter. Someone tries that trick on her, she's going to laugh and say, 'You want two black-buttered eyes?'"

Well, maybe Tiare won't have to do that, Tamatoa elaborates, because she will already have a reputation, she will be
known as that girl who takes *merde* from nobody, not even bossy
boys who steal Twisties. She will have muscular arms, and eyes
that fear nothing. She'll never cry because a boy took all her
marbles — nobody will be touching her marbles, it's simple.

She won't ever cut a lock of her hair to give to a boy who
doesn't even like her, and she will NOT follow a boy into the
school toilets to show him her private parts just because he wants
to see and she thinks he'll like her after she does what he wants.
If a boy ever asks Tiare to show him her private parts, she'll
laugh and say, "Ah, you want to see my private parts, eh? Well,
here's my private parts." Bang, she'll knock that stupid boy's
teeth out.

Pito is starting to wonder how much of this is coming from
Tamatoa's personal experience, but his son is not finished. Tiare,
he announces, will not be wasting time doing a boy's homework just because he said, "You're so pretty, can you do my
homework?" She'll be doing her own homework and get good
marks like her Auntie Leilani. And she will be strong like her
Auntie Leilani. She will say what Leilani used to tell boys: "I'm
not a servant in my own house, why should I be in yours?"

So this is Tamatoa's plan. He will never ask his daughter to
get him a beer out of the fridge and turn her into a servant.
He will never tell his daughter that she's ugly, like the father
of one girl he knew, who was willing by seventeen years old to
do anything (and by *anything* Tamatoa means *anything*) a boy
asked her in return for a small compliment. He will never tell
his daughter that she can't do this, she can't do that, because
she's a girl...

"In short," Tamatoa continues, "I'm going to raise my daughter like you raised my sister."

"Eh?" As far as Pito is concerned, Materena is responsible for Leilani's raising.

He did very little with his daughter. He never took her to a soccer match. Never took her fishing. Leilani was always stuck at home with her mother. "Like I raised your sister?" he says.

"You never treated her like she was your servant," Tamatoa says. "And you've never told her that she couldn't do this, she couldn't do that, just because she was a girl, and look at Leilani now. She's strong, she takes *merde* from nobody."

And before Pito can say, Look, I appreciate the compliments and everything, but the person you should really be complimenting here is your mother, Tamatoa steps in. "I had a really good weekend with my daughter, Papi . . . Thank you for opening my eyes."

He continues to talk about the girls he met and who grew up without a father, and how insecure they were. "Papi, there was this girl," Tamatoa says, "she was mad, but my God, she was beautiful, a *canon!*"

Tamatoa loved walking with that girl in public. Everyone would look at her, and Tamatoa would laugh in his head, "Bad luck for you! She's with me!" But she asked the stupidest questions. "Would you still find me beautiful if I had no toes?" *Oui*, Tamatoa would say. "Would you still find me beautiful if I had only one eye?" *Oui.* "One arm?" *Oui.* "No fingers?" *Oui, oui, oui,* shut up and take your clothes off.

"Then one night, we were at a restaurant, just about to order, and she says, 'It's the end of the world, and you can have only one more kiss. Who is it going to be with?' and I said, 'Isabelle Adjani.'"

That name flew out of Tamatoa's mouth before he could think because . . . well, he wouldn't mind kissing Isabelle Adjani before he dies. What a way to go! She's more than a *canon*, she's a goddess! Anyway, no sooner had Tamatoa given his answer than his mad girlfriend flicked her glass of water at him, stood up, gave Tamatoa a long look, and said, "How could you ever be the father of my children?" Then she left, just like that!

"You didn't go after her?" Pito asks.

"Would you have gone after her?"

Pito thinks about this. "I don't think she would have been with me in the first place."

Tamatoa shakes his head and half cackling says, "I don't know why I attract girls who don't have a father. I must have a tattoo on my forehead or something." Anyway, Tamatoa's point for today is that daughters need a father, and he's persuaded that the reason why Miri is crazy in the head is because she grew up without a father.

"There's her childhood too," Pito reminds Tamatoa. He won't go into Miri's childhood — well, the little he knows (and guessed) from Miri's short letters full of self-pity.

"*Ah oui,*" Tamatoa admits. "She did have a...colorful childhood." Meaning, drama galore.

"And you're being careful with your seeds at the moment?" Pito asks.

"Papi, don't worry, I'm *paranoid* about my seeds now."

"Be careful," Pito repeats.

"It's registered, Papi," Tamatoa says. "The last thing I want is a girl to come up to me in twenty years and say, '*Bonjour,* do you remember my mother?' One daughter is enough for me. I don't need more responsibilities." Then, sighing, he whispers, "But I really feel sorry for daughters who don't know their fathers...that's sad."

And in that very moment Pito knows exactly what he has to do.

Pito's Contribution

Mama Roti is out of the house, playing bingo with her sister-in-law Rarahu, so Pito (who took a day off today) has decided to use her telephone for a few hours.

Well, talk about luck! First number on the list, and bingo!

"One second, Monsieur," the nice woman who answered the telephone said. Then, "Papa! Telephone!"

"Who is it?" A grumpy voice in the background.

"I don't know, he just asked to speak to you."

"*Oui?*" The voice is very terse.

"It's you, Tom Delors?"

"Who wants to know?"

"Me."

"Me who? And how did you know I was here?"

"I just called the number on the list."

"What list? Who the fuck are you? How fucking dare you call me on my daughter's phone?"

"I didn't know it was your daughter's phone, I just called the number on the list." *Purée,* Pito tells himself. No wonder I can't stand French people. Arrogant pigs.

"What fucking list?" Tom Delors asks again with that tough-guy voice gendarmes in the movies use to intimidate people.

"The fucking list from the fucking telephone books." That man isn't intimidating Pito at all.

"What the fuck is this?" Now Tom Delors sounds confused.

"Oh, Papa." His daughter has had enough, Pito can hear in the background. "Stop swearing!"

"Did you do military service in Tahiti forty-two years ago?" Pito fires away his first question. There's no need to talk to this arrogant man any longer if he's not the Tom that Pito is looking for.

"Who needs to know?"

"Give me your answer first and I'm going to tell you who needs to know, I'm not going to give you any information if you're not the Tom Delors I'm looking for. My wife's story isn't for the whole population. *Alors?* Did you or did you not do your military service in Tahiti forty-two years ago?"

"Why should I answer your question?"

Pito grinds his teeth. But he can see that man's point of view. If he ever got a call from someone asking him if he did military service in France, he'd immediately get on the defensive. He was just a kid back then, not even nineteen years old, and he did do a lot of *conneries.* Pito is not talking here about the (very careful) sleeping around he did; he's talking about stealing a car, driving it around for two days, and abandoning it in the middle of a street when it ran out of petrol. Pito has more stories like that, all to do with breaking the law.

"Do you know Loana?" There, how about that question. It might be easier for Tom to answer.

"Loana Mahi?"

Bingo.

*   *   *

There are two queues at the Faa'a International Airport, one for the foreigners, and one for the French citizens. Tom Delors, traveling with daughter Térèse, heads to the French citizens' line — he in front, barging; she following and struggling with her two items of hand luggage. At the counter, a friendly Tahitian customs officer stamps the Frenchman's passport and asks him what business is bringing him to Tahiti.

"Mine." Tom wasn't always this way — abrupt, short, impatient. But forty years as a gendarme putting scums behind bars has changed him, and turned him into an intense, private individual, suspicious and sometimes unreasonably intolerant. He's never had his tongue in his pocket anyway.

"*Bonjour,* Monsieur!" Térèse is just the opposite. Friendly, too friendly, so friendly that anyone she talks to immediately falls under her spell.

"Are you here on holidays?" the customs officer politely asks, stamping the *jolie mademoiselle*'s passport.

"Familial visit."

"*Ah oui?* You have family here in Tahiti?"

"My big sister lives here."

"And she's pretty like you?"

"I can't tell you, Monsieur, I've never met her, it's —" But her father is waiting, and the story would take far too long to tell, so, thanking the customs officer profusely — that's the only way Térèse thanks people, profusely — she moves on.

"Must you chatter to everyone?" her father complains, heading to pick up his luggage.

"Oh, Papa," Térèse laughs. "You really regress when you're nervous."

"I'm not nervous," Tom corrects. "But my patience has limits."

She brushes her shoulder against his, he brushes his shoulder against hers, she elbows him, he elbows her back, and Tom cracks up laughing — loudly, as he always does. Heads turn to this unusual couple; the tall buffed-up intimidating-looking man with the broken nose who must be — what? — in his fifties? And the tall expensive-looking blonde, maybe twenty or twenty-two. For the record, he is sixty-two and she is thirty.

He has two pieces of luggage, she has four, he is staying for six days, she is staying for three months. He's here to briefly meet his other daughter, she's here to connect with her only sister. He retired two months ago, she hasn't had a holiday for almost ten years. Mind you, she's been planning a three-month holiday for the past four years; she has simply changed the destination from Corsica to Tahiti.

Térèse glances at her father's golf clubs and sighs with disapproval. She's already done this checking in at the Charles de Gaulle Airport. She still firmly believes that her father should have left his golf clubs behind. He's not in Tahiti to play golf. He's here to meet his daughter.

"Papa," Térèse says, "you're not here to —"

"They have the best golf course in Tahiti!" Tom immediately guesses what his critical daughter is criticizing. "One game, just one game."

They walk through the door, he pushing the luggage trolley, she lovingly brushing hair off her father's forehead. Hundreds of people are ready to greet their loved ones (a few are already crying); two mamas, clutching onto flower wreaths, are anxiously waiting... Tom and Térèse detour to the right to avoid this mass of human emotion. She's the first to notice the Tahitian man with the white flower pinned to his shirt.

"Oh, this must be Pito," she says, waving.

Pito hurries towards them, closely followed by Ati, the best friend and, for today anyway, the designated chauffeur. Hands are shaken, introductions are made, the young, pretty woman gets her kisses (two only are required in Tahiti, not four, as they do in France — "Oops, sorry," laughs Térèse). But welcome to Tahiti, and please accept these flower wreaths, and how are you, how was your flight et cetera, et cetera...The car is there, not far away, follow us.

Father-in-law and son-in-law lead the procession, not speaking a word but throwing the occasional furtive glance at each other and smiling half smiles. It must be stressed here that Pito has never had to deal with a father-in-law before, so he really doesn't know the protocol. He didn't have to ask that man for his daughter's hand. He didn't have to pass the father's test.

For now, all Pito can do is be polite. Tom is feeling the same. Polite and calm, it is definitely not the time to get aggravated because the car is parked so far away and that damn trolley has squeaky wheels.

Behind, though, a lively conversation is unfolding with questions and answers flying backwards and forwards between the inquisitive, smiling Frenchwoman and the Tahitian man who's made it his lifetime mission to despise French people (those wicked *popa'a,* those invaders, thieves, arrogant pricks, et cetera). But for the moment, Ati, gallantly carrying Térèse's hand luggage, smiles his *uh-huh* half-sexy smile that he does when in the company of a woman he likes. With each step he takes in her company, each word she says, he feels drawn to her for no other reasons than pure chemistry. And the fact that she's Materena's sister, perhaps, too.

The drive to the Hotel Maeva Beach, where Tom and Térèse are staying for a week, goes in a flash. Two miles, it is short.

"*Bon,*" Tom says with his serious voice, rubbing his hands. "*Merci...alors,* see you for lunch, *oui?*"

"Will you be coming too?" Térèse asks Ati.

"*Euh...*" Ati hasn't been invited.

A smile. "I'm inviting you."

Pito is taking his wife to the restaurant for lunch at the Hotel Maeva Beach, and Materena didn't even ask the reason behind this unexpected invitation to eat. When Pito made the announcement, "*Chérie,* I'm inviting you to the restaurant," Materena exclaimed, "*Eeeh!* That's so nice, *chéri.*"

Wearing a beautiful dress, makeup, and new shoes, and with flowers in her impeccable *chignon,* Materena confidently reverses her car. Pito looks on, wondering if he's done the right thing interfering like this. Perhaps he should tell Materena the news now; that way she'll have some time to get herself prepared in her head.

And she should definitely know that her father is a pack of nerves before meeting him. Rude too, a swearer, abrupt...a retired gendarme, so what do you expect? But Pito is not complaining that his father-in-law used to be a gendarme. It's a useful job, putting scums behind bars. Maybe Tom could talk to his grandson Tamatoa about that.

Tom declined Pito's invitation to stay at the house because, well, because he doesn't like to stay at people's houses, and he insisted that the meeting takes place on neutral ground. But Tom, keeping his identity secret, did go to that bookshop in Paris where his granddaughter works, bought a book she recommended ("highly, Monsieur"), and bought a plane ticket for Tahiti hours later. This shows that he cares a bit, *non?* And the sister is very nice. Ati is already crazy about her.

Materena stops her car at the petrol station to wave to Cousin Loma walking to the Chinese store. "*Iaorana,* Cousin!" Materena calls out, smiling.

"*Iaorana,* Cousin!" Loma calls back, so happy that Materena is waving at her in such a friendly manner. "Where are you two off to?"

"Pito has invited me to the restaurant!"

"Ah, that's nice."

Okay, since the news has been delivered, Materena can go on with her driving. Cousin Loma will make sure to pass the news about Pito's sweet invitation to the restaurant to the family. Materena doesn't mind the whole population knowing this.

They are now at the hotel, and Materena parks her car, whistling a happy tune. She switches the engine off and turns to her husband, sitting quiet. He looks a bit sick. "Are you all right?"

"*Oui,*" Pito is quick to reassure Materena.

"You've got enough money to pay?"

"*Oui,* don't worry about that." Pito gets out of the car, a forced smile on his lips.

"What is it?" Materena is not being fooled by her husband's fake smile. "Listen, if you don't want to eat at the restaurant, it's fine with me." She knows all about Pito's ridiculous fear that the chef will spit or cough on his food.

Pito gives Materena a long look and takes her into his arms. Right there in the parking lot, in front of people driving and walking by.

"Pito —" Materena cackles, "you're a bit bizarre today."

Pito gently pulls away and, taking Materena's hand, he starts to walk.

"Eh, that's Ati's car," Materena says, noticing the black Suzuki with the number plate ATI. "He never rests!" Materena automatically assumes that he's romancing with a girl in her hotel room.

They walk into the lobby.

"You reserved the table?" Materena asks just to make sure. Pito doesn't have experience eating in restaurants. "Lots of people eat here, and if you don't reserve the table, it's not guaranteed that —"

"There's somebody here who wants to meet you." Here, Pito spilled the beans.

"Somebody?" Materena asks, casually slowing her steps. "Who?"

"Actually, there are two people who want to meet you."

"Two? Who? I know them?"

"I can't say that you know them, but you've heard about them, I mean one of them."

Materena stops and faces Pito. "Who are they?"

"It's your father."

Materena turns pale. "Pito, don't make fun of my head."

"And your sister."

"What?" Materena puts her hands to her mouth. "Pito, this is not funny." Her eyes fill with tears.

"They arrived this morning."

"Pito, I'm warning you, if this is a joke —"

"They're with Ati, he likes your sister, and they're waiting for you at the restaurant."

And with this, Materena, bawling her eyes out, runs towards the restaurant.

Very slowly and pushing disturbing thoughts out of his mind, Pito chews the piece of steak *grillé* in his mouth, concentrating on the wonderful flavors, the spicy sauce, the tenderness of the meat. He chews on while trying hard, extremely hard, let's be honest here, to chase away images of the chef coughing on this very piece of steak.

Twice he attempts to swallow the steak, which is by now, he can picture it, a gray blob of unflavored thing, but it just won't go down. Ah, there, done, Pito forced it down his throat.

Next piece of steak...and the nightmare continues. Again, Pito pushes disturbing thoughts out of his mind, chewing for longer than necessary.

Nobody at the table seems to be noticing Pito's show. Words are flying nonstop between Ati and Térèse, Materena and Térèse, Tom and Materena, Tom and Térèse...words, laughter, just your ordinary family enjoying food and one another's company. Now and then, a hand reaches to the other for a touch, a magic touch, a loving squeeze. And under the table, Materena's foot is lovingly rubbing her husband's.

Three Days Later...

As expected, the news about Materena's father and sister being in Tahiti was on the coconut radio quick-smart. This explains the gathering of hundreds of Materena's relatives at her fibro shack behind the petrol station not far from the church, the cemetery, the international airport, and the Chinese store.

Poor Tom Delors looks bewildered. He came here to meet his daughter — not her entire tribe! But as they say in Tahiti, this is family.

The last time Tom was in Tahiti, he didn't get much attention. Actually, the last time he was here, Tahitian people only gave him quick glances. Sometimes the glances were despising, other times angry — especially when he was in the company of his beautiful Tahitian girlfriend, Loana. But back then, he was just a nobody *popa'a, farani taioro* in Tahiti for military service, giving local women a bad reputation.

He is now Materena's father, half the reason she is on this earth today. He is the grandfather of Tamatoa, Leilani, and Moana. He is the great-grandfather of Tiare. He is *somebody*.

Materena's tribe want to touch Tom now, kiss him, hold him tight, make him feel welcome, look him right in the eye and remember him until he dies, even years after. Forever, actually. This is how Tahitian people remember their loved ones — forever.

As for Tom's youngest daughter, Térèse, she is Materena's sister. There's no half-sister in the story, because here in Tahiti siblings are siblings full stop. They are not halves. And of course, everyone present agrees that Térèse is beautiful. She is beautiful because she smiles a lot, kisses the children with affection, and holds the hands of the elders with respect.

Tom is a bit more reserved, he took half a step back when Mama Teta threw her arms around him as if she knew him well. But give Tom a few more days and he'll be throwing his arms around Mama Teta like a long-lost friend because by then he *will* know her well. She will have told him the whole story about how she lost her husband very young and raised their four boys on her own, how none of her boys has ever done time at the five-star hotel.

Unfortunately, Pito's mother, present today representing the Tehana tribe, can't say the same, but that isn't the reason why Mama Roti didn't throw her arms around her daughter-in-law's French father. For some reason, Mama Roti — who has never been shy in her entire life before — got a bit embarrassed before the tall, handsome Frenchman. She gave him two shy kisses and then scurried away to the kitchen to help Moana with the food preparation.

Next in line to meet the famous Tom Delors was Materena's favorite cousin, Rita.

After Rita greeted Materena's father, she introduced him to her heavily pregnant (as usual) cousin Giselle. Well, Tom couldn't hide his look of horror when Rita told him that she and her man, Coco, were going to adopt Giselle's new baby because they couldn't have children, while God is giving Giselle a child every year.

"What?" asked Rita when she saw Tom's expression. Was it fine for his people to come to Tahiti to adopt Tahitian babies but shocking for Tahitian people to offer each other their children? Ah, if only Tom was staying for longer, he'd understand that Giselle's gift was one of love.

For Giselle is not discarding her child, *non,* she is offering her child with all her heart and soul so that her cousin's life doesn't remain empty.

Giselle knows that this child in her belly is about to embark on a wonderful journey as Rita and Coco's child. And she is so tired... And since she's bound to fall pregnant next year because all she has to do to fall pregnant is look at her husband for two seconds, and since Rita and Coco want two children, then Giselle is likely to offer them her next child too.

If people are going to have two adopted children, they might as well be siblings. That is Giselle's thinking anyway, she explained to Tom.

When Tom shook Loana's hand, he did it the way *popa'a* do when they want to say, Pleased to meet you, how do you do? But then again, Loana didn't lean forward to offer her cheeks for the two kisses that say, So pleased to see you! And how *are* you? You're good, my friend? Those two just shook hands and shyly smiled. You'd never know they'd once seen each other naked and done all the intimate things lovers do in the throes of passion.

But give Tom and Loana a few hours alone together and who knows what might happen? Or anyway, so say Mama Teta and her gang of *memes* all dressed in their pretty floral dresses. That Tom Delors, they say, he's nice to look at and so is Loana. Put one and one together and magic might happen again, as it did forty-two years ago on the dance floor at the Zizou Bar.

And even if none of that sort of magic happens, there will be a strong connection between those two now, the connection a man and woman feel whenever they talk about their child. And of course Tom will laugh at the stories Loana will tell him about his daughter as a very curious child asking couples in the truck, "Are you two married?" And he will, for certain, feel a twinge of sadness that he wasn't around to tell his daughter that worms have no eyes, two plus two equals four, and that *A* is for *arbre.*

Perhaps too he'll ask Loana why she didn't tell him about their daughter earlier, and she will shrug, as Tahitian people do, meaning, I didn't think to do that, I just moved on with my life. He might then say, But I could have helped you... financially, and Loana is sure to get her claws out. "What are you saying?" she will bark. "My daughter never went hungry! She never had to walk around naked!"

It will be in Tom's best interests just to concentrate on what a wonderful, wonderful job Loana has done raising their daughter.

Well, anyway... finally all the introductions to the Mahi and Tehana clans are complete, and it is time to pose before Pito, designated photographer.

"Photos?" asks Tom, sounding surprised. "With all these people?"

Well, *oui,* with all these people. Why do you think they're all wearing their best clothes? To go for a walk?

"How will we all fit in?" Tom, sounding even more surprised, asks.

"We're going to take turns, that's all."

Okay, everyone, ready?

First photo session, and Pito tries very hard to focus on the people he's about to immortalize, but really, what's with Loana now? Smile! She looks so uptight. Mama Teta still has her famous bright smile on now for the camera. You can always count on Mama Teta to smile, and her smile is so real, unlike Pito's mother's smile. Then again, Mama Roti might still be feeling shy. Mama shy? Pito laughs in his head. What's next? Chicken with teeth?

Allez, time to get serious...ah, Pito is so happy for his wife, and she is so beautiful, and look at her father holding her the same way he's holding his other daughter, the daughter he raised on his own. And Ati eh, it's clear to see that he likes Materena's little sister...well good luck to him!

Next to Ati is Pito and Materena's son-in-law, Hotu, looking a bit gaunt, a bit sad. *Eh bien,* Hotu has just come back from his trip to France to see his girlfriend, Leilani, and he must be missing her already. A lot of people are missing Leilani, it's not just her lovesick boyfriend, who jumps on the plane to France every three months for a short reunion with that girl he can't get out of his mind.

It would be so wonderful to see Leilani home, but Leilani has a rule. She will not come home until she finishes her studies. She's afraid that if she comes home, she won't want to leave...and then will live her life with regrets. *Aue,* children, eh?

Ah, and there's Pito's little angel, his ray of sunshine, the apple of his eye, his beautiful granddaughter, Tiare, laughing her head off because she's sitting on her father's shoulders and he's bopping around — and she's so scared of falling off but it's so fun, Papa! Again!

And it's great to see Moana, that boy has sure grown, he's a man now, a happy man too, for the woman he loves loves him back with the same passion. Pito, his eyes darting back to his wife's, thinks, I'm a lucky man too.

"Ready?" he calls out.

"*Oui!*" everyone shouts back.

"Okay, say *fromage!*"

"*Fromage!*" they call back, laughing, Hotu included.

Pito raises the very expensive Canon camera he borrowed from Ati, and the thought that comes into his mind, right now, right this second, is...

Life can't possibly get any better than this.

Acknowledgments

This book, which is about the relationship between a man and his granddaughter — his redemption, his chance from the sky to become a better man — was a lot of fun to write.

I'm a great-auntie, though I'm not even forty years old yet! To watch my male cousins become grandfathers is just amazing — sometimes it's hard to recognize them from the coconut heads they were as boyfriends, husbands, and even fathers. I'm told this wonderful transformation isn't just typical of Tahitian men...

My eternal gratitude goes to my very good friend and agent-with-a-mission, Louise Thurtell, for her huge support with my writing and many other parts of my life. One thing is for sure, Louise, we will remember 2005 forever!

Special thanks to my dedicated editor, Amanda Brett. This is our second novel together, and we survived! The editor-writer relationship can be extremely challenging, as writers are often very sensitive about their work. Amanda, you are a professional with great people skills. I'd work with you anytime, baby.

My publicist, Gemma Rayner, the one and only, you are just sensational, girl. That taxi ride in Melbourne was very interesting indeed!

Michael Heyward and the whole Text team, thank you so much for launching me onto the international stage.

And as always, a big MAURURU to my family and friends for their undivided attention whenever I passionately go on (and on and on) about my fictional characters as if they truly existed.

And finally, to a very special little girl, Jenna Mack, who provided much inspiration for my portrayal of Tiare in these pages. Jenna, you brighten up my life, sweetheart!

Reading Group Guide

Tiare in Bloom

A novel by

Célestine Vaite

Célestine Vaite

on why Pito's voice had to be heard

When we meet Pito in *Breadfruit,* he's in his thirties. In *Tiare in Bloom,* Pito is in his forties, and it's time for some serious changes.

The idea to write my third novel in the Materena trilogy from Pito's point of view came to me after one of my closest friends asked, "What's your next book about? What about Pito? Will we ever hear his voice? What's in his head? Sure, he's sexy, but what else have you got, Pito? Talk to me, Pito."

And I thought, Of course! I will put myself under Pito's skin and write from his point of view. I will redeem him. I will make him shine!

The next question was, How?

Pito likes to go out drinking with his *copains,* well, not anymore, Pito, because I'm breaking one of your legs. That way, you're going to be bedridden and see what a loving wife you have looking after you and everything. But I could see Pito hobbling out of the house with his other good leg, so I broke both his legs.

There.

So here was Pito, stuck in bed and talking a lot of wind talk to Materena, and after two chapters, he got on my nerves.

Time to get out of bed, Pito!

Next, I thought that a separation might work better. I wrote the chapter of the separation, with Materena banging pots and pans and chucking Pito out with his ukulele, lots of drama, as you can imagine, but I'm Tahitian, I can do drama easy.

Poor Pito, here he was, sobbing on his mother's sofa, but next he was having a party, going on, Woohoo! I escaped! *Vive la liberté!*

Pito's redemption looked like it wasn't going to work, so I put the idea aside, gave my house a big cleanup, and opened myself to the universe.

Not long after, I went home to Tahiti for my family injection and work, and who do I bump into by the side of the road but my cousin George with his newborn granddaughter, and what a transformed man my cousin was! Long gone was the tough coconut-head George, who wanted nothing to do with his children because beer with his *copains* sounded so much better and because that's what *real* men do.

And because our culture allowed him to. It's almost like, as a grandfather, a man is finally free to show his sensitive nature, it's culturally acceptable, people aren't going to think he's a *mahu*.

Cousin George wasn't the only man transformed in my neighborhood. I was, at the passionate age of thirty-eight years old, a great-auntie to a few *bébés*.

I came back to Australia thinking, That's it! Pito, my friend, you're going to be a grandfather.

Next question was, Okay, which one of his three children is going to have a baby?

It couldn't be Leilani, *non,* she was busy studying, and I had other plans for her, no way I was going to make her fall pregnant, and it couldn't be Moana, he's such a sensitive character. I just couldn't picture Moana as an absent father. This meant that Pito wouldn't have much to do at all, except say, "Here I am, give me the baby, I'm going now, here's your baby back."

Tamatoa, then? In France doing military service...

I was very conscious to be careful with Pito's transformation. It had to be gradual and real. None of the "he wakes up one sunny morning and he's a new man" kind of thing. It had to be believable, and that is why his granddaughter, Tiare, arrived in his life the way she did. She couldn't have arrived any other way.

And I knew, I knew in my heart, my soul, right down to my blood vessels, that I was on the right track when I burst into tears writing the scene when Pito puts his three-month-old granddaughter to bed.

That was the moment I said to myself, "Girl, you're falling in love with Pito here, keep writing..."

Tiare in Bloom was the easiest of the three books to write; nine months compared with three years with *Breadfruit,* and two with *Frangipani.*

And I sure had a lot of fun.

Questions and topics for discussion

1. *Tiare in Bloom* is a novel built around relationships—between husbands and wives, fathers and children, family members near and far, and friends. Which relationship did you find the most compelling? Were any reminiscent of the relationships in your life?

2. We watch many men transform and mature throughout the novel. Can you identify a turning point for each male character? What made Tamatoa take responsibility for his daughter, or Ati reclaim his life? Why did it take a grandchild to make Pito see the error of his ways?

3. Tiare, the author tells us, is Tahiti's national flower. What is the significance of Tamatoa's daughter's being named Tiare? Why do you think the author chose the title *Tiare in Bloom*?

4. How would you describe the author's writing style? Did you find anything striking or unusual about the way the story unfolds? Can you think of any moments in the book where the voice is deceptively simple?

5. *Tiare in Bloom* is told from both Materena's and Pito's point of view. Talk about the differences and similarities in each character's attitude and voice. How do Pito's chats with his male friends differ from Materena's conversations with the women on her radio show? Whom do you identify with more?

6. At one point in the novel, Materena and her friends confess the crazy things they've done for love—dyed their hair blond, walked twenty kilometers to see a man, sneaked out of a bedroom window at night, given up a favorite pastime. What's the craziest thing you've done for love? Was it worth it?

7. What lessons do you draw from Pito in the novel? And from Materena? Think of these characters in terms of both their individual qualities and the ideals they represent.

8. In the chapter "Breathing like you want," Materena speaks about what it means to be a Tahitian. Did you find any of these things surprising or, in your opinion, particular to a Tahitian way of life? Are these qualities you had expected Materena to point out? How would you describe *your* heritage or culture?

9. What do secondary characters such as Leilani, Ati, and Lily bring to the story? What do you think the author is hoping to show through each of these characters?

10. What did you know about Tahiti before reading *Tiare in Bloom*? How does the novel change or shape your understanding of Tahitian culture?

Following is an excerpt
from the opening pages of

Célestine Vaite's

Breadfruit

A Love Movie

Materena likes movies about love.

When there's a love movie on the television, Materena sits on the sofa, her hands crossed, and her eyes focused on the TV screen. She doesn't broom or cut her toenails, she doesn't iron, or fold clothes. She doesn't do anything except concentrate on the movie.

Movies about love move Materena and sometimes it happens that she imagines she's the heroine.

The love movie tonight is about a woman who loves a man with a passion, but, unfortunately, she has to marry another man — it's the plan of her parents. Her future husband is not bad-looking or mean. It's just that she feels nothing for that man. When she looks at him, it's like she's looking at a tree — whereas when she looks at the man she loves, her heart goes *boom, boom,* she wants to kiss him, and she wants to hold him tight.

The woman in the movie meets the man she loves one last time — it is a day before her grandiose wedding, and he's leaving for a faraway country, never to return, because it's too much for him to bear to stay in the neighborhood. It's easier for him to just disappear.

The lovers meet behind a thick hedge. They kiss, they embrace, then he falls to his knees and declares: "I will love you till I die, till I die, I swear to God, you are the center of my universe, my guiding light, the only one."

The heroine hides her face in her gloved hands and bursts into tears. There's violin music, and a tear escapes from the corner of Materena's eye. She's sad for the woman. She can feel the pain.

"Poor her," Materena sighs.

"Zero movie! What a load of crap!" This is Pito's comment.

In his opinion, there is too much crying in that movie, too much carrying-on, no action. And the man, what a *bébé la la* — wake up to yourself.

"Well, go read your Akim comic in the kitchen." Materena wipes her eyes with her pareu.

But Pito is too comfortable on the sofa, and he wants to watch the end of that silly movie. Materena wishes she could transport Pito somewhere else. He's been annoying her ever since the movie started with his comments and sighs.

Pito doesn't like movies about love. He prefers cowboy movies, movies with action and as little talking as possible.

The movie is near the end and Materena hopes Pito is not going to spoil it with a stupid remark. Materena needs complete silence. The end of a love movie is very crucial. There's a lot of tension. In Materena's mind, the heroine will be reunited with the man she loves, but love movies don't always end the way Materena would like them to end.

There's the grandiose wedding and it is clear to Materena that the bride's thoughts are not in the church. She keeps looking back, waiting for the man she loves to appear and rescue her. Materena can guess it. Materena expects the man to barge into the church at any second too, but he's far away, riding on his horse. Materena says in her head, Eh, go get the woman you love, you idiot. But he keeps on riding that horse.

And meanwhile, to Materena's sadness, the heroine becomes the wife of the man she doesn't love.

Confetti greets the newlyweds outside the church and doves are set free. The heroine watches the doves fly toward the gray sky.

It is the end of the movie and Materena is really annoyed, she prefers happy endings. She listens to the soft melody of the piano during the credits and reads the names of the principal actors. It reminds her that the sad story is only a movie and not the reality.

After the final credits have finished, she switches the TV off.

"Zero movie!" Pito gets off the sofa like he weighs over two hundred pounds.

Materena tidies up the living room.

"Zero movie!" Pito is now making himself comfortable in the bed.

Materena pulls the bedcover her way and rolls to the far side of the bed.

"I tell you, Materena, if I was the man in the movie, I tell you, if it was I, the man..." Pito says he would have snatched the woman and escaped with her on the horse.

"Yes, okay. Good night." Materena is not listening to Pito anymore.

She closes her eyes and drifts off to sleep. And she dreams she has to marry the man in the movie, but the man she loves is Pito. She's in the church, about to pronounce "I do," when the door of the church swings open. It is Pito. He is on a horse and he's wearing cowboy clothes and a cowboy hat.

People stare as Pito makes his way to the altar, they also stare at the horse.

Pito grabs Materena by the waist and he says to the man she's supposed to marry, "Listen, that woman, she's for me — you go look for another woman, okay?" Pito has a fierce look on his face. Pito and Materena ride out of the church, they ride far away, far away, to the desert.

When Materena wakes up, she's laughing.

About the Author

CÉLESTINE VAITE was born in Tahiti. The daughter of a Tahitian mother and a French father who went back to his country after military service, she grew up in her big extended family in Faa'a-Tahiti, where storytelling was part of the everyday life, and women overcame obstacles with gusto and humor. Her first two novels about the Mahi and Tehana families, *Breadfruit* (which won the 2004 Prix littéraire des étudiants) and *Frangipani* (which won the 2006 Prix littéraire des étudiants), have been published in the UK, the United States, Canada, Italy, Spain, Norway, Sweden, Finland, the Netherlands, Brazil, France, Germany, and French Polynesia. *Frangipani* was short-listed for the 2005 NSW Premier's Literary Awards. Célestine now lives on the south coast of New South Wales. *Tiare in Bloom* is her third novel.